DEATH
BREAKS
THE RING

VIRGINIA RATH

DEATH BREAKS THE RING

VIRGINIA RATH

COACHWHIP PUBLICATIONS
Greenville, Ohio

DEATH BREAKS THE RING

PART ONE

"Oh, I've rid from San Antony
Through the mesquite and the sand,
I'm a rarin', flarin' bucko,
Not afraid to play my hand."

The Killer

I

William Travis Logan went swiftly up the stairway from the second to the third floor and on toward the back room he shared with the night desk clerk. Even in the hall it was unpleasantly warm on this top floor at two o'clock of an August afternoon.

The bedroom Logan entered, after listening for a moment outside its door, had its one window closed against the sun. The night clerk was sweating and fretful, knotting his tie in the glare of an unshaded light bulb.

"Oh, it's you," he said ungraciously. "I've given up trying to sleep in this oven. But I don't see what you want up here at this time of the day."

"I wouldn't have woke you even if you'd still been asleep," Logan said.

The night clerk grunted. It was true the fellow walked like a cat, and though Logan was already known to the guests and other employees as "Tex"

and well liked by most of them Mr. Pruett resented him.

For one thing, after nearly a month Logan
was still unclassified on the Summit House pay
roll. He wasn't drawing a large salary, but no one
seemed to know exactly what he was supposed to
do to earn it.

He went swaggering around in boots and riding trousers, bright silk shirts and a ten-gallon
hat. Almost, Pruett though disapprovingly, as if
he were a guest himself. Of course he was good
looking in a flashy way, so he could get away with
anything as far as the women were concerned.

"I wanted to get some of those trout flies I tied
myself," Logan went on, sitting down on the bed,
"but, as long as I'm here, reckon I'll change my
shirt too."

Pruett felt that Logan was waiting for him to
go and decided testily that he would not be driven
from his own room until he really wanted to leave.
So he combed what hair he had again, polished his
shoes with a towel and finally put on his coat.

"You'll roast in that," Logan commented.
"What's the idea? Makin' yourself pretty for our
angel?"

"Angel?" Pruett repeated blankly.

"Didn't Bernard Gould put up most of the
money to build this joint and get it runnin'?"

"Yes. Everyone knows that," Pruett said patronizingly. "I did or I might have hesitated to take a job in a new hotel like this even if I did want to get out of the city this summer. A man with my experience don't have to take just anything. But, while the average San Franciscan thinks of Gould just as one of these Texas oil millionaires, I happen to have it on very good authority that he's financially interested in several hotels and night clubs in the city."

"Sure 'nuf? Well, you may have faith in him as a financial backer, but I kinda thought he got in your hair when he made the grand tour of inspection last week end." Logan grinned irritatingly. "He sure don't miss much."

Mr. Pruett frowned. Bernard Gould had arrived at Summit House last Saturday, a week ago today, in time for a late lunch. He had driven away on Sunday afternoon, leaving the hotel staff feeling, if nothing worse, very much out of breath, and, departing, had left behind his wife and his wife's sister, Miss Lawton, to spend this week at Summit House.

It was simply not good business, Mr. Pruett thought, to have the wife and sister-in-law of the hotel's financial angel occupying one of its best rooms during the rush season. Besides, on Wednesday a young man named Peter Wallis had turned up, announcing himself a friend of the Goulds, though in a few hours everyone in the hotel knew it was Bettina Lawton who had drawn him here.

At least Mr. Wallis hadn't made any complaints about his room or the service or asked for a rate— yet. But on Friday a Mr. and Mrs. Farnham and their small daughter, Patricia, had arrived. Mrs. Farnham immediately let it be known they were also well acquainted with the Goulds.

Raymond Farnham was a lawyer—Bernard Gould's lawyer, Pruett supposed. Farnham had come to fish and he was fishing indefatigably. He'd been out today since before sunrise. Unfortunately he had not taken his wife and daughter with him.

Mrs. Farnham had already been heard to say at least six times: "I shall certainly tell Mr. Gould what I think of the service in this hotel." As for Miss Patricia— Mr. Pruett, who had had a varied experience with children in hotels, was inclined to close his eyes and shudder when he thought of Miss Patricia.

And it seemed the Gould circle wasn't complete yet. Thursday night a wire had come asking them to reserve two rooms for tonight for a Mrs. Alling and a Geoffrey MacNair who were also friends of Gould's. That meant that, altogether, six rooms would be occupied by—

Mr. Pruett turned and looked at Logan apprehensively, suddenly recalling his: "Makin' yourself pretty for our angel?"

"Do you mean," he said, "that Bernard Gould is going to be here this week end—again?"

"Again and too. I understood he wasn't comin' back until maybe in September. But he'll be here tonight with a guy named MacNair and a Mrs. Alling."

"Oh, they're expected. Gould reserved rooms for them last Thursday but he certainly didn't intend then to come back so soon himself."

"He made up his mind kind of unexpected like," Logan drawled. "He phoned this mornin' to say he'll arrive with MacNair and Mrs. Alling. He said him and MacNair wants to go fishin' tomorrow morning. Coakley says Mrs. Gould seemed just as surprised as he was himself that Gould's comin' up here again."

It was Pruett's opinion that Coakley, the hotel manager, was apt to speak too freely to his employees, so he merely sniffed disparagingly and went out. As soon as he had closed the door Logan rose quickly and locked it.

From a bureau drawer he took a sheet of the hotel stationery and a pair of scissors. He cut a strip of paper, roughly, eight by three inches, and laid it on the bedside table before he turned the

water on over the washbowl, took off his green
silk shirt and laid a purple one ready on a chair.

That done, he found a pencil in one pocket, sat
down on the bed again and pulled the small table
up between his knees. It was a poor substitute for
a desk, but Logan worked quickly, apparently un-
disturbed by the heat though sweat glistened on
his brown shoulders.

He stopped once to push the big Stetson back
on his forehead, whistling softly through his teeth.
One corner of his mouth curled into a smile as he
bent over the strip of paper again. . . .

He had just finished when someone tried the
locked door and then knocked loudly. "Are you in
there, Tex? It's me—Coakley."

"In a minute," Logan said coolly. "Soap on my
hands—"

He went over to the bureau, separated three
gay-feathered trout flies from a small heap in the
corner of the top drawer and hooked them neatly
through the strip of paper. He even took time to
look approvingly at his work before he sealed it
into a long envelope and put that into a trouser
pocket.

"Coming," he called soothingly, turned the
water off, threw his hat on the bed and unlocked
the bedroom door.

"Sorry to keep you waitin'. I thought I'd wash
up and put on a clean shirt."

"That's all right." Mr. Coakley looked a little more than usual like a well-intentioned but worried walrus. "Only, why lock the door?"

"I didn't want to be disturbed," Logan said truthfully. "You know I rode herd on that Farnham brat this mornin', and she took quite a shine to me. I locked the door in case she came lookin' for me."

"I don't blame you. The mother's worse than the kid," Coakley said. "I finally had to give her a new room—she made so much fuss. And now Bernard Gould's going to be here and will want to go in with his wife, so we'll have to put Miss Lawton up here on this floor. For tonight, that is. I imagine they'll all be leaving tomorrow."

"MacNair and the Hon MacNair and Mrs. Alling too?"

"Yes. I guess they're only coming to take Miss Lawton and Mrs. Gould home. It hasn't been announced yet, but Bernard Gould told me Miss Lawton and this MacNair are engaged," Coakley said importantly. "He seemed pleased about it. So I take it MacNair and Mrs. Alling—she's MacNair's sister—are good friends of the Goulds."

Logan whistled. "I'll say it hasn't been announced yet and I know one guy that isn't going to be pleased about it."

"Peter Wallis? No, I guess he won't be. I suppose he knows MacNair. But I came to tell you those women from Sacramento want to get a last ride this afternoon. I'm sorry—"

"Hell, I can take it if the horses can," Logan said, tucking his shirt into his trousers.

Mr. Coakley smiled sadly. "Yes, but I'd hoped they'd just rest for the dance tonight. There are still so many things to be attended to that—"

"That you figured you'd like to have me aroun'? Well, I'll try to get them big Berthas back early— if the horses don't give out on us. I reckon the fishin' party will be late getting in."

"Yes, they were going all the way to Downie-ville. That means we may have to keep the dining room open later than usual."

"You wouldn't dare close it, anyways, till Gould and his party gets in," Logan remarked. "No one 'll expect the dancin' to begin too early. I'll get them dames on their ponies, and we'll get going."

II

From the foot of the stairway Logan could see his charges waiting on the porch: three large fortyish women crammed into riding trousers. Two were giggling while the third admonished them: "Now, girls! Girls, I don't know what's come over you two!"

Mr. Logan spat neatly and derisively into the nearest spittoon. He dodged quickly across the lobby toward the small bar, feeling for the envelope in his trouser pocket.

The bartender, Augustus Leiber, was polishing glassware. Gus's hair was his own but it looked more like a wig than any wig ever made. Ladies and gentlemen under the influence had been known to try to snatch it off his head as final proof that it was a wig.

This probably accounted for Gus's habit of smoothing it apprehensively back from its oily center part every minute or two. It was certainly in no danger of attack from Peter Wallis, who was drinking beer and had taken half an hour to consume half a glass.

Logan, seeing Peter's red head and broad shoulders bent over the bar, shrugged and took his hand out of his pocket.

"Rye, Gus. I need fortifyin'. I'm about to take two tons of female out to see nature from a horse," he said.

Gus grinned appreciatively. "Maybe Mr. Wallis would like to come wit' you," he suggested. "I been sayin' a husky young guy like him hadn't oughta be stayin' inside all day."

Logan's black eyes glinted maliciously. "Just what I was thinkin'. I'm surprised you didn't go fishin' with Farnham and the rest of 'em."

Peter looked away from the mounted stag's head over the bar, glanced at Logan and decided he preferred the stag, glassy eyed though it was. Mr. Wallis shared Mr. Pruett's wonder as to Logan's exact status and duties—when he considered him at all.

That was seldom, for Peter was living in a two-directional world, bounded on one side by himself, on the other by Bettina Lawton. He had been thinking, when Logan came in to the bar, that he might as well have stayed in San Francisco and the good graces of his immediate superior in the firm of architects he worked for.

But when Bettina told him that she and her sister, Stella, were coming up here with Bernard Gould Peter's one idea had been to get to Summit House before their week here was over. He had managed that, and the setup should have been perfect—no other young men in the hotel, warm, clear nights, unlimited grounds to stroll about in. . . .

But Bettina had avoided being alone with him. Inside the hotel every old gossip, male or female, was watching them interestedly, and at night they seemed always to find themselves playing bridge with someone. Until last night. . . .

It was so warm inside that Bettina had finally agreed to go out with him. They'd sat down on a rustic bench off to one side of the hotel. No one had come along the path, and Bettina had suddenly leaned back against him and drawn his arms about her.

"Don't—don't talk," she said. "It doesn't do any good to talk."

They'd stayed that way for half an hour, his cheek against her hair. He hadn't even asked just what she meant by "It doesn't do any good to talk." But at last he kissed her temple softly, then her cheek and closed eyes. That was when she sat erect, pulling away from him.

"We shouldn't have stayed so long," she said. "It isn't fair to. . . . Let's go in."

Before he could stop her she was half running along the path to the hotel. Today he'd seen her only in the dining room at lunch time.

"Waitin' at the gate for Katy?" Logan said.

"Katy? What do you—? You mind your own business, will you?" Peter said rudely.

"Sure. I was just going to give you fair warnin', but if you say not to that's O.K."

Logan nodded to Gus and started toward the door. Peter stared after him. "What do you mean?" he asked, against his better judgment.

"Oh, all I know's what I hear," Logan drawled. "But if you're waitin' for Miss Lawton you might have a long wait. She may have a lot of primping to do, what with the dance tonight and her fiancé being expected and all."

"Her— What did you say?"

"The guy she's going to marry—this Geoffrey MacNair. Coakley got it from Gould himself," Logan said. "I'll be seeing you."

He went out, and feminine squeals from the porch indicated his riding party was receiving him with enthusiasm. Peter stared at the defunct stag, and the stag stared glassily back at him.

"I know just how you feel," Gus said sympathetically. "I felt that same way when my second wife went off with a vet'inary."

"But she can't—" Peter began, and stopped, scowling at Gus helplessly.

Bettina mustn't marry Geoffrey MacNair or anyone but Peter Wallis. But when you got right down to it MacNair was pleasant enough, still in his thirties, not bad looking, apparently well off. And of course he was head over heels in love with Bettina. He'd been hanging around her for a year, and Bernard Gould would approve of Bettina's marrying him, while he had always turned a very frigid shoulder in Peter's direction.

All very good reasons why Bettina should marry Geoffrey MacNair, but love, Mr. Wallis thought sagely, had nothing to do with reason. And he was unshakably certain Bettina didn't love Geoffrey.

She didn't have to marry anyone she didn't want to. Girls didn't do that nowadays, even a girl like Bettina who hated to quarrel with anyone.

For an instant Peter was ready to dash upstairs and insist on talking to her, but she had promised to meet him in the lobby late this afternoon and she shared a room with Stella Gould. She probably wouldn't let him in if he did go upstairs.

"More beer?" Gus suggested. "That's pretty flat."

"Scotch!" Mr. Wallis snapped. "And leave the bottle where I can reach it."

III

It was a tribute to her husband's driving that on a mountain road like an interminable corkscrew Valerie had been half asleep for the past hour. What thoughts she had were longingly of food. When she realized Michael had stopped the car she sat erect, expecting to see some roadside filling station, hoping she could buy at least a handful of candy bars.

But it seemed they had stopped simply because they had to. The road narrowed at this point, and there was a long black car standing across it. There was still a faint golden light over the tops of the pine trees, but the sun had already begun its toboggan slide down the mountains.

The road and the forests stretching away on either side were in cold purple shadow. It was easy enough to see that of the three people hurrying toward them one was a woman and two were men but not to make out their features.

"Is—is it a holdup?" Valerie whispered.

"I wouldn't know," Michael said discouragingly. "What their intentions are, that is."

He set the brakes with one hand while with the other he yanked down the door of the small compartment in the dashboard where they carried road maps, dustcloths, cigarettes, Kleenex, sunburn lotion—and a small automatic.

The taller of the two men approaching them broke into a long-legged trot, waving an urgent arm. He reached the car, stopped to take breath and then seemed to lose it again when he saw the gun in Michael's hand.

"Is this a holdup?" he said finally, coolly enough.

"I don't know," Michael said with a greater degree of coolness. "Is it? Why is that car across the road?"

"Oh, I say! We aren't holding you up," the man protested.

He was tall, very thin and so blond his hair had the gleam of silver where it was clipped close at neck and temples. His eyes were a light grayish blue, and the rest of his features paid proper deference to a long, well-shaped nose. He turned toward his companions.

"Maria! These people think—"

"That we're highway robbers," the woman said calmly. "I expected that. I— Damn, I've got to get this blasted rock out of my shoe. Barney got us into this. Let him get us out."

"I got you into this! That antediluvian monster is yours, not mine. You said its gas gauge could be trusted, or we would have taken on gas in Nevada City and not be stalled here."

"Out of gas?" Michael said, without taking his finger from the gun's trigger. "Did you lose control of the car when it expired, so that it sprawled across the road?"

The man called Barney glared at him and then laughed. "Five cars whizzed by us, and we didn't want to stay here all night. I suggested we push the car across the road to block it. Maria said the first passerby would feel just as you do. But we're harmless. This is Geoffrey MacNair, and that's his sister, Mrs. Alling, back there, and I'm Bernard Gould, if that means anything to you."

"Should it?" Michael said. I wonder, his wife thought admiringly, why people don't hit him when he speaks like that. "My name is Dundas, if that means anything to you? It doesn't? Then we are back where we started."

"Don't be pompous, Barney," Mrs. Alling advised before Gould could speak. "Yours isn't quite a household name yet."

She finished tying her shoelace and reached the car in half a dozen long strides. "I do think, though, that Mr. Dundas should know by looking at me that I'm no gangster's moll."

Michael grinned briefly and put the gun back in the dashboard compartment. The countenance Mrs. Alling thought he should find reassuring brought that of an amiable and sagacious mule to his mind. Yet, item by item, her features were those of her brother, except that Geoffrey's slight, pallid mustache did make his long upper lip at least appear shorter.

Michael guessed Mrs. Alling to be in the neighborhood of forty-five, perhaps ten years older than Geoffrey and five years younger than Bernard Gould. Not that many people would at first glance give Gould fifty years.

He had a powerful chest and shoulders and more than merely the remains of a waistline and hair. His tan had the patina of a genuine antique, and the lines about his eyes seemed more the result of squinting into the sun than of middle age. But though he'd chosen to give the impression Gould's name meant nothing to him Michael knew quite well who Gould was and that he must be in his fifties.

"I'm sorry if I seem overly suspicious," he said, addressing Mrs. Alling, "but a friend of ours was recently held up on one of these mountain roads, and I'm a timid soul."

"Really! I thought the finger on that trigger remarkably steady and I also rather fancied you're simply in a very bad humor."

Valerie laughed. "That is putting it mildly, though I don't really blame him, and it's my fault that he is."

"Precisely. We have been visiting friends in Brookdale, which is over on the Feather River Highway. You might well ask what, then, we're doing here on the Yuba Pass," Michael said, "and why, when we wanted to return to San Francisco, we didn't take the shortest route home."

"And why didn't you?" Geoffrey said politely.

"Because Mrs. Dundas wanted to view a little more of the infinite monotony of mountain scenery. She wanted to see Sierra City and Downieville. So we spent several hours wandering back and forth between two supremely unimportant hamlets known as Calpine and Sierraville, looking for the Yuba Pass road. It seems," Michael continued, getting his teeth into the subject, "that the repair or oiling of unpaved roads is always carried on during the summer months. Except when the roads are unrepaired and unoiled and never in this world will be—"

"We are both tired and famished," Valerie said. "We're going to stop overnight in Auburn. Can we take you there or drop you off at Nevada City or Grass Valley if you'd rather go there?"

"We're bound in the opposite direction," Mrs. Alling said. "We were going to Summit House."

"The hotel about fifteen miles back? Off the main road, of course, but I seem to remember signs advertising it."

"You should if you hadn't been half asleep," Michael said. "There were at least ten miles of them, each one larger and more lurid than the last. Little as I care for the so-called scenic beauty of the mountains, I do prefer it unadorned."

Gould cleared his throat explosively, and Mrs. Alling grinned. "Barney is part owner and guiding genius of Summit House. He wants to inspect his enterprise again. Isn't that what you said, Barney?"

Malice was not a quality you'd expect to encounter in Maria Alling, and, as usual, her voice was brisk and forceful as a slap on the back. But Michael thought Gould glanced at her speculatively—with a "how-much-do-you-know?" look—before he said flatly:

"No. Oh, I do want to keep an eye on the place, because only time will tell what sort of resort we'll be able to make of it—a luxury or a quiet family hotel. Just now it's neither one nor the other. But I want to get some fishing tomorrow. I was too busy to go out at all last week end. Besides," he continued, looking to Valerie as a more sympathetic listener than her husband, "they are having an old-fashioned square dance at the hotel tonight.

"My wife and her sister, Bettina Lawton, have been spending this week at the hotel. I didn't leave our car for them, so someone had to see they get back to the city. I suppose we will arrive before the dancing is over if you'll send someone with gas from the first filling station you come to."

Michael looked at Valerie and then shrugged resignedly. "You win, Mr. Gould. I knew mine was a lost cause as soon as you mentioned square dancing to my wife."

"Well, I didn't like to suggest you turn back with us, but, since you aren't going on to San Francisco tonight, does it matter whether you stay in Auburn or at Summit House?"

"I suppose not," Michael said ungraciously. "And Valerie will turn cannibal if she isn't fed soon. We'll take you to Summit House, but you'll have to get that car to the side of the road before we go. If you have a tow rope I suppose I can pull it to a safe place. Though," he added candidly, "it would give me great pleasure to see you try to push it."

IV

When they were finally on the way toward Summit House Maria Alling planted her feet on her suitcase and found a cigarette and a kitchen match in a pocket of her tweed jacket.

"Your name is familiar to me, Mr. Dundas," she said, snapping the match expertly against a thumbnail. "I'd swear I've seen and talked with you before."

"I've talked to you, without introduction, in the paddock at Bay Meadows and Tanforan. You are known to your friends as the 'Honorable Maria,' though you aren't an honorable, are you? You're Canadian born and you married a Richard Alling who was a minor ornament of peninsula society. He's not living. You have a—well, I suppose you call it an 'estate,' near San Mateo or Redwood City."

"I call it a farm. You didn't get all this from the *Racing Form*."

"I suppose I picked it up at the tracks. Do you still raise blooded stock? You haven't entered horses at any racing meetings for some time."

"My racing stable was an expensive luxury," the Honorable Maria said grimly. "I never saw any prize money. My Starfleet and Dusty Rose should have won, but I was always unfortunate in my trainer or jockeys. I sometimes acted as my own trainer, but my size, if not my sex, kept me from seeing to it personally that my horses got a good ride."

"My sister thinks she is an excellent judge of character—and she is very often," Geoffrey said. "But she'll give any vagabond who tells a plausible or pathetic story a trial. The place is overrun with men like that. If they don't pinch the silver they spend half their time loafing."

"If some of them are malingerers I can always stir them up when necessary. I've learned to be careful whom I employ about the stables, even if I have given up racing. Well, your information so far is accurate, Mr. Dundas. Are you certain you don't know as much or more about Barney here?"

"Certainly, though I wouldn't pamper him by saying so when he flung his name at me in lordly fashion. Mr. Gould is an entrepreneur—if you don't object to that term, Mr. Gould?"

"I don't pronounce it quite like you do, but it's good enough, though I don't know why you use it."

"From what I've heard, or anyone seems to know, of your activities in San Francisco and this state, 'enterprises' is the only word that covers them," Michael said. "Of course, I do know you are supposed to have started life as an oil driller and wildcat operator and that you eventually struck it rich."

"That's right," Gould agreed. "I still spend as much as four months a year in Texas and Oklahoma."

"And your wife has been called the most beautiful woman in San Francisco," Valerie said.

Gould shrugged. "She'll pass in a crowd."

"And I've heard a great deal about Bettina this last six months. And about your wife—incidentally."

"Who do you know that knows us?" Gould asked.

"A young man who works for the firm of architects that drew the plans for our house. Though he looked at me in horror when I told him I was going to have a paneled dining room with a plate rail even if it didn't happen to be architecturally the fashion we've become rather good friends. He steers me into corners at parties and talks to me about Bettina Lawton."

"That," Gould said bleakly, "would be Peter Wallis."

"I think you've just thrown a brick, my dear," Michael said.

"So do I, though that certainly was not my intention."

"It's only that Geoff and Bettina are engaged," the Honorable Maria said. "And I'm afraid Bettina's so softhearted she hasn't given Peter his walking papers yet. He'll probably cut up rough when she does, but I think Barney is a little severe with Peter. And I've placed you now, Mr. Dundas. You own that specialty shop called Gisele's. You're rather famous as a couturier all along the Pacific coast."

"If having your best designs copied—badly—is fame, yes," Michael agreed.

"And," Mrs. Alling went on, "you are forever getting mixed up in murder cases. A woman named Amalia Landreth was killed last November, and her murderer took a shot at you—"

Michael moved his right shoulder reminiscently. "I recall the incident. And I've decided that the amateur detective isn't needed—or wanted. Do they give many old-fashioned dances in this part of the country, Mr. Gould?"

"What? Oh—Coakley, the hotel manager, is a local man and he says some of the young folks that come to the hotel dances are interested in the old country dances. Texas people around El Paso weren't doing much but square dancing last summer, but I don't know if the craze ever really hit California."

"I don't think it has," Valerie said. "There's a dance hall down on Polk Street where they have old-fashioned dances sometimes. We like to go there, but Michael taught me the steps. He'd learned them in Wisconsin in a lumber-mill town years ago. Of course, all old-fashioned dances aren't square dances, though most people think they have to be."

"That's true," Gould said. "A lot of the most popular old-time dances are contrys, not square dances at all. Did you ever do one called Hull's Victory?"

"'Turn your opposite twice around, kick her in the shins and knock her down'?" Michael said. "Yes. And I used to be able to dance any sort of polka and even a five-step schottische. Those dances were still popular with the Poles and Scandinavians when I was a boy."

"I know. I was born in New England. Well, if you have a good prompter and know what's meant by all emande right, chassé left, dos-à-dos, form a basket and so on you can dance anything even if you've never tried it before—"

"We'll be quite a family party," Mrs. Alling said abruptly. "Did you know that Ray Farnham is at Summit House, Barney?"

"Certainly," Gould said emphatically. "They told me so at his office Friday. I recommended the place to him, as I have to everyone I know."

"Who is Farnham?" Michael asked. "There is a rather well-known lawyer by that name—"

"That's the man. Very clever fellow. I've known him socially and in a business way ever since I established residence in San Francisco."

"I like Ray Farnham," Mrs. Alling said. "I pity him—and his wife, though I can't like her. She has the disposition of a jealous hyena with an inferiority complex. I doubt if anyone could make a success of marriage with her, and the situation is complicated by a child. One never knows at any given time if Ray and Lilian are living under the same roof. They may be undergoing a brief separation—"

"Not just now, old girl. Mrs. Farnham and the youngster are with Ray at Summit House," Geoffrey said. "I ran into Farnham Thursday night, and he told me they were all three going."

"Oh. I didn't suppose— Well, I hope, for Ray's sake, she hasn't insisted on going fishing with him," Gould said. "We'll be at Summit House in a little while now, and I'm sure you people won't regret having turned back with us. . . ."

V

Bettina Lawton sat down at the dressing table and began to take hairpins from the curls massed on top of her head. Since her hair was naturally curly and she wore the standard long, casual bob, washing it was an easy task. It had been dry for more than an hour, and there was no reason why she shouldn't have gone downstairs long before this.

Instead, she had played maid to Stella, since there was no beauty shop in the hotel. Stella took a long nap every afternoon and she was still lying on one of the twin beds, her hands with their freshly varnished nails lying limply along either thigh.

A towel covered her hair, and a thick mask of beauty clay her face. The "beautiful Mrs. Gould" was far from lovely at that minute. Still, a stranger, seeing her slim body in its thin robe, would probably think that even if there was only a run-of-the-mill face attached to it Stella would still get by very nicely.

In its way Bettina's figure was as satisfactory as Stella's, though it was a smaller, less spectacular way. Her hair was the color of honey, her face heart shaped and always a little wistful. For an instant she sat staring into the mirror, at her own and her sister's reflection in it. Stella parted her lips very slowly and carefully.

"Do you remember how long ago it was that we first went down to see that farm of Maria Alling's?"

The effect was rather as if she had managed to breathe the words down her nose. It robbed them and her voice of any expression, but the surface of the beauty mask remained uncracked.

Bettina, considering what she would say to Peter Wallis, needed a minute to switch her thoughts to this new track. Then:

"Wasn't it last September?" she said. "We hadn't known Geoffrey and Maria very long before Maria asked us down there."

"I guess it was September. Maria insisted on showing us the place—"

"I remember. Of course, you didn't really want to tramp about and look at horses and stables," Bettina said, smiling. "You came in very hot and cross, though no one would have guessed you were. But does it matter how long ago that was?"

"Um-m," Stella said unsatisfactorily. "I was just wondering how long— No, it doesn't matter."

"Then why did you ask me—?" Bettina began, stopped, shrugged imperceptibly and picked up a comb.

Although most people spoke of them as being "such devoted sisters," she and Stella did not always confide in each other. That was impossible so long as Bernard Gould was the third of their family trio. Even when he was away from home they were conscious of him as a presence off stage.

Besides, Stella and Bettina had never really known each other until two years ago. They didn't often bother to explain that Stella, the oldest of

a family of five, had been brought up on various
army posts, while Bettina had spent most of her
life with a grandmother in Santa Barbara.

Mrs. Lawton had been well occupied with three
sturdy, martial sons. She wasn't interested in
daughters and had been glad to be rid of Bettina,
who at four years old was labeled "delicate." Probably Mrs. Lawton hadn't been interested in Stella
either. At any rate, Stella had married Bernard
Gould thirteen years ago when he was thirty-eight
and she was only nineteen.

Bettina was fourteen when Lieutenant and Mrs.
Lawton died in the same year. Stella and Bernard
Gould had still been flitting about Texas, Oklahoma and even Mexico then. But when the grandmother Bettina lived with died, five years later,
her death almost coincided with Gould's sudden
decision to buy a home in San Francisco.

So the Goulds had swept Bettina under their
wing and on up to San Francisco with them. But
all she knew of Stella's girlhood or the first years of
her marriage was just what Stella chose to tell her.

Nevertheless, they usually understood each
other very well without words. They often formed
a strictly defensive alliance against Bernard Gould
without ever admitting they did or discussing him
even when they were alone.

Undoubtedly Stella had been wondering, just as Bettina had, why Gould had decided to come up here this week end, because he'd said he couldn't when he left them here last Sunday. Some geologist was to arrive in San Francisco today, and apparently Gould had been very anxious to talk to him—then.

But still, Bettina thought, she and Stella had spent the afternoon together without mentioning Gould. And now—well, it was no use trying to guess why Stella had suddenly wanted to know when they'd first visited Maria Alling's peninsula home.

If you knew what Stella had been thinking for some time before she spoke you might know what prompted that apparently trivial question. It might even be that it wasn't trivial at all. . . .

Stella cautiously opened her lips again. "Have you talked to Tex Logan very much?"

"Why—I went riding with him and some others one morning, you know. He's inclined to be rather—presumptuous. Most of the women in the hotel encourage him to be, and he doesn't like it when one doesn't. Why, Stella? I didn't think you'd had anything to do with him. Do you—do you think you've seen him somewhere before?"

"You never can tell," Stella said languidly.

"But he is from Texas, and I've heard him mention San Antonio when he was talking to some of the guests. Wasn't Papa stationed at Fort Sam Houston quite a while before you married Barney?"

"Yes, but there are a lot of people living in San Anton'," Stella said impassively. "And I shouldn't talk when I have this clay on my face. You'd better get downstairs before Barney and Geoff and Maria get here."

Stella could be stubbornly silent when she put her mind to it, and Bettina had no time to try to find out what was really in her sister's mind. Talking to Peter was going to take more than just a few minutes. She closed the bedroom door and started downstairs.

Peter was not in the lobby or outside on the porch. Bettina looked toward the bar as Tex Logan came into the lobby from the back of the hotel, hat pushed back from a damp forehead.

"Good evenin', Miss Lawton." His voice and the way in which he snatched off his Stetson were so unnecessarily deferential as to be merely mocking. "Has Mr. Gould and party arrived yet?"

"No," Bettina said shortly.

"Oh. And do you happen to know if the fishin' party is back yet?"

"I really couldn't say. I haven't been watching for them," Bettina said, and walked past him toward the bar.

Logan grinned and followed her. "Wallis was here when I left and he's likely still here, though he probably ain't still drinkin' beer."

Peter had moved down to the far end of the bar and was staring morosely into an empty whisky glass. Bettina stopped near the door, and Logan sauntered on up to the bar.

"You're kinda late getting back," the bartender commented. "You look tired."

"The horses look worse 'n I do, and I don't guess any of those dames will be wantin' to dance tonight—not if they're sore as I think they are."

"That Farnham kid was lookin' for you this afternoon."

Logan grimaced. "I've had enough of her for one day. Oh, Mr. Wallis—"

"So it's you again?" Peter growled.

"If you don't mind my mentionin' it, I think there's a lady would like to speak to you."

"What?" Peter turned and saw Bettina. "Oh. Did you want to talk to me?"

"If—if you're not busy."

"Oh, I'm very busy." Mr. Wallis was elaborately ironical. "But I can spare a few minutes."

He took two careful steps away from the bar, watching Logan truculently. But there was nothing in Logan's expression to suggest he thought Mr. Wallis must be finding the floor a little unsteady beneath his feet. He turned and planted his elbows on the bar and spoke to Gus as Peter joined Bettina.

"I'm going to be pretty busy from now on, Gus, and I'm not aimin' to get up early in the mornin', so I'd like you to . . ."

"Well, where shall we go?" Peter asked ungraciously. "And I'm not tight. I just, as Logan would say, needed fortifying."

"Oh," Bettina said. "Then you—you know—"

"Yes. Nice to get a piece of news like that from the hired help. We'd better go outside."

Two elderly ladies sitting on the porch regarded them with sympathetic smiles. Peter looked at them with open aversion and guided Bettina down the steps toward a graveled walk that led to the grounds at one side of the hotel.

Except on this walk, trees and mountain shrubs had been left as they grew. The bench where Peter and Bettina had sat last night was nailed to the largest of a group of pines, facing another path that led to the side door of the hotel's ballroom.

Peter stopped before they reached the bench, at a point where still another path branched off from the one they were on.

"I'd rather not go where we were last night. I suppose it doesn't mean anything to you—"

"It does, but perhaps I'd rather go there alone. Women are foolish enough to make themselves miserable with memories or keepsakes," Bettina said. "Men are—are sensible enough to avoid things that will make them remember."

Peter groaned. His reaction was so entirely spontaneous that he would have been furious had anyone told him how much he resembled a ham actor playing the "great renunciation" scene. The resemblance was intensified when he managed the difficult feat of setting his jaw grimly and at the same time speaking through his teeth.

"We'll take this path. It goes off to the other side of that clump of trees where the bench is. There is a sort of pool back here. Have you been there?"

"Mrs. Farnham and I brought Patty over here yesterday afternoon." Bettina went ahead of Peter along the hard path. "Patty was restless, you know."

They stopped where a large concrete basin had been sunk into the ground. It was fed by a tiny stream that showed signs of going dry. The pool was bordered with marigolds, and a small stack of planks against a tree indicated another bench was to be built there.

"I suppose this was one of your brother-in-law's bright ideas," Peter said. "But he'll soon have to find water for his pool somewhere else."

"Don't try to be casual, Peter. I know I've treated you badly. Who told you I'm going to marry
Geoffrey?"

"That fellow Logan. He got it from Coakley,
and Coakley had it from Gould."

"Oh. Barney shouldn't have— That is, I'm sorry
you had to hear it from Mr. Logan."

"He has the nerve of a brass monkey. Seems
to me he's pretty interested in the Gould family.
Have you ever seen him watching Stella?"

"Most men watch Stella," Bettina objected half-
heartedly.

"I know, but— Well, I did know he was telling
the truth about you and MacNair. That accounted
for everything."

"I know I should have told you at once, Peter.
But Geoffrey and I only became engaged two days
before I came up here. And when you came I—I
didn't want you to go away again."

"Then why are you marrying MacNair? WHY?"

"Peter, please don't shout. I'm very fond of
Geoffrey. I am of you too. But I didn't ever say I'd
marry you if I—if I could."

"No, because if you said that you know it would
make me feel worse. You're being forced into this
marriage—"

"Peter, you know that's ridiculous. How could
anyone force me to marry Geoffrey?"

"That's what I'd like to know. But you don't really deny it. Go on—look me in the eye and tell me you're very happy!"

Bettina raised her eyes as high as his collar and then turned aside. "Oh—I've told you I'm really fond of Geoffrey—"

"And you'll try to make him a good wife!" Peter finished savagely. "Why is Gould so set on your marrying him? He is, isn't he?"

"Y-yes," Bettina admitted.

"Well, I just don't get it. I know MacNair has more money than I have, but what's that to Gould? If you don't care that I have just a salary, why should he? Maybe he thinks MacNair is more settled and dependable than I am, but, even if he does, why should he get paternal about you all of a sudden?"

"But he has always been very generous to me. You know I haven't enough money of my own to live on—just the little my grandmother left me— and I won't pretend I'd like to have to earn my own living. And you do antagonize Barney, and he doesn't like to be opposed or—or thwarted."

"Is that all?" Peter asked grimly.

"There's Stella. She's absolutely dependent on Barney and she's so much younger than he is and almost too beautiful— Oh, I know I don't make sense! But I can't say anything more, Peter."

She turned quickly and started back toward the hotel. "I thought I heard a car drive up a few minutes ago. It may have been Maria and Barney—"

"You go on. There are two guys I don't want to see right now, and MacNair and Gould are both of them. I'll stay here for a while. . . ."

VI

If Bernard Gould had not been so briskly executive, Michael thought unappreciatively, they might all be in their rooms by now. But he had personally ushered them into the lobby after pointing out that the hotel was constructed of huge reddish logs and that architecturally it very slightly resembled a French château.

Once in the lobby he called its best features to their attention and gestured toward social hall, dining room and bar. "And where," Michael inquired, "is the public bath? That is, if we can't have private ones?"

Mr. Coakley said soothingly that he could give Mr. and Mrs. Dundas a very good room on the third floor.

"Why not the second?" Gould demanded. "It may be rather warm on the third floor. That roof must be insulated before next year. Here, Pruett! Let's see where you're putting all of us."

After five minutes' critical scrutiny of the arrangements already made Gould handed down the opinion that Mrs. Alling had better have the room reserved for her brother but admitted the Dundases would have to go to the third floor.

"What we all need is to wash up and get outside a big steak," he said with what Michael considered an excess of joviality. "Then we— Oh, Stella, my dear."

Stella Gould smiled at them limpidly and presented a smooth ivory cheek for Gould's husbandly peck. A good many yards of sheer black only drew attention to the fact that she was encased in a carefully fitted under-slip. Under the lights her hair was palest gold, her skin flawless.

"'Icily regular, splendidly null,'" Michael murmured, regarding her without enthusiasm. Valerie thrust an admonitory elbow into his ribs and said: "How do you do?" as Gould introduced them.

Gould chose that moment to explain again why they had been delayed and did not omit the detail of Michael's having "pulled a gun on us. And he took his time about putting it back in the car. I've been called a highway robber but— Well, Bettina! I wondered where you were."

Bettina's smile could only be called dutiful, Valerie decided. She kissed Mrs. Alling's leathery cheek, and she and Geoffrey shook hands formally.

"Hullo, my dear. We finally got here," he said, which seemed to Valerie as inadequate as Bettina's polite:

"I'm so glad you did. But don't you want to go to your rooms and then have dinner?"

"If you only knew," Valerie began plaintively, "how much we do want to do both—"

But this was smothered by the Honorable Maria's sudden: "Is there any telegraph service here?"

"Oh yes. You have to use the telephone in my office," Coakley said. "But they take any message in Nevada City and also phone in any wires sent in care of Summit House."

Michael stooped and picked up their bags. "Would it," he said to Pruett, "be within your power or province to produce a room key? Almost any key will do, and we won't ask that you give us even a vague hint where this elusive room may be."

Mr. Pruett, a true desk clerk, was always impressed by rudeness. He promptly selected a key from the board behind him.

"I'll take you up myself," he said. "There isn't an elevator—just these stairs."

When he left them in a large front room, cool enough since the sun had set, Michael cast himself, full length, on one of the twin beds.

"*¡Dios!* What a day," he said briefly.

"Y-yes. Though this last hour or so has been rather interesting—except that it was tiresome of Mr. Gould to fuss so about unimportant details and want to show off his hotel."

"Besides holding court in the lobby, surrounded by his submissive family and admiring retainers," Michael said acidly. "I suppose it was to be expected that his ego would reassert itself speedily. Out there on the road it rested with me, not him, whether he sat there waiting for someone to bring gas to them or arrived here in time for dinner. Though he did make certain no more cars could ignore their distress signals."

"You didn't care much for his methods, did you?"

"I did not. If someone had come too fast around that curve he might have smashed into Mrs. Alling's car before he could stop. But Mr. Gould is an Important Man and mustn't be kept waiting by the roadside. If you want your dinner you'd better dress."

"I'm so hungry I'm not hungry any more." Valerie frowned into the suitcase she had packed assuming she would be at home tonight and wouldn't need anything that was in it. "I don't know what I'll wear. Everything's crushed or dirty."

She disappeared into the bathroom with a handful of clothing that was nothing worse than wrinkled. Michael closed his eyes but he did not doze and when Valerie turned off the water in the bathroom got up and began to unbutton his shirt.

Someone tried the bedroom door and then knocked. Michael jerked it open and found himself facing a thin, dark-haired woman. In spite of a look of frailty she would have been attractive if her expression had not been almost perpetually one of aggrieved discontent.

"Oh, so they put you in this awful room?" she said. "I suppose you're Mr. Dundas, the man who pulled a gun on Mr. Gould?" She laughed unpleasantly. "I'd like to see Barney explaining at the point of a gun. I'm Lilian Farnham. We had this room until this morning, and I think I left my compact here."

"Will you come in and look for it? We haven't really taken a good look about the place yet."

"Oh, of course we had the smaller room on the other side of the bathroom for our little girl," Mrs. Farnham said quickly, as if she considered it important that he should understand they were not people who must economize in any way. "But the compact wouldn't be in there. I suppose they've locked it off by now. I think Bettina Lawton is going to sleep there tonight. If you don't mind my looking in the bureau . . ."

She walked toward it but not so quickly that she did not have ample time to look over Valerie's toilet set and the lingerie and dresses she had tossed on chair and bed. She found a red compact in the top bureau drawer and held it up for Michael to see.

"It matches the dress I want to wear tonight. I suppose you will be down for the dance?"

"I have no hope that I won't."

"I'm sure Mr. Farnham would rather go to bed early. He isn't even in from fishing yet and expects to go out again tomorrow with Mr. MacNair—and I suppose Barney Gould, since he's turned up. But it's about time the management did something to entertain us. Why anyone would want to build a hotel in this God-forsaken spot—"

"It is near some rather interesting old mining towns," Michael said. "Columbia, Rough-and-Ready, San Juan—and not too far from Sierra City."

"Yes, they'll take you to those places, but who wants to look at that sort of thing? And the hotel is wretchedly run. But I suppose you want to get down to dinner, Mr. Dundas. I'll see you later."

"'Jealous hyena with an inferiority complex,'" Michael muttered, closing the door. Then he eased it open again as he heard Mrs. Farnham's voice from near the stairway.

"Well, Barney! What are you doing here?"

"I wanted to see if the Dundases are comfortable. I didn't know you were here with Ray, Lilian."

"I meant, what are you doing here at Summit House?—not, what are you doing on the third floor? I take it if you'd known I was here, too, you wouldn't have bothered to come up to keep an eye on Stella?"

"Don't be a fool—again," Gould said.

"I'm not but I'm not foolishly trusting either. I haven't, for instance, gone off to Palm Springs for two months this summer even if I should have for my health's sake. But your wife and my husband have been perfectly circumspect. I'll see you later—downstairs. . . ."

Michael closed the door hastily and locked it. When Gould knocked he said: "Who's there?" and let Gould make his inquiries from the hall.

"We are quite comfortable," he told him. "The room is satisfactory—or would be if we had it to ourselves. And we're dressing for dinner. . . ."

                                VII

He had just finished shaving when Valerie, struggling into her slip, invaded the bathroom to say that someone was trying to unlock their door.

"With a key," she specified. "Do you think—?"

"I think we'd have more privacy in the East Bay Terminal," Michael snapped. "A key, you say?"

He slung his shirt over his shoulders and opened the door again. Their third visitor was a man of about forty with a thin, clever face and dark, peaked eyebrows that gave him a look of rueful humor.

"Oh, I'm sorry," he said. "I'm Raymond Farnham—"

"And you thought this was still your room," Michael finished. "According to Mrs. Farnham, it was yours until this morning."

"I see." Farnham shrugged and put the room key into one of the wide pockets of his fishing jacket. "I've been fishing all day. Our party only got in and went straight to the bar as we always do. No one thought to tell me Mrs. Farnham has moved into different rooms. I suppose you don't know where they are?"

"I'm afraid I don't, except that they are probably on the second floor."

"Undoubtedly," Farnham said dryly. "Aren't you Michael Dundas? Some other lawyer introduced us once. It was— Good evening, Wallis. You should have come with us today. We all got the limit."

"I got the limit, too, right here." Peter's enunciation was a trifle fuzzy. "And all the poor fish aren't in streams. Hello, Michael. You're a hell of a friend, you are!"

"If you'll excuse me?" Farnham murmured, backing away from the door. Without waiting for an invitation Peter pushed past Michael into the bedroom.

"A hell of a friend," he repeated. "If it hadn't been for you old Gould and MacNair would still be sitting by the roadside."

"The story seems to be common property by now."

"Oh, sure. Gould makes out he thinks it was funny, you pulling a gun on him, but I'll bet he was plenty burned. He's a bloated plutocrat and a petty tyrant, that's what he is."

"Having given Mr. Gould such a good character, would you mind removing yourself? It's very nice meeting you here so unexpectedly—"

"But I'm not too surprised that he is here," Valerie said from the bathroom. "Go away, Peter. I wouldn't come out if I had a dress in here and could. We know Bettina is going to marry Mr. MacNair, but I'm too weak with hunger to care."

"Very well," Mr. Wallis said sadly. "I'll go."

"I have never heard that ancient line better delivered anywhere on stage or screen," Michael said. "And, for God's sake—do go!"

He slammed the door on Peter's heels, put on his shirt, combed his hair and slipped into a coat.

"You're as beautiful as you need to be, Valerie. Come here." He picked up the full-skirted silk jersey she had chosen to wear and slid it over her head.

"This isn't a room—it's a race track." He dealt quickly with the small covered buttons that ran all the way down the back of her bodice. "There. If I ever need a job I could no doubt qualify as a lady's maid on your recommendation."

He turned her about, straightened her belt and suddenly pulled her close and kissed her. "Because you don't talk to me when I'm in a bad humor, even if you do drag me off onto uncharted and perilous country roads— No, you don't need powder, and I do need black coffee—about four cups."

They were almost the last to leave the dining room. Gould, Stella and Bettina, Geoffrey and his sister were finishing their dinner as Michael and Valerie ordered theirs. When they came back into the lobby Gould had gathered his family and relatives, presumptive about him there.

The other hotel guests eyed them curiously and kept their distances, but the Honorable Maria, seeing Michael and Valerie, boomed out a hearty: "Come over here and sit down." She made room for Valerie between herself and Bettina on a large chesterfield, but Michael refused to sit down.

He leaned against a pillar where he had an excellent view of the entire group. The interest of the hotel's guests was naturally extended to include these new additions to the Gould party.

"Such an unusual-looking man," a graying but dreamy-eyed lady murmured to her companion. "So very dark, but that white triangle in his hair—I think he has *suffered*, don't you? And, my dear, those eyelashes!"

Fortunately Michael did not hear this or he would undoubtedly have at least severely wounded the romantic lady with a single look. He was watching Stella Gould. She was sitting in a high-backed chair, and, though you didn't feel she was consciously posing, any orthodox portrait painter could have set to work immediately without asking that she change her position in any way.

When a woman was as beautiful as Stella she was usually enclosed in an invisible picture frame, Michael thought. That is, if her beauty owed nothing to vivacity—and Stella's certainly did not. She smiled receptively whenever anyone threw a remark in her direction but returned nothing more than a throaty "Yes" or "No."

He glanced from Stella and Stella's black gown to the Honorable Maria and grinned. Mrs. Alling had donned what could only be called an evening garment. In color it was pale peach. It had

shoulder straps and it covered her. The same description would have applied equally well to a
nightgown.

"Yes, Mother, Geoff and I lived in Toronto the
year around," she was saying to Valerie. "My father was lucky enough to file claim to what turned
out to be several quite rich gold mines in the Por-
cupine and Kirkland Lake districts. One of them
was called the Golden Hope—"

"Oh, I see," Valerie said. "I'd heard your place
down the peninsula is called Esperanza de Oro
and I wondered—"

"That's it. Sheer sentimentality on my part. But
I was frightfully homesick for so long after I married Alling. Well, he was tubercular, poor chap.
Didn't live long, but by the time he died I'd got to
feel Esperanza de Oro was home. Then Geoff came
down to be near me after his— That is, about ten
years ago. He came to like California, and we're
both American citizens and— Hullo there, Ray.
Come over and sit down, you and Lilian."

Unfortunately her "Lilian" sounded merely a
polite afterthought. Mrs. Farnham blinked resentfully and said she didn't really think she cared to
sit down but was appeased when Geoffrey promptly gave up his seat to her.

"I have to go upstairs to see if our terrible
infant is really asleep," Farnham said. "I don't

want her sneaking downstairs when she hears the orchestra begin to play."

"Ray is determined Patty shan't be underfoot during the dance," Mrs. Farnham said. "Though I hope I've brought up my child to behave properly. . . ."

Farnham grinned. "I've been hearing how she indulged in a little archery practice in here yesterday with the bow and arrows I was foolish enough to give her. I understood she made a bull's-eye— with the night desk clerk for a target."

"Oh, he wasn't really hurt. And I don't see why she shouldn't watch the dancing for an hour or two. She's a talented little singer and dancer—"

"She's a precocious brat," Farnham said pleasantly. "And, while her parents may appreciate her talents, they shouldn't inflict them on anyone else."

"Really, Ray! Patty comes by her talent naturally. I would have gone on the stage if I hadn't married so young. I'd already gotten bits in Hollywood, because I lived there, though I always preferred the legitimate stage. And— Well, good heavens! Will you look at that?"

Michael looked at "that" and saw a muscular, tanned man coming down the stairway, wearing tight black trousers, a black silk shirt and half boots trimmed with silver.

"All he needs is a white horse to double for Hopalong Cassidy," Valerie murmured. "And two guns, of course, one on each hip—"

She stopped as Logan came up to them. "Hello," he said to the group in general. "The musicians are here. They're a local-talent gang, but I reckon they'll do. We expect several parties from outside and when they get here maybe we can get going."

"Yes—yes, of course," Gould said rather absently. "That's quite an outfit you have on, Tex."

"If Coakley wants me to play master of ceremonies I might as well dress the part. I'll see if I can herd some of these folks into the ballroom. It might encourage 'em if you-all made the first move."

"You see?" Mrs. Farnham said as Logan walked away. "He gives the impression he's your equal and has known you for years. He does seem to know you, Barney."

"Of course he does," Gould said impatiently. "I was here last week end. I agree with Coakley that Logan's a useful man to have around. This year, at least. You can't have too large a staff in a hotel like this its first season and expect to break even."

"According to the other men here, Logan is a Jack-of-all-trades but master of a surprising number of them," Farnham said. "An excellent fisherman and horseman, among other things. I haven't talked to him much myself—only yesterday afternoon when he took some of us fishing. I got the idea he may have done some soldiering—"

"Oh, a soldier?" Mrs. Farnham looked thoughtfully at Stella Gould. "That's—interesting, isn't it?"

"Very likely I'm mistaken about that," her husband said hastily. "Men like Logan aren't often
communicative about themselves, except indirectly. And I must go upstairs and pacify that youngster if she is still awake."

Mr. Coakley came out of a door across the lobby marked "OFFICE."

"Here's a telegram for you, Mr. MacNair," he
said, holding out a yellow envelope. "I took it
down over the phone. I put it in an envelope to
make it look businesslike," he added naively, "and
in case I couldn't locate you right away."

"Thank you." Geoffrey took the envelope, hesitated briefly and ripped it open. "Will you excuse
me?"

He turned his back on the group, and they
were immediately bound by one of those silences
that come when everyone is trying so hard not to
appear curious that no one is able immediately
to fabricate any harmless small talk. Finally the
Honorable Maria looked away from her brother's
tweed shoulders and addressed Gould.

"I'd like to have a look at the nearest of those
old mining camps we were talking about."

"You might find Columbia interesting," Gould
said. "It—"

Geoffrey turned to face them again, looked at his sister, nodded slightly and thrust the telegram into a pocket.

"I'd like to take a turn about the grounds before the dancing begins," he said abruptly.

"May I come with you?" Bettina asked.

"Of course. But shouldn't you have a wrap? It may be coolish outside."

"I'll be warm enough." Bettina slipped her arm through his. "We won't stay out too long."

They went off together. Valerie got to her feet in time to see Peter Wallis, standing at the foot of the stairway, scowling after them.

"I'm going to our room for a while, Michael," she said. "Do you want to come with me?"

Michael nodded and when they had reached the stairway remarked: "Peter went into the bar after registering grief and despair. I suppose that by the time the dancing begins he'll be—"

The lobby was suddenly invaded by seven or eight couples, few of them older than twenty, and all of them very noisy. The girls wore full-skirted cotton frocks, the men tight blue jeans and gaudy shirts. They swarmed about Mr. Coakley, clamoring to know when the dancing would begin.

Michael, watching them from the stairway, sighed. "The young are so exhausting. These may not know the steps but they will certainly like the exercise."

VIII

At a little after eleven o'clock Mr. Coakley came up to Michael and Valerie where they were sitting near the ballroom's side door.

"Mr. Gould thinks it would be nice to show these youngsters a dance or two done like it really should be done."

"Why?" Michael said. "The youngsters seem to be enjoying themselves. If they don't mind that they seldom manage to follow the prompter's instructions, why should we?"

"Well"—Coakley looked over his shoulder at the dancers waltzing to the strains of "Love's Dream After the Ball"—"yes, but Mr. Gould thinks it would be nice. Mr. and Mrs. Farnham, Mrs. Gould and her sister know what it's all about. Gould says you two do, too, and so does Mr. Wallis."

Coakley lowered his voice, worrying his walrus mustache. "Wallis says he was in New England once and knows all the contry and quadrille steps. So maybe it's better not to try to keep him from dancing. That makes seven, and Tex Logan will fill in, and Mr. Gould will call. So if you'll come over—they'll help us out, Mr. Gould."

"Well, what will it be?" Logan said. "Sally Goo-din? Down the Center and Split the Ring?"

"We danced Sally Goodin in El Paso last summer," Bettina said, "but it's rather complicated—"

"Well, how about Ring, Ring?" Logan said. "It's simple. Maybe we better cut out the preliminaries —you know, 'Honor your partner, lady on the side' and so on. They're supposed to come before every dance, but it might just mix these amatoors up."

"All set?" Gould said. "Music!" He began in the stentorian singsong of the practiced caller:

"First couple out to couple on the right form a ring! Ring, ring, pretty little ring! Break that ring with a corner swing! Ring, ring, pretty little ring! Break that ring and your partner swing! Circle four! Two little ladies dos-à-dos! Half promenade and circle four! Pick up six. . . ."

They began sedately enough, but the music, the cadence of the prompter's voice and the precise movements of the dance slowly took hold of them. By the time Gould stopped for breath and the musicians dropped their instruments half the audience was stamping and clapping in time to the music.

"Good!" Gould said. "I never saw it better done by the Ranger Club in El Paso."

Farnham bowed ceremoniously. "But we'd do even better if Stella didn't have a little trouble making up her mind which is her corner and which her taw," he said teasingly.

"Taw?" Stella repeated.

"Your partner, dear," Lilian Farnham said condescendingly. She had already proved herself to be a much better dancer than Stella. There was color in her sallow face, and at the moment she looked neither peevish nor discontented. "'Seesaw your pretty little taw.' Or 'do the same to your own little doll.' I was at Storowton in Massachusetts one summer and heard Happy Hale call. He's supposed to be one of the best in the country and he called a quadrille—"

"Whatever your partner is called, I still have to look to see which hand my wedding ring is on to tell my left hand from my right," Stella said.

"Her left hand knoweth not what her right hand doeth," Logan drawled. "Want to try another?"

"I like Cast Off Six," Mrs. Farnham said. "Or Morning Star or Portland Fancy—"

"I don't know them last two," Logan said indifferently. "Guess they never got down our way. How's about Sashay Halfway Round?"

Michael dropped back from the group and lighted a cigarette, waiting for them to come to some agreement. He was instantly aware that

Bettina and Peter were standing behind him, talking together, though Bettina's voice was always soft and very low and Peter was trying to maintain a cautious whisper. This put him at a disadvantage, as he always assumed that he could win any argument by talking loudly.

". . . no reason why you can't. No one will notice," he said. "And you aren't a child to be sent off to bed if people don't like what you do. And for two cents I'd tell 'em so!"

"That's what I'm afraid of. It won't do any good, Peter, but I'll try to slip out if you'll try to—to be discreet."

"All right. I'll wander off, and everyone will think I'm in the bar. The musicians should take a rest around midnight, and maybe there will be something to eat then. You should be able to get away—say, a few minutes after midnight. I've thought of something since this afternoon that might—"

"We'll make it a waltz quadrille," Gould announced. "You and Geoff get in this one, Maria."

"I rather fancy I remember the old waltz quadrille," Mrs. Alling said. "Come on, Geoff. I'll be your partner."

"Give us a good waltz," Gould told the orchestra. "All set? Now you waltz down the center and now you divide! The lady goes right, and the gent the other side! Now honor your partner and don't be afraid—to swing on the corner with a waltz promenade! Come on! Next couple out. . . ."

Gould and the musicians seemed tireless, and it was Stella who finally put an end to the dance by dropping out of it.

"I'm too tired to go on," she murmured plaintively. "I want a drink, Bernard."

"What? Well, it is warm work," Gould conceded. "Maybe Mr. Dundas will take you to get a drink, and I'll organize these young people."

"I'd be glad to," Mr. Dundas said untruthfully. "Will you come with us, Valerie?"

"I want fresh air, not a drink." Valerie smiled at him unsympathetically and moved toward the door. She was surprised to find Tex Logan at her elbow.

"Maybe you'd like to set outside awhile?" he said. "There's a bench out that-a-way. . . ."

"It sounds inviting but as if it might very probably be occupied."

Logan grinned. "Later on, I reckon. The gang is still interested in dancin' now."

Gould's voice, calling "First couple out, balance and swing! Down center and split the ring," floated after them as they walked around the curve of the path from the side door of the ballroom to the bench against the pine tree.

"They haven't put up lights here," Logan said. "But they'd just draw a lot of insects anyway."

"I like it best this way." Valerie sat down on the bench and leaned back against the tree trunk. She was again surprised when Logan remained standing.

"Won't you sit down? Though I suppose I should allow you to remain in that respectful attitude?"

Logan laughed and sat down. "Thanks. I reckon somebody's said I'm not too respectful. It ain't in me, for one thing, and it's part of a job like this to hand out a line to the women. But you aren't the kind of girl that would ever chase after lifeguards or dude wranglers or hotel musicians. And I know a thing or two about husbands and I wouldn't want to tangle with that one of yours."

"Why?" Valerie said. "You're taller and much larger than he is."

"That don't count in the long run. I'd size him up as the kind that wouldn't mind layin' for you five years as long as he got you in the end—maybe because I got a long mem'ry, too, and don't mind evening up old scores when I can."

"In that respect you resemble each other. What part of Texas are you from? I suppose you're tired of being asked that, but, even without knowing your nickname, I'd still know you were from Texas. We've been visiting the Allans in Brookdale. He's sheriff over there but he was born in Texas."

"Sure 'nuf? Does he spell his last name with two
*a*s? There was an old fellow in Gillespie County
named Robert Edward Lee Allan—"

"That's Rocky's father. Did you know him?"

"No, what I recollect him by was that they
struck oil on his place where oil shouldn't have
been at all. I reckon ever'body aroun' San Anton'
knew about that."

"I know the Allans went to San Antonio often.
Do you know it well?"

"Oh, I've been in and aroun' it a lot."

"Isn't that where Fort Sam Houston is?"

Logan eyed her thoughtfully. "Sure, Fort Sam's
there. Best army post in the U.S. If you want to
know about Fort Sam— But why would you? I was
born in Amarillo but I've been lots of places since
then: United States, Mexico, even Canada."

"And had different jobs in all of them?" Valerie
suggested.

"Just about. I've even been a cowboy extra in
Hollywood, besides workin' in hotels, garages,
gamblin' joints. As a matter of fact, I haven't been
in Texas for quite a spell. I'll be headin' back
someday. It always seems kind of funny to me
when people just stay put where they was born. I
guess it runs in our family to have an itchin' foot.
One reason I came out here— Seems like your
husband's huntin' for you."

"I thought you'd be somewhere outside," Michael said, appearing around the curve of the path. "Will you come in, my dear, so that I won't have to dance again with Mrs. Gould? She is a very beautiful woman, but, as you so suggestively remarked, Mr. Logan, her left hand knoweth not what her right hand doeth."

"Why 'suggestively'?" Logan asked, unabashed.

"Isn't the left hand the one on which her wedding ring reposes? However, if you would substitute 'feet' for 'hands' I'd agree with you. And Coakley wonders where you are. It seems our audience would like to see us do Ring, Ring again."

"You do me a good turn and tell Coakley you didn't see me? I'll set here and smoke and then maybe I'll feel like dancin' some more. I've had to go the rounds, seein' there's too many extra women. And, speaking of feet, the Honorable Maria may be light on hers but she sure is heavy on yours."

"The— Yes, I've noticed that too," Michael said.

He took Valerie's arm and walked with her back to the hotel without saying anything more. She saw, as they stepped into the brilliantly lighted room again, that he was frowning.

"What is it? I assure you Mr. Logan was nothing more than entertaining."

"What? Oh, then it wasn't around the corner and under the tree the gallant cowboy made love to me? That hadn't occurred to me, and if it had, I'm quite certain you're perfectly capable of taking care of yourself. What time is it?"

"Almost midnight. Will they feed us?"

"There will be light refreshments in the dining room whenever the musicians decide to rest."

"Good. Let's dance this—"

The orchestra was playing another waltz, and the younger set and a fair number of hotel guests were dancing. Peter had disappeared along with the Goulds, the Farnhams and the Honorable Maria. Only Bettina and Geoffrey were still in the room, sitting the dance out.

That much Valerie noted as they circled the floor once. A minute later two couples near them suffered a rear-end collision. Immediately one of them raised the cry: "Boops-a-Daisy!" It was enthusiastically echoed by all the younger dancers, and in five minutes everyone was booping vigorously.

Even guests who had so far been merely onlookers were whisked from their seats and persuaded to boop. The floor became crowded, and the dance degenerated to the point where it consisted mainly of forcible collision with anyone who was in a position for a rear-guard action. This impromptu shindy lasted perhaps ten minutes and ended as suddenly as it had begun.

The elderly and middle-aged staggered weakly to their seats while the young leaned on one another's shoulders and giggled. Michael, having found Valerie again, assured her Coca-Cola was to be had at the bar and started her toward it.

The lobby was nearly deserted. An elderly bellboy was dozing in a corner, and Mr. Pruett was not behind his desk. The front doors onto the porch were open, and Peter Wallis came through them before Valerie and Michael had turned into the bar.

Peter had his arm about Bettina Lawton, half carrying her. His hand left a red smudge on her white dress.

She looked down at it, shuddered, and her head fell forward as Peter shouted:

"That fellow Logan's been stabbed out there by that pool. He's lying face down in it. . . . For God's sake, why doesn't somebody do something!"

PART TWO

They called Bean to view the body.
  First he took a drink of toddy,
Then he listed all the things the dead
  man had.

* * *

Said Roy Bean: "You'll learn a lesson,
  for you have a Smith and Wesson,
And to carry implements of war is
  wrong."

Roy Bean

I

The county sheriff, Alfred Payne, was in his late forties, tall, but well upholstered with solid fat. His first remark to Mr. Coakley was: "Shucks, Ben, it's too bad anything like this had to happen," and his second: "Did you move the body?"

"No," Coakley said gloomily. "The fellow that found it did—a little. I guess you want him to tell you about that himself. You want to see the body first?"

"Might as well. You know Doc Hill, the cor'ner, Ben? Come along with us, Doc. You two"—he spoke to two young deputies—"go inside and talk nice to people. Tell them we'll turn 'em loose or let them go to bed soon's we can. All right, Ben."

They were standing on the porch. Coakley turned and led the way down the steps, explaining:

"This path goes round the side of the hotel like you see, through the trees here, and there's been no lights put up on this side yet. . . ."

"Yep, I see." Payne produced a large flashlight. "An' the path divides here—"

"Yes. If you take this right branch you come to a bench in a bunch of trees. That's where Logan was last seen. A Mr. and Mrs. Dundas left him sitting there. There's another path that leads from the bench to the side door of the ballroom. But you can't see that door from the bench—or the bench from the door—because there's a little curve in the path."

"But he wasn't found dead at this bench?"

"No. This left branch of the path leads to a pool, and you'll see how it's located in reference to that bench where Logan was last seen. And here he is."

Logan's body lay face down, head and neck in the water. Payne's flashlight picked out the dark handle of a knife between Logan's shoulders.

"Nice, neat job," he commented. "Any idea where the knife came from?"

"From a display we've got on one of the walls of the lobby. Anyone could get at it, with the lobby almost empty since the dance began. The knife was there at five this afternoon. I was looking over the display with one of the guests then."

"Well, I'll leave you here, Doc," Payne said. "I'll send one of the boys out to help you. Where you want us to put him, Ben?"

"We can spare the ballroom better than any other room, and you can carry him in at the side door. Now look, Fred. This pool is about on a line with that bench I spoke of. And the bench is going to come up in people's stories. . . ."

He pointed to the trees and shrubbery at the right of the path where they stood. "It's only about a hundred yards through there to the back of the bench. We haven't cut a path through, but you can tell people have broken a trail through there from the bench over to here."

"Just tonight, you mean?"

"No, I noticed the other day they had done that and thought we'd better cut a path through to save folks steps. The way it is now, if you don't want to go through the brush, they got to go back to where the path divides to get from that bench to this pool."

"Well, I guess I got the necessary g'ography in my mind," Payne said. "Let's go inside."

"We've already roped off the people from outside the hotel," Coakley said as they turned back. "They're mostly just kids—about twenty-eight of them, mostly from Grass Valley and Nevada City, so you'll know a lot of them."

"I probably won't have to keep them more than a minute or two. Where can I set up shop?"

"My office—no, that's pretty small. You'll be wanting coffee and sandwiches, and there's plenty of those in the dining room. You'd better move in there."

"All right. Send the gang from outside in, about ten at a time," Payne said, stepping into the lobby and beckoning to his deputies. "Dodge, you go help Doc Hill. You come with me, Briggs."

Bernard Gould got up from the lounge where he had been talking to Farnham. "Well, Coakley? Is this the sheriff? I hope he approves of the way I've—we've—handled matters?"

"Uh—yes, of course." Coakley glanced uneasily from Gould to the sheriff, as if uncertain to which he owed allegiance. "Fred, this is Mr. Gould. Sheriff Payne, Mr. Gould."

"Yes. I wanted a word with you about my young sister-in-law. . . ."

Gould accompanied the sheriff, Coakley and the deputy, Briggs, into the dining room, and the doors closed behind them. Presently Coakley came out, but not Gould. Coakley went into the bar and reappeared in an instant, herding some ten or twelve of a rather subdued younger set toward the dining room.

"I think," Michael said, "that we will soon be ushered into the presence. Remember what I told you?"

"Wide eyed, girlish and rather dumb," Valerie said. "Don't volunteer any information. Yes, I remember. But is that an order?"

"That's an order. This is one of those times when you are supposed to remember that I'm nine years older than you are and that the word 'obey' was not omitted from our marriage service."

"But you're not unreasonable enough to refuse to tell the reason for your order?"

"You should guess that I don't much like your having been the last person but one to talk to Logan."

"If you leave yourself out of it. But I don't see that anything he said could be important or incriminate anyone."

"Perhaps not," Michael said. They had one corner of the lobby to themselves. It had been some time since anyone had tried to discuss the murder with them, as there was no one in the hotel quite hardy enough to be impervious to Michael's unadulterated rudeness. He went on:

"But if it's known he talked to you about his past life someone might get the notion he told you more than he did or be afraid that in time you might suddenly realize you'd overlooked some significant remark of Logan's."

"It's possible. Murderers do get panicky. I did ask Mr. Logan about Fort Sam Houston because I wondered if Mr. Farnham was right in thinking Mr. Logan had been in the army."

"Yes, that was 'interesting'—as Mrs. Farnham remarked, looking at Mrs. Gould. Because I remember now that, according to Peter, Stella and Bettina are army brats."

Valerie nodded. "Only, Bettina lived with a grandmother in California until about two years ago. How old do you think Mr. Logan was?"

"Oh, at least thirty-five. And the sovereign state of Texas does keep cropping up. It's a pity I interrupted you just as Logan was, apparently, about to tell you at least one reason why he happened to wander into this state."

"I thought he also started to tell me to ask someone here about Fort Sam Houston if I wanted to know more about it," Valerie said. "Stella Gould, perhaps? But, of course, it isn't just the Texas connection you have to consider if you're looking for connections."

"No. Logan told you he'd even been in Canada, didn't he? Besides having done time in Hollywood, where Mrs. Farnham once lived. He didn't say how long ago he was there. But, speaking of Canada—"

"Yes?"

"Oh, you were watching MacNair and the Honorable Maria when he read that wire. I thought they both found it a trifle upsetting. Apparently just a nod from him was enough to tell her what was in the wire."

"And isn't there something else—that you noticed before I did?"

"The fact that Logan referred to Mrs. Alling as 'the Honorable Maria'?" Michael said. "Yes. She hasn't been here long enough for the nickname to be common property, since it isn't a name you ever use to her in direct address. But if she and MacNair knew Logan they gave no sign they did when he came over to speak to all of us this evening."

"Neither did he give any sign he knew them. And Bettina strikes me as being in love with Peter but engaged to Geoffrey, and that doesn't make sense. Very likely it isn't important, so far as the murder is concerned," Valerie said. "But if Geoffrey had been killed instead of Mr. Logan you'd think it was all very simple."

"Yes, or if Gould, Farnham or even either of their wives had been killed it would still be fairly

simple. From overhearing Mrs. Farnham talking
to Gould, I take it those four might be arranged
in various ways to form a triangle. But it was
Logan who was killed, and offhand you can't think
of any motive for his death except that he was
blackmailing someone here. And perhaps had been
doing so even before he came here."

"Well, perhaps the sheriff will discover that one
of the maids here had come to love Mr. Logan not
wisely but too well," Valerie said. "That would be
simple and easy. . . ."

"I imagine the sheriff will try to take the easiest way out. Logan was no one of importance.
Gould is, and the sheriff and Coakley seem to be
old friends. I don't think Payne will try to hold
everyone here for several days while he checks
and double checks their statements. He might get
somewhere if he did, but I—"

Coakley approached them apologetically.
"Would you step into the dining room now?"
he asked. "The sheriff would like to talk to you
next. . . ."

                              II

"We've got your name," Payne said, "but not your
occupation and address."

Michael hesitated, glancing toward Briggs, a
husky towhead who was acting as stenographer.

Briggs's shorthand was the muscular variety, achieved by the sweat of a furrowed brow and with his tongue between his teeth. It was doubtful that the word *"couturier"* was included in his vocabulary or that he could spell it if he knew its meaning. Michael smiled sourly and yielded to necessity.

"Dressmaker," he said.

"Hunh?" said Mr. Payne.

"Dressmaker. I own a shop called Gisele's. G-i-s-e-l-e. In San Francisco. Residence, 75 Russian Hill Place. It was my pleasure this afternoon to play good Samaritan to Mr. Gould, Mrs. Alling and Mr. MacNair. We were coming from Brookdale by a roundabout route. In Brookdale we had visited the Rocky Allans, or, if you prefer, the N. B. Allans. We—"

"Shucks, why didn't you say you was a friend of Rocky's?" Payne broke in. "I know now who you are—the guy that helped him break the Armstrong kidnaping case back in 'thirty-eight."

"He says I did. But I wasn't certain you aren't the sheriff he doesn't get on with."

"Naw, that's old Fordley. Him and Rocky had a little set-to over a question of jur'diction once. Well, of course you never seen Logan before you come here this afternoon. By the way, Ben, how did you happen to hire Logan?"

"We needed someone to help keep the guests amused," Coakley said glibly. "We feature riding, not having put in a swimming pool yet, so we wanted someone who knew horses and maybe was a good mechanic, besides acting as a guide, fishing and hunting. And if we keep open this winter, like Mr. Gould thinks maybe we will, with the interest there is in winter sports now and the Auburn Ski Club just down the line—"

"Yeah, you'll need someone who can ski too," Payne said patiently. "Anything else?"

"Oh, we wanted someone who could get people to dance and lead singing and— Well, I ran into Logan in Grass Valley. He'd come up looking for work in the mines. I got to talking to him, and he seemed just what we needed, so I took a chance and hired him. His real name was William Travis Logan, but we all called him Tex. He was here a little over three weeks, and all he ever really told me about himself was that he was born in Texas," Mr. Coakley said firmly.

"Don't you get the names of your employees' nearest relations, Ben?"

"Well, I should and I intended to but I just never seemed to get around to it," Coakley said apologetically. The apology was for Gould, who was looking at him disapprovingly.

"I see," Payne said. "Well now, you and your husband seem to be the last people who talked to Logan, Mrs. Dundas. What 'd you talk about?"

"Oh, the dancing," Mrs. Dundas said vaguely. "And about there not being any lights outside."

"Was that all?"

Valerie pouted. She thought she did it rather well, though she saw Michael flinch, watching her.

"He paid me a few compliments as part of his regular routine. Then my husband appeared, and we went back to the dance and left Mr. Logan sitting on the bench. That was just before midnight. I remember that because," Valerie said plaintively, "I was hungry then."

The sheriff grinned. "Have a san'wich now." He gestured toward a long table. "There's heaps there, and coffee keeping hot. Will you get this young Wallis and Miss Lawton, Ben? Now, Mrs. Dundas, why didn't Logan go back to the dance with you?"

Valerie returned to the official table with the sandwich of her choice. "He said he was tired."

"Then you didn't have any idea he might be waitin' to meet someone at that bench?"

"Not then," Valerie said thoughtfully.

"But you have since? What do you say, Dundas?"

Michael poured a second cup of coffee. "It seems possible now that he may have expected to meet someone at that bench—but he wasn't killed there."

"He could 've got over to the pool in less than no time, even goin' the most roundabout way," Payne said. "If he went the nearest way—through the trees and brush back of the bench—there may be some leaves or somethin' sticking to his pants."

"But you left him a little before midnight? Say, five minutes to? And I understand from these kids I let go home that about midnight they started some fool dance that lasted over ten minutes."

"'Boops-a-Daisy,' they called it," Gould said. "I'd been in the bar and when they began shouting that I glanced into the ballroom—"

"And seeing how eagerly the lobsters and the turtles all advanced, did you wait upon the shingle or did you go and join the dance?" Michael said.

Payne grinned. Mr. Gould did not. "No, I went out and around to the garage by the driveway on the other side of the hotel than the one where the pool is. I wanted to see if the men we sent for Mrs. Alling's car had returned with it. There was no one on duty at the garage. We must investigate that, Coakley. There should have been a man there."

"Surely," Michael said blandly, "Mrs. Alling's car must have been salvaged and in the garage long before midnight. I asked if you joined in the Boops-a-Daisy because I noticed before it began that you and Mrs. Gould, Mr. and Mrs. Farnham and Mrs. Alling were not in the ballroom."

Gould scowled at him. "I suppose, since we weren't on the dance floor, we must account for ourselves. My wife, Mrs. Alling and Farnham went upstairs to their rooms after we all left the ballroom together about eleven-fifty."

"Not to go to bed?" Payne asked.

"No. Mrs. Alling wanted to get her knitting. British War Relief, you know. And, I suppose," Gould continued, striving hard for joviality, "my wife thought she needed to powder her nose. She complained she'd gotten hot dancing. She doesn't like that.

"Well—Farnham went to look in at their youngster. Mrs. Farnham said she was tired, so she sat down in the lobby. The desk clerk, Pruett, was in the office, I believe. There was a bellboy over in one corner, but he was half asleep—"

"And ever'one else almost was dancing, and the floor was crowded," Payne said. "But when did you-all come back to the lobby?—or did you?"

"Mrs. Gould didn't come down at all. She can easily spend half an hour powdering her nose. Mrs. Farnham says she got tired of waiting and decided to go upstairs after all. She and Farnham came back down together, and Mrs. Alling just after them. That was just after I got back. I came up the front steps hardly a minute after young Wallis brought my sister-in-law in and began shouting that Logan had been killed. And it seems to me about time you talked to—"

Peter came in, alone and sober, though the scent of Four Roses hung round him still and his hair glistened as if he had spent some time under a water faucet.

"I suppose you want my story?" he said truculently. "Though Gould took it on himself to question me—

"Oh, you'd better tell it to me yourself, son," Payne said, mildly. "Go ahead."

"Well, I left the dance floor about a quarter of twelve. I went in the bar and had a drink. That took about ten minutes. Gould came in—so I went out. I came through the lobby, went outside and just walked around."

"Where?" the sheriff asked. "I take it you ended up at the pool?"

"Well, I was a little high. I thought I'd better walk and take my time. I went around the other side of the hotel back to the garage and stables."

"You had the start of me, but it's odd I didn't see you," Gould said. "Was there anyone about the garage when you were there?"

"I didn't see anyone. I just kept on going, all the way round the back of the hotel. That will finally bring you to that bench, you know. I went past that and on down to where the path divides and along its left branch to the pool. Where else is there to walk around here except—?"

"He was going to meet me at the pool," Bettina said, coming into the room.

She had taken off the white dress Peter's hand had stained but hadn't bothered to renew her make-up. Even her lips were pale, and the muscles under her eyes nervously tense.

"Peter probably thinks he is protecting me," she went on, "but I had to have some reason to go to that pool—alone—didn't I?"

"Bettina! Look, I didn't think about that. I mean, I thought maybe you wouldn't want me to say—"

Bettina glanced at him enigmatically, took the chair Coakley presented and turned it so that her back was to Peter.

"Peter asked me to meet him outside when I could leave the dance floor without its being too—too noticeable. We thought the dancing might stop at midnight, but it didn't. But Peter had said a few minutes after midnight. So," Bettina said, flushing, not looking at Gould, "I asked my fiancé to go up to my room and get a wrap for me so we could walk about outside.

"It—it wasn't a nice thing to do, because I told him my room wasn't locked, and it was. But he went. I told him I'd wait outside the ballroom door but I didn't. I ran along the path to the bench. I'm sure there was no one there. I was afraid Peter was waiting and would—would—"

"Get impatient and come and drag you out by the hair," Mr. Wallis growled. "Well, I could hear the music still playing and I walked to give you time and keep from getting impatient. I know I was making a pest of myself," he added repentantly.

"If you think it is important to verify the fact that these two did agree to meet outside, I can do that," Michael said. "I overheard them arranging to do so."

"Well, then! I think Bettina's part in it is certainly clear enough," Gould said. "And she's already had about all she can stand tonight."

"I'm not half so fragile as people seem to think. I'm all right!" Bettina said with surprising impatience. "I only fainted because I saw the mark Peter's hand made on my dress, and you know I get sick when I see blood. I was going to tell you that I ran past the bench, down to where the path divides and to the pool that way. When I got there—"

"When she got there I was kneeling down and had just pulled Logan out of the water by his shoulders," Peter said. "I said: 'He must have had some kind of fit.' Then I saw the knife. I had sense enough not to touch it but I got blood on my hands. His shirt was—wet. But it was black, you know. I eased him back into the water and said: 'He's been stabbed. Let's get out of here.' Is that right?"

"That's exactly as I remember it," Bettina said.

"What about Mr. MacNair?" Payne asked. "When did he come downstairs again?"

"Bettina's room is on the third floor," Gould said quickly. "It must have been after midnight when you sent him to—uh—get your wrap, Bettina."

"I—I suppose it was. Y-yes, it must have been—"

"The—uh—Boops-a-Daisy began about midnight," Michael said helpfully.

"Oh, of course. Yes, it had just begun, and I saw they wouldn't be stopping for a while, so I thought I'd better not wait. That—that was what you meant, Barney? I'm a little confused. . . ."

"Yes, that was what I meant." Gould rewarded her with a paternal smile. "Geoff probably had quite a time getting out of the ballroom if that dance had begun and—"

"You must have watched the dance only just an instant yourself or you'd have been apt to see if he did," Payne said with what Michael was beginning to consider deceptive mildness. "I'll talk to MacNair later. I suppose there's some back stairs to this place?"

"From the second to the first floor," Coakley said uneasily. "They end in a sort of linen-and-supply room—"

"I'll get around to that later. And there's all the hidin' places in the world outside," Payne remarked. "All you got to do is step off the paths and keep quiet."

He eyed Peter benevolently. "It's just as well Mr. Dundas heard you arrangin' to meet Miss Lawton, son. Because I can't imagine you makin' a date with Logan for the same place. Did you like the guy?"

"No. And if he knew Bettina and I were going to meet outside and where I wouldn't put it past him to snoop around just on general principles."

"What do you think about that, Miss Lawton?"

"I—I don't know. He was inclined to be impertinent. And he was curious. He asked me questions about the Farnhams after they arrived and about my sist— Oh, nothing important."

"What did he want to know about Stella?" Gould demanded.

"Oh, j-just was she much older than I am," Bettina stammered. "He'd heard someone say she was.

Of course he had no right to ask, but—but people can't believe she's in her thirties."

"I haven't seen Mrs. Gould yet," Payne said. "But—well, you can go, Miss Lawton. You, too, Mrs. Dundas. And Mr. Wallis. I'd kind of like to have you stick around awhile, Mr. Dundas. I like all the help I can get."

"If Mr. Gould doesn't mind, I'd like to," Michael said. He added to Valerie as he opened the door for her: "Lock the bedroom door, my dear. And don't wander off into dark places alone."

III

Valerie locked the bedroom door, investigated the windows and saw that there was no ledge under them to give anyone a foothold there. She turned down the beds and went into the bathroom.

She had just finished washing her face when she remembered that Mrs. Farnham had said that she thought Bettina was sleeping tonight in the room the Farnhams had had for their daughter. It would be on the other side of this bathroom, and the door into it must be locked off, though she hadn't tried it at any time when she'd been in the bathroom.

She tried it now cautiously. Some of Mrs. Farnham's complaints regarding service in the hotel seemed justified. The door was not locked, though after it had slid open perhaps three inches it struck some sort of barrier.

Valerie closed one eye and put the other to the gap. She saw what she thought was the back of a bureau and its mirror and guessed that the furniture in the room had been rearranged before Bettina moved into it.

But what interested her more was the fact that Geoffrey MacNair's voice came to her so clearly. ". . . hear that noise?" he was saying.

"I didn't hear anything. You're a bit nervy, old boy. I am myself and have been for days. And I'm old enough that I should have known there's no use planning too far ahead. Human nature doesn't change, and you certainly can't know what a—a madman is going to do."

"But we hoped, even when we had the first letter, that it would never come to this. And after all these years—"

"It was always possible it might happen, though we never talked of it," the Honorable Maria said. "And I'd nearly forgotten. You are thinking of Bettina, too, aren't you?"

"Well, I do love her—very—very much, you know. I'm certain I could make her happy, though I know she isn't too keen on marrying me. But now— We don't know how this will turn out, though there seems no immediate danger that—

Isn't that someone in the hall? Perhaps Barney is coming to bed. . . ."

"Whoever it is has gone on. But we'd better take Bettina's things down to Stella's room. Barney didn't like it too well when I said Bettina shouldn't be alone tonight and he'd better sleep here—at first. When he thought it over he agreed with me heartily. Take the suitcases, Geoff. Careful—they aren't well packed. I'll carry her dresses."

They moved toward the door, but apparently Geoffrey stopped his sister before they reached it.

"Maria, what did you do after you left the dance and came up to your room?"

"I looked out for my knitting and washed my hands, to put it politely. And thought a bit. I was in no hurry to get back to the dancing."

"Oh. Well, I fancy I'm going to be asked why I was so long coming downstairs when I found at once that Bettina's door was locked and I couldn't get her wrap. I realized then that she must have wanted to get me out of the way. She needn't have done that, but young Wallis was making a nuisance of himself. I thought I'd allow her to handle things her own way and didn't hurry downstairs again. Besides, I had a beastly headache and stopped in my own room for some aspirins."

"Did you?" the Honorable Maria said politely. "I didn't hear you. But I daresay I can forget to

tell the sheriff that when he sees that our rooms
are next door to each other. Bring those suitcases
along down, and if Bettina doesn't need me again
I'm going to turn in. . . ."

Valerie closed the bathroom door, locked it and
went back into the bedroom. She sat down at the
writing table, found the usual wobbly pen and
bottle of pale ink and jotted down every word she
could remember of the conversation she had just
overheard.

She regarded the result discontentedly, though
she thought it was a sufficiently accurate report of
the MacNair-Alling dialogue.

"If I'd only begun to listen in five minutes
earlier," she muttered. "And it seems to me that
the first and last parts of their conversation don't
match. I'm not certain why. Perhaps Michael can
tell me."

She put the notes under her pillow, undressed
swiftly and in five minutes was asleep.

Michael, who had remained with the court of
inquiry mainly to annoy Gould, was soon regret-
ting this laudable impulse. Payne remarked:

"I take it Miss Lawton's engaged to MacNair and
Wallis ain't too happy about it?" And when Gould
nodded he began questioning Coakley about the
servants.

Mr. Coakley hastened to assure Mr. Payne of the collective virtues of the hotel staff, also to explain that only Pruett slept in the hotel.

"There's very nice quarters built onto the garage, but Pruett seemed to think it wasn't dignified for him to sleep out there with the rest of 'em. So when Logan came I put him in with Pruett. And we haven't any waitresses under forty, and none of them good looking," Coakley added practically. "Even if they weren't all good, respectable girls."

"You mean Logan wouldn't have wasted any time on them?" Payne asked.

"That's it. Of course, you'll have to question them, but I imagine the ones on duty must have been working together, and those that were hanging round just to watch the fun would be in the kitchen or dining room too."

"Well, I'll stay the night here so's I can get at them and the guests early tomorrow. Only, it's really today I mean, isn't it?"

The coroner, a small man, dry and brown as a dead leaf, came in with the other deputy, Dodge.

"There wasn't anything in the guy's pockets but the usual odds and ends," Dodge said. "But he did have two hundred bucks in twenties in his billfold. I put it all in envelopes. No prints on the knife."

"But a few bits of brush sticking to Logan's pants," Dr Hill said. "He may have gone through the brush to get from that bench over to the pool."

"Plenty of marks of feet, but you can't make anything out of 'em," Dodge contributed gloomily.

"Well, Logan was alive at five of twelve," the sheriff said. "He was dead by twelve-fifteen, and I know you'd never try to set the time of death any closer than that, Doc."

"No, I can't help you along those lines. Shall we take him on down to the morgue?"

"Guess you'd better. You help him, Dodge."

"Sure thing. Only there *is* all them different ways to get to that pool, Fred. None of them takes any time at all—I mean, to get to the pool *or* back. And if you heard someone coming you'd just step into the brush or behind a tree and hide—"

"Fred knows all that," the coroner said dryly. "There's a few people hanging around the lobby that say they want to go to bed. But some of them seem to want you to know they've got alibis or maybe some of them think they have something to tell you."

Payne sighed. "Well, you better bring them in, but if they really knew anything they'd have busted in here to tell it before now. I'll see you tomorrow, Doc."

"And I think I will go to bed," Michael said. "But I'd like to know if we're going to be able to leave here by this evening."

"This evening? Oh, sure—Sunday evening. No, we probably won't get the inquest over before Monday sometime," the sheriff said.

"Then I'd like to make a long-distance call."

"Go ahead. You tell him where, Ben, and then send some of those folks in."

Coakley glanced anxiously toward the guests waiting in the lobby and turned Michael over to Pruett. "Telephone? This way."

Pruett came out from behind his desk and opened a door close to it.

"This is the office. It isn't an ideal arrangement, but we haven't room telephones this year, though I believe they may be put in next season— if there is another season after what's happened. Well, just take off the receiver and when Nevada City answers ask for long distance."

Michael sat down at the square desk and picked up the telephone. When he had long distance he gave the number of his shop on Sutter Street.

"You'd better ring back, operator." This was for Pruett's benefit, since, going out, he had not quite closed the office door. "It may be some time before anyone answers. I'd be unpleasantly surprised if anyone did," he added under his breath, and turned his attention to Mr. Coakley's desk. What he had hoped to find was lying on top of a mass of papers: a pad of yellow telegram blanks.

There was still a sheet of carbon over the top page and underneath that, in Coakley's handwriting, a copy of the message he'd handed to Geoffrey MacNair before the dancing began. It read:

G. A. MacNair c/o Summit House, Nevada County, California. Last facts re T. confirmed. Situation grave. Can only repeat what I said at our last conference. Jones.

IV

"Jones," Michael muttered disgustedly. He picked up the telephone with one hand and turned Mr. Coakley's papers over with the other while he listened to the operator's report.

"If you can't raise anyone cancel the call," he said loudly. "And put through another for me: Prospect 19041. That's right."

Most of the papers in the desk were bills and statements or had to do with the hotel in one way or another. Michael glanced through them rapidly, at the same time repeating to himself Mr. Jones's wire to Mr. MacNair. He was about to close the desk drawer when he saw a single sheet of paper covered with sprawling, almost childish writing.

He closed the drawer quickly and put his elbow and the telephone over the letter as Pruett looked in.

"No luck?" Pruett asked.

"No, but the telephone is some distance from our maid's room, and she's probably sleeping soundly."

"Well, let me know if I can be of any help."

Pruett went back to his desk, and Michael pulled the letter closer. "Dear Coakley," it began. "I think you can make use of the bearer, Tex Logan. He knows horses and he's a fair mechanic. In fact he can do a little of everything and from your letters that's what you need.

"It might be best not to tell anyone I sent him. He's an independent kind of cuss and if they don't like his manners the other help might think he thought knowing me gave him some special privileges. He says he'll behave and I've told him this is the last job I'm going to get for him if he don't. He's not apt to stay long anywhere, anyway. I'll be seeing you in the next few weeks. Till then—Bernard Gould."

"What a fluent liar our Mr. Coakley is," Michael murmured. "Though very likely only his delivery was fluent and it was Gould who gave him his lines. And probably Coakley thinks he didn't keep this."

He returned the letter reluctantly to the desk as the telephone rang again.

"Summit House? I have your party," the operator said. "Go ahead, San Francisco."

"Patton? I'm sorry to get you out of bed at this ungodly hour—"

"That's quite all right, sir," their admirable maid said. "I own I was a little startled when I realized the telephone was ringing. I hope nothing has happened?"

"Merely murder. But don't be alarmed. This murder is none of our business, and we will leave here as soon as possible, because we know you wouldn't approve if we had our names in the newspapers."

"You will have your little joke, sir," Patton said placidly. She had grown sufficiently inured to her employer's eccentricities not to protest at his joking on long-distance rates. "When may I expect you home?"

"Monday afternoon or evening. I'm sorry I can't be more definite. And since they can't raise anyone at the shop—"

"But why ever in the world would they at this hour, sir?"

Michael laughed. "I was usefully employed while waiting for a report to that effect. You call the shop and tell them I won't be there until

Tuesday. We're at a place called Summit House if anyone needs to get in touch with us."

Having been told what the charges were, he stopped to pass the information on to Pruett, who at once made a note of the amount.

"I should think you'd be wanting to get to bed, too, Mr. Dundas. You won't get much sleep, though the dining room will stay open till eleven tomorrow morning, since everyone's been up all hours."

"Eleven? And what time, *por Dios,* does it usually close?"

"By nine-thirty or ten on Sunday mornings. There was a fishing party to go out before sunrise—Mr. Farnham, Mr. Gould, Mr. MacNair and some other gentlemen. I don't suppose they'll be going now. One of the deputies just went up to look over things in my and Logan's room—"

"You did share a room with him, didn't you?"

"Yes, we were supposed, with our hours what they were, not to get in each other's way. I'm usually up by three or four in the afternoon, but yesterday he came up there before then. I was awake, but he really drove me out, sitting down and acting almost like he was waiting for me to go. I suppose he could have found those trout flies and changed his shirt in my presence."

"What trout flies?" Michael asked.

"Some he'd wrapped himself that the fishermen here think are pretty good. When he saw I was up he said he thought he'd put on a clean shirt and he took his time about it, because Mr. Coakley finally went looking for him. Oh well, he did talk to me for a while. Told me Mr. Gould was expected with MacNair and Mrs. Alling. He evidently hasn't known the last two were coming and he seemed—well, interested."

"Yes?" Michael said encouragingly.

"Well—of course, I knew Mrs. Alling and her brother were coming up. But we—uh—hadn't expected Mr. Gould to come back so soon. Logan remarked that Coakley said Mrs. Gould also seemed surprised to learn he'd be here. But then," Pruett said disapprovingly, "Logan was like that. Curious, I mean."

"Weren't you?" Michael said, smiling. "Curious about him, that is?"

"Oh"—Mr. Pruett looked down his nose—"I was curious because he seemed to consider himself a privileged character. I wondered if Mr. Gould could have sent him here as a spotter—a spy, you know. But I doubt if it was in Logan to be very respectful to anyone. He always seemed to be laughing at people—to himself, that is."

"A very annoying characteristic," Michael said solemnly.

"Yes, it is. Though he was vain, too, and he didn't like it when Mrs. Gould and Miss Lawton didn't encourage him like some women in the hotel did. But I never really learned anything about him. I had very little sleep today, which turned out to be unfortunate—because I'll admit I went into the office before midnight because I could doze in there."

"So you can't say who passed in and out of the lobby or went upstairs and came downstairs again between eleven-fifty and twelve-fifteen?"

"No," Pruett said regretfully. "I did doze and jerked up when Mr. Wallis began shouting. The bellboy in the lobby was practically asleep and sitting in a corner. He isn't much force anyway."

"I wonder if Logan had any close relatives," Michael said. "Did he write or receive any letters?"

"I can't say, because he almost always was the one to go to Nevada City every day to take the mail in and bring it back. I never saw any letters about the room."

"Well, I'd better get to bed. But I think I'll have a nightcap first."

Michael walked toward the bar, thinking rather fretfully: Why do people tell me these things? Well, Pruett had probably been unprofessionally expansive because he didn't like Gould and considered Mr. Dundas' attitude toward the hotel's "angel" pleasingly irreverent. But he'd also questioned Pruett as questions occurred to him. . . .

"It's a vice," he muttered, put his elbows on the bar and ordered brandy. But even if he had not been disgusted with himself for having talked so long to Pruett it would not have occurred to him to talk to the bartender.

Gus looked as if he were longing for bed but still, Michael thought, as if he'd been drawn for a Gay Nineties scene by John Held, Jr. He drank his brandy quickly and left the bar without speaking to Gus again.

Unfortunately, neither did it occur to anyone else to question Gus—or, at least, to encourage him to remember all he could regarding Logan's various visits to the bar on that last day of his life.

The emphasis was on time and the period from eleven-fifty to twelve-fifteen. When, he was asked, was So-and-So in the bar and for how long? Striving to answer these questions accurately, it was small wonder Gus forgot or didn't realize it might be important that on one occasion Tex Logan had come in to the bar with something besides a drink in mind.

V

Michael had been drowsily aware that at some hour he would have pronounced uncivilized Valerie was up and dressing and that before she left she kissed him and said softly:

"If you're awake enough to hear me—I'm putting something under your pillow. Read it when you wake up if I'm not back before then. . . ."

That had been some time ago, and there was no reason why he shouldn't have gone sound asleep again. He had been pleasantly on the verge once but now he began to feel uneasily that there was someone in the room—someone staring at him.

He sighed, turned so that he was facing the other twin bed and unwillingly opened his eyes. Then he covered them hastily with his fingers, counted ten and looked at the bed again.

The apparition was still there, sitting cross-legged on the bed, regarding him with round blue eyes. Michael sat erect and returned the stare.

"My God! What have I done to deserve this visitation at this hour of the morning?" he protested.

The visitation giggled. It was one of those reprints of an early Shirley Temple offered to the public as first editions by fond mammas. The dimples were an original creation, but the smile that displayed them to best advantage was strictly a copy. So were the curls, a trifle stringy and in need of combing and probably owing a good deal of their color to golden-glint rinses.

"I'm Patty," the child said. "I'm seven, going on eight. How old are you?"

"Thirty-three, scarcely going on anything as yet. Patty what? Farnham?"

"Um-hum. You're nice and brown, aren't you? I can see your ribs," Miss Farnham said interestedly. "But I guess you've got some muscles too. But what's that funny thing on your shoulder?"

"That's the souvenir of a gunshot wound. To what am I indebted for this pleasure?"

"I came to get my dolly. I left her in the bottom dwarwer of the bureau, and she was lonesome without me."

Patricia picked a large doll, flaxen haired, arrayed in pink, from the bed. She planted a kiss on its face and displayed her dimples. Michael shuddered.

"'Speak gently to the little child, Its love be sure to gain. . . .' No, Patricia, I do not think you are cute or that you really care two cents about that doll."

"Dolls are kind of silly," Patricia agreed cheerfully. "I like my bow and arrows better. I hit Mr. Pruett in the lobby yesterday. He yelled very loud. Would you like me to sing you a song? I can dance too."

"If I can guess two of the songs you know will you let me off?" Michael said anxiously.

"You mean, not sing? We-el. What do you guess?"

"'On the Good Ship Lollipop' and 'Santa Claus is Coming to Town.' Right? Remember—it was a bet, and I won. You don't sing. Or dance. Where are your father and mother?"

"Downstairs," Patricia said vaguely. "Daddy was mad when I woke him up but he took me to breakfast. He said he didn't have any sleep. I heard him and Mommy talking when I woke up and wanted a drink. They were fighting again," Patricia said casually. "They're always fighting."

"Oh, are they?" Michael said blankly.

"Yes. About me—a lot. They both want me."

Michael hesitated. Then: "What the hell!" he thought. "She undoubtedly chatters like this to everyone. . . ."

"But they both have you," he said.

"I mean, they both want me all to themselves if they ever get a divorce. Daddy has plenty of money for all of us but he says he wouldn't ever turn me over to Mommy to bring up alone. I mean, it isn't just that he don't want to pay alimony, though he'd have to if Mommy got a divorce, because she hasn't much money. And Mommy says she'll never give me up, so he can't divorce her, and she can't divorce him."

"Good lord! Do they discuss these things be-fore you?"

"Daddy don't want to but he can't stop Mommy. Nobody can stop her talking when she gets mad."

Michael stared at the child and then shrugged. He should know a youngster who was witness to its parents' quarrels was usually a precocious brat. He couldn't remember how old—or how young—he had been when he first knew his mother and father were not faithful to each other. Perhaps that was what had prejudiced him in favor of monogamy.

"But sometimes they're nice to each other," Patricia went on. "Daddy always tries to be. Then Mommy makes him mad, and he says, 'What's the use trying to reason with a jealous woman?'"

"None, so far as I know."

"Is your wife jealous too?" Patty asked sympathetically.

"She might be if she came in and found me entertaining a young lady in our bedroom."

Patricia giggled. "You talk funny, but I like you. I like Bettina too. She took me walking and she'll play with me sometimes. But Mommy don't like her. She says Bettina can get away with anything just 'cause she has a baby face and makes men feel like they want to protect her. She's jealous of her but not as jealous as she is of Stella. I like to look at Stella, don't you? She's nice, too, but I guess I like Pearl best of all."

"Who is Pearl?"

"She's our colored girl, so it's funny she's named Pearl, isn't it? She takes the most care of me, because Mommy has nerves. Only, Pearl's sister was having a baby again, so she wanted to stay with her two or three days. Her sister's always having babies," Miss Farnham remarked thoughtfully. "I think black ones are the cutest kind, don't you? They're so shiny."

Being unable to think of any sensible answer to this observation, Michael changed the subject. "It's been nice meeting you, but hadn't you better run along, *niñita?*"

"That's what Tex called me once. Except when he called me 'chatterbox.' He said I ought to be branded with a box C, and that could stand for 'Chatterbox.' I didn't know that—"

"Do you mean that Mr. Logan played nurse-maid to you?" Michael said sharply.

Patricia tossed her head. "I'm too old for a nurse. Mommy got nerves yesterday morning and asked Tex to amuse me. He took me down to town to get the mail. I liked him. But where's he gone? Daddy says he's gone away—"

"I don't know where he has gone," Michael said truthfully. "But a car did come for him. Did—had you ever met Tex before?"

Patricia frowned. "I don't remember if I did. I like cowboys though. When Mommy and I were at Palm Springs we used to see some cowboys. From ranches, you know?"

"Dude ranches, you mean? Well, suppose you look about for new fields to conquer. I want to dress."

"Haven't you got on anything at *all?*" Patty asked, eying the sheet that covered him from the waist down.

"I'm wearing enough that I can leave my bed to pluck you off that one—if necessary."

"You mean you'll put me out if I don't go? Then I will," Patricia decided. She slipped off the bed, straightened her brief, frilled pink frock and did a few dance steps. "See—I can dance. Mommy says I'd be in the movies now if Daddy would let her try to get me in. Good-by. Someday I'll sing for you."

"I'm very much afraid you will if I'm around long enough. Close the door when you go out."

Patricia shut the door, but Michael did not get up. He closed his eyes and leaned back against the pillows, frowning. Valerie found him so when she came into the room fifteen minutes later, carrying a cup and small pot of coffee.

"I brought this up, since the hotel staff seems to be rather disorganized this morning. What's the matter? Have you read my notes?"

"Notes? What notes?"

"Under your pillow," Valerie said disgustedly. "I didn't wake up when you came to bed last night—"

"Then who was that man you let into this room?"

"I was walking in my sleep. Besides, the notes could wait. But read them now. . . . Well, what do you think?"

"That your ears have suddenly grown very long," Michael said, looking at Valerie's digest of the conversation between Geoffrey and Mrs. Alling. "How did you happen to hear this?"

Valerie told him. "But that isn't important. What do you—?"

"Oh, they'd certainly have some explaining to do if the 'Law' had heard them. There may be some very harmless explanation. They may not have been discussing the murder just before you began listening in."

"But who is the 'madman' Mrs. Alling referred to? Mr. Logan certainly didn't seem to me a person you'd call mad."

"Some people think anyone who won't see things their way or, as they say, 'see reason,' must be a little insane," Michael said, not knowing how nearly the solution of this case rested upon the correct interpretation of that word "madman."

"I'm rather more interested in MacNair's saying: 'But we hoped, even when we had the first letter, that it would never come to this.' Could I have some of that coffee?"

"He also said: 'And after all these years.' Do you remember," Valerie asked, handing him the coffee cup, "when Mrs. Alling started to say something like: 'Geoff came down to be near me after his—' and then changed it to 'About ten years ago'? I wonder what she was going to say and why she didn't?"

"I have no idea, my dear. The mention of a letter is interesting because it makes you think of blackmail again. And 'first letter' suggests there was more than one letter received. Coakley made a carbon copy of that telegram he gave MacNair, and I turned it up in his office."

Valerie grinned. "What was in it?"

"'Facts re T. confirmed. Situation grave. Can only repeat what I said at our last conference. Jones.'"

"Oh. 'T.'?"

"Yes. 'T.' for Tex and Texas. But I do think it is more natural to use the initial of a man's last name if you want to refer to him by initial."

"Well, I know we aren't going to take any action—any more than you've already done, snooping around Mr. Coakley's desk. But we can take an academic interest in the case, and is there anything about that conversation that strikes you as peculiar?"

"Yes. They seemed to be talking with perfect confidence in each other until Geoffrey asked his sister to account for her movements during the critical twenty minutes. After that—constraint. And an unduly lengthy explanation by Mr. MacNair of his own movements."

He held out his cup, and Valerie emptied the coffeepot into it. "During my snooping, as you so disrespectfully call it, I also found the letter Gould wrote Coakley and gave Logan when he sent him up here. Mr. Gould seems to have known Logan well enough to have found more than one job for him."

"Oh! Why, he probably told Mr. Coakley what to say before the sheriff got here. Are we going to let him get away with that?"

"I don't promise I won't do my best to cause Mr. Gould some slight uneasiness, should the opportunity present itself," Michael said. "But we'll keep our information to ourselves, because if we don't we might have to stay here several days more. Besides, I wouldn't be surprised if the sheriff doesn't suspect Coakley lied. Do I seem the sort of person who would take pennies from a blind man's cup?"

"Oh, not ordinarily. Why?"

"I feel as if I'd done something of the sort. Getting information from a child. . . ."

"Patty Farnham? When? What is she like?"

"When she is imitating a child screen star she is god-awful. Otherwise, seven at times, and a very wise fourteen or so at others. She prattles merrily of divorce, alimony, her mother's jealousy. Apparently Mrs. Farnham finds her a convenient audience, and that type of child records and reproduces as faithfully as a phonograph record.

"I'll tell you about my encounter with her," Michael added, getting out of bed. "But from now on we are going to spend a quiet and blameless Sunday, marking time. . . ."

VI

By midafternoon the shouting and the tumult had lessened and a large number of guests had departed from Summit House. Some had always intended leaving today, while others decided abruptly that they had vacationed quite long enough—here.

A handful besides what Michael thought of as the "Gould claque" remained at the hotel, with nothing to do but eat, sleep and gossip. Sitting in the lobby, which was the clearing house for fact and surmise, Michael learned that Miss Lawton was "prostrated" and keeping to her room. He also gathered that when Mrs. Gould was not putting cold cloths on Miss Lawton's head Mrs. Alling was administering sedatives while Mr. MacNair sat by the bedside and held his fiancée's hand.

Several middle-aged ladies ventured a word of sympathy for Peter Wallis, but the general sentiment was against Mr. Wallis. This might have been because he alternated between sulking in his room and striding defiantly across the lobby toward the bar, with an almost visible chip on his shoulder.

Mrs. Farnham was also staying in her room, suffering from a sick headache. Mr. Farnham had asked and been given leave to put his daughter in his car and take her off for the day—which, as someone remarked, was not only so much the best thing for the child but everyone else.

Mr. Gould's activities were not mentioned—specifically. But, hearing that Pruett had offered his resignation, that one maid had had hysterics and two others were still sniffling, Michael judged Gould had not been inactive.

Pruett's resignation had not been accepted, but the man in charge of the garage was under notice to leave. As he was the cook's cousin, various items on the luncheon menu had been under- or overcooked, too well seasoned or not seasoned at all.

These were facts, but neither did the company lack theories. One group inclined to the belief that Logan had been a gangster, fleeing mob vengeance that had finally overtaken him in the dark at the hand of the usual mysterious stranger.

The more prosaic were willing to believe that Logan had been killed by: (a) Peter Wallis, simply because Mr. Wallis had found the body, or (b) by the garage-man, plainly an untrustworthy character, or (c) by any member of the hotel staff who had no alibi. And what did Mr. Dundas think about it? Was it true that he'd had some experience with this kind of thing?

Mr. Dundas thought it was a pity they had to include the garageman among their suspects, because if his cousin, the cook, got wind of that dinner might be worse than lunch had been. He left them looking gravely apprehensive and went over to the office as the sheriff, standing in its doorway, crooked a finger in his direction.

"Come on in," Payne said. "Thought you might like to know what we've been doing."

"Completely demoralizing the hotel staff, apparently," Michael said. "And, since you've made no arrest, I take it your efforts have been wasted and Mr. Gould is still lacking a scapegoat."

Payne grimaced. "He ain't very tactful. But you're right—all the help's pretty well accounted for, includin' this fellow Gould fired. He's supposed to look after the garage, but Coakley says he ain't been very satisfactory. He's careless—though, as the guy says, 'Who's going to steal anybody's car in a place like this?' He didn't see no reason why he shouldn't sneak in to look at the dancing and get a bite to eat."

"So he wasn't in the garage when Gould went out there or when Peter Wallis passed by it?" Michael said, sitting down.

"No." Payne settled himself behind Coakley's desk. "Well, there was just Logan's clo'es in his room besides his shavin' outfit and things like that. No letters or anything to tell us if he has any relatives that should be notified. From what he said to a lot of the guests, he'd been pretty near everywheres, and it's been my experience guys like that always travel light."

"Of course you are sending his fingerprints to Washington?" Michael said.

"Sure. That's been tended to, but what makes you think about that right off?"

"Oh, Farnham rather thought Logan might have done a hitch in the army. And if he did his prints will be on file even if he has no criminal record."

"Well, I hope they are so's we can get a line on his past life. Here's something funny," Payne added, pushing half a dozen sheets of the hotel stationery across the desk toward Michael. "We found these in his room. He drew pretty good, didn't he?"

Michael turned over the papers which were covered with crude but vivid sketches of the hotel's guests. Logan had had the gift of seizing upon his subject's most prominent or least admirable feature and subtly distorting it.

Most of those subjects were unfamiliar to Michael, but Gould was there, chesty as a bullfrog and more than a little Napoleonic. And Bettina, looking wistful and as appealingly helpless as a wounded doe. But Stella's perfection of feature had defeated Logan. He had finally drawn her face as a mask, but it was a beautiful mask. Peter was all shoulders, jaw and hair, with the lines of the jaw suggesting pigheadedness rather than true strength.

"He was clever," Michael agreed. "I'm as well pleased that he didn't get around to me."

"Or me, neither," Payne said, caressing one round, prominent ear. "He didn't get round to the Farnhams or Mrs. Alling and her brother, neither—they been here such a short time. Kind of a mean sense of humor he had though. I get the feeling he wouldn't mind making people squirm if he had a chance."

"You think he might have found blackmail rather amusing as well as advantageous financially?"

"I got no proof he did," Payne said cautiously. "All I got to go on now is that there's eight people here that ain't got alibis. I guess you know who they are?"

"The Goulds and the Farnhams, Mrs. Alling and her brother, Peter Wallis and Miss Lawton?"

"Yep. But I don't know any motive any of 'em had for killing Logan. He could 've been killed within two minutes after you and your wife left him by someone lyin' in wait for him already. Because six of them eight had left the dance floor by eleven-fifty. Three of them went upstairs right away—Mrs. Gould and Mrs. Alling and Farnham. Mrs. Farnham says she went up after them about twelve-five or -ten. But the windows at the side of the lobby were open, and there's no one to say she didn't go in and out of it that way if she didn't want to use the front door to get outside."

Michael nodded. "I noticed that those windows reach all the way to the floor and open out. It's a very short drop to the ground outside. Go on."

"Well, that's the people who left the dance floor early enough to be already waitin' for Logan when you left him. Farnham, Mrs. Gould or Mrs. Alling

could 've gone down the back stairs and out that
way. They come out into a room where they keep
linen, brooms, pails and stuff like that. One door
in that linen room opens into the laundry and it
has a door onto the back yard. And none of the
hired help was in the laundry at that time of night."

"And no one who went upstairs came down again
until after Peter had reported Logan's death?"

"Nobody saw 'em if they did. Gould and young
Wallis admit they was outside and they could
either one have got to that pool in a few minutes,
even going the long way around by the garage.
MacNair would have been later getting to the pool
than anyone else if it was him killed Logan. I'd
like to know just what time Miss Lawton really
did send him off. No one can say—"

"Bernard Gould did."

"He certainly tried to prompt Miss Lawton on
that question," Payne admitted. "And she tried to
play up to him. I got an idea it was closer being just
midnight than some time after when Miss Lawton
sent MacNair off, though him and Gould—and
her, too—have had time to get together on their
stories. But, however early or late he started up to
get Miss Lawton's wrap, MacNair had time to slip
out and kill Logan.

"Mrs. Farnham says she was sitting in a chair
with its back to a pillar, facing the windows

instead of the stairway, and that she had her eyes closed because she already was getting a headache. If that's the truth she couldn't have seen anyone go upstairs or come down again and slip out the front door. And she says she didn't see MacNair go upstairs at all."

"You're eliminating Miss Lawton as a possible killer?" Michael asked.

"I am not," Payne said decidedly. "She had the best chance to kill Logan quick and easy—except maybe young Wallis. But all she had to do was go out the side door of the ballroom like she did and make it to that pool in no time at all. The only thing is that she did make a date with young Wallis to meet him as near midnight as possible."

"Yes," Michael admitted. "And it was Peter who set the time, but she made no objection. And if she intended dealing with Logan at the pool she needn't have agreed to meet Peter there."

"In any case, there was a lot of people running around and just missing each other," Payne said gloomily. "Some of them must be telling the truth. *Some* of them must 've been in their rooms like they say, where they couldn't see anything. Only thing is, I ain't so certain they'd tell if they had seen anything suspicious. People like them are apt to stick together against outsiders, which they consider I am.

"But," he added, "as far's people not runnin' onto each other outside, that's all right. As my deputy, Dodge, keeps telling me, it 'd be the easiest thing in the world to hide outdoors—to wait for Logan or to hide if you heard someone comin'."

He leaned back in his chair, balancing it precariously on two legs, and eyed Michael thoughtfully.

"You're probably thinking: 'This is all very well, but what's he going to do about it?'"

"No," Michael said, smiling, "I think I know what you're going to do and I don't blame you."

"Well, what can I do? I can't keep these folks here forever. Sure, I'm going to keep on digging away, trying to find out something about Logan. But that all takes a lot of time."

"Are you also going to come back to talk to the servants—after Gould has left?"

Payne grinned. "What do you think? If they know anything I can get it out of them finally. I want to know all they can tell me about Logan since he came up here. But I can't hold people here just because I want to do that. I don't want to make things tough for Ben Coakley. All his life he's wanted to get this hotel built here and he's got his own savings in it. I can see he don't want to offend Gould, though Ben and me is due to have a little talk when Gould's gone," Payne said mildly. "And I guess you 'n' me understand each other, because I ain't blamin' you neither."

"Why should you? I've done nothing but mind my own business."

"But you don't always, do you?" Payne retorted. "And your wife is about the last person that talked to Logan, which might be dang'rous."

"You don't miss a great deal, do you?"

"I try not to," Payne said complacently. "And I figure if you had any idea who killed Logan you'd tell me. You haven't and you don't want to stick around here. That's all right. But if I turn up anything interestin' in the next few days maybe you'd like to hear about it? It might just happen to fit in with somethin' you noticed here."

"That's always possible," Michael said cautiously. "I'll leave that to your judgment. If you want to get a line on Logan's very early life try Amarillo, Texas. Let's say that's just a—hunch? And now I suppose, since there's nothing else to do, that I might as well go upstairs and take a nap."

VII

Michael often commented, half admiringly, half resentfully, upon Valerie's "infinite capacity for sleep." Though she'd passed half the afternoon sleeping she announced herself ready for bed at ten o'clock.

"There's nothing else to do," she said reasonably. "And everyone else seems to have gone to bed. I suppose they're bored too. However, I may read for a while until you come up."

"Then you'll read for several hours. I should have known better than to nap this afternoon."

"I should have known better than to let you. It's just beginning to be safe to talk to you. Oh well, sleeping in the daytime does make people cross," Valerie conceded. "And you're a night-blooming Cerberus anyway."

"Cereus, darling—if you don't mind? A species of cactus rather than a three-headed dog."

"I don't mind. And, as the dog was a snappy old thing and cactuses have prickles, either is appropriate," Mrs. Dundas said sweetly, and departed for their bedroom.

Michael grinned appreciatively, picked a magazine off one of the tables in the lobby and sat reading it and smoking for more than an hour. Mr. Pruett, who had had very little sleep today, was nodding behind his desk.

The sheriff had gone back to Nevada City, leaving Dodge and Briggs at the hotel. Briggs was in the lobby, also obviously in need of sleep, while Dodge had disappeared in the direction of the kitchen some time ago. Michael found himself increasingly bored with his magazine. It was not even a much-needed soporific. He had never been more wide awake in his life. "Desperate diseases," he muttered, got up and went out onto the hotel's wide front porch.

He stopped there, thinking that if he was going to take the sort of walk that might help him to sleep he had better take it along the road that led from the hotel to the main highway. Still, fresh air and a harmless amount of exercise were surely obtainable without walking ankle-deep in dust along a dark road. . . .

Oh well, why not admit he was interested in the locations of the stables and garages and also in the garage attendant who'd allegedly been discharged for incompetence? And, admitting this, he wasted no time in self-justification but went down the steps and turned to his left.

This was the route Peter claimed to have followed. Michael wondered as he walked along the driveway leading to the garage how Peter had managed to take fifteen minutes to reach the pool on the other side of the building. However, when a man was not only fairly well sozzled but also in love he might very naturally stop now and then to howl at the moon.

Or, lacking a moon, to consider his miseries and, in Peter's case, what he was going to say to Bettina. No one had asked what, specifically, he had meant to say to her. But when he had shaken off his present mood of truculent sulkiness he would undoubtedly crave sympathy. Probably he would come seeking it from Valerie when they were all in San Francisco again.

Michael had reached the back of the hotel by now and found that the garage, servants' quarters and stables were separated from it by perhaps three hundred yards of no man's land. It had been only partially cleared of trees and brush, but there must be paths crisscrossing it, besides the driveway that ended at the garage.

Light glowed yellow in what he supposed were kitchen windows, and he thought he heard a man laughing. He walked on toward another light, a faint pin prick against the dark bulk of a building shaped like an L turned upside down.

This was the garage; the light a small shaded globe to one side of the big double doors. There was a small bell button under the light, with a sign advising that one "Ring Bell for Attendant."

Michael hesitated, looking at the sign. Probably the attendant was in bed by now. All cars must have been in and accounted for since Farnham returned with a daughter mercifully so weary that she fell asleep over her dinner.

Very likely all the servants were quite as weary as Patricia and sleeping soundly by now. At any rate, there were no lights showing in their quarters at the back of the building where it jutted out from the garage proper or any sound to be heard except a horse's soft whinny off to the left.

Then, looking more closely at the double doors, Michael saw that they were not locked. One swung a little open. But surely the attendant hadn't gone to bed and left them that way. If he had gone to bed . . .

He put his finger on the bell button and held it there a full half-minute. Somewhere in the back of the garage a buzzer whirred raucously. He waited for some time after the sound ceased, but no voice, however sleepy, answered, nor was there any sound of footsteps coming toward him.

Definitely uneasy now, he put his shoulder to the door and slipped through into the garage. "Is anybody here? I want to get into my— Ugh!" said Mr. Dundas, and went down like a log on the garage floor.

"Want to—get—into my—car," he muttered presently, and began to fight his way through a warm, smothering darkness that smelled of rubber, grease and gasoline. It took time, but he finally pulled himself to his knees.

For an instant he was afraid his head would explode and then he was afraid it wouldn't. Gradually it shrank to its proper size, and he was left with nothing worse than a violent headache and a lump over his ear. He got to his feet and steadied himself against the garage door as he heard voices coming gradually closer.

"Even if you have been fired, you hadn't ought to leave the garage unlocked," the deputy, Dodge, was saying. "Not that you'll be much force as a watchman tonight. I'll just see if everything's all right out here before I— Jeez! Is something wrong, Mr. Dundas?"

"Oh no—I do this sort of thing for my insomnia," Mr. Dundas said. He looked at the man with Dodge, a squat, unshaven specimen with a strong whisky breath. "I rang your bell, Whatever-Your-Name-Is."

"Harmon," the man said, and added placatingly: "sir."

"When you didn't answer and I saw the doors were not locked I was overcome with anxiety as to your whereabouts—dead or alive. Dead, I was afraid." Mr. Harmon turned green. "So I entered the garage, as you see."

He indicated the door he had pushed open. "I entered, hailed you in a loud voice and was promptly conked over the ear by someone who must have been waiting for me behind the door I did not open."

"Oh." Dodge inspected Michael's head. "Say, you have got a lump. What do you suppose they used? And why—?"

"Why? Presumably because I was blocking the exit. And knowing what I was hit with wouldn't cure my headache. However, I'd say it was something not too heavy, because— Good God!" He turned on Harmon. "Are there lights inside this place? Well then, turn them on!"

"Y-yes sir." Harmon flung both doors open, found a light switch inside the garage and pressed it on. "There you are—plenty of light."

"Yes. And here is my car."

Michael strode over to it, twisted the door handle savagely and jerked the door open. He pulled down the lid to the dashboard compartment, found Kleenex, road maps, sunburn lotion—everything, in fact, but his gun.

"Laid out with the butt end of my own automatic, no doubt. And where, Mr. Harmon, are my car keys?"

"Right there in the ignition. Right where you put 'em when you left your car in front of the hotel for me to drive it back here yesterday."

"Since I left my car and its keys in your care, *por Dios,* why didn't you use them? Don't you ever remove keys from the ignitions and lock the car doors?"

"N-no, not often," Harmon stammered. "Who'd want to get in anyone else's car—?"

"*¡Jesús mil veces!* You unmitigated idiot," Michael said without raising his voice. "You addlepated anthropoid—"

"Here!" said Mr. Harmon feebly. "Who you calling names? Who's a—a—?"

"Oh, shut up! Your brain must be filled with cream cheese."

Dodge was grinning but he said mildly: "You didn't tell Harmon you had a gun in your car."

"If I had told him that I was carrying the British crown jewels in a side pocket do you think it would have made any great difference? Of course, I may not be the only person who carries a gun in his car. But I'm the only one who pulled a gun on Mr. Gould yesterday and had the story broadcast over the entire hotel."

"Oh. I did hear something about that. Well, it's gone and— Look, you go to bed, Harmon."

Mr. Harmon closed the doors very quickly and could be heard locking them before he stumbled away across the garage.

"He's pretty dumb and he polished off nearly a bottle of corn tonight," Dodge said. "He came in the kitchen looking for something to eat. He was there about twenty minutes while I gave him some coffee. Then I brought him back out here."

He debated whether to offer Michael a supporting arm as they started back toward the hotel and decided it might be just as well not to.

"Hell, I'm sorry about this," he went on. "Not that there seemed any reason we should watch the garage, but I don't see how anyone got out there. Of course, there's the back stairs and—"

"I'm not particularly interested in knowing how the person who hit me got in and out of the hotel. What matters is that someone did."

"I couldn't lock off the back stairs," Dodge said defensively. "You can't risk doing anything like that—in case of fire."

"I hadn't thought of that," Michael said more reasonably.

"You got to think of it up here. If you come down those back stairs you have to go through that linen room first, and there's a door from it to the kitchen as well as one into the laundry. I had that door part open but I can't say I was watching it every minute. Someone could have slipped past it into the laundry and through the laundry door into the back yard."

"Oh, don't let it worry you. The front stairs may have been used, too—to enter the hotel again— because very likely both Briggs and Pruett are fast asleep in the lobby by now."

His prophecy was correct except for the minor detail of Mr. Pruett's having retired to the office to enjoy his nap in dignified seclusion. Briggs started up guiltily, protesting that he'd only "closed his eyes for a minute." He listened to Dodge's story while Pruett hurried to open the bar and get the bottle of whisky Michael demanded.

"We'd better call Fred," Mr. Briggs said. "I mean, if we want to search the joint we'd better ask him about it first."

"That's what I think. People ain't going to like it," Dodge said. "Well, I'll call him. Look, Mr. Dundas, maybe you'd better talk to him."

"With pleasure." Michael followed Dodge into the office and sat down at the desk, placing the whisky bottle within easy reach. "Have you any aspirin, Pruett?"

"I'll find some. And here's our first-aid kit. That place on your head is bleeding. I'll be right back."

"Fred? This is Dodge. Look—Mr. Dundas has something to tell you. . . ."

The sheriff, hearing Michael's tale, swore in a grieved sort of way. "You're sure everyone knew you had that gun in your car?" he asked.

"Mr. Gould told the story of the holdup to a fairly large audience, not omitting the fact that I carried the gun in the car. Peter and Mrs. Farnham weren't there but they knew the story when I saw them later," Michael said, vaguely aware that Dodge was hovering over him solicitously. "No doubt the story was passed on to Farnham too."

"We'll have to search the place. But what do you think? It 'll cause an awful rumpus if we jerk people out of their beds right now."

"Oh, I don't think—" Michael rose, quite involuntarily, half out of his chair. He turned and glared at Dodge. "What the bloody hell—"

"I just put some iodine on that place. You hadn't ought to let it go."

"Will you take that iodine and put it— Oh well, the harm's done. No, I wasn't talking to you, Payne. But that last statement is true."

"Yeah. The gun's probably been thrown away by now. And you tell them deputies of mine to camp on the front and back stairs—right on 'em—and stay there. I'll be with you early in the morning, and we'll search the place."

"You'd better search all the luggage that's leaving the hotel too."

"What's up?" Bernard Gould demanded, coming into the office with Pruett and a bottle of aspirin just behind him. "You look the worse for wear, Dundas. Run into a door in the dark?"

"Oh-oh-h!" thought Mr. Dodge in pleased anticipation. "Now he'll get some of that language."

But Mr. Dundas merely looked at Mr. Gould and finally smiled. It was, Dodge decided, a damned nasty smile. Mr. Dundas got up and handed the telephone to Mr. Gould.

"The sheriff may have something to say that will interest you," he said. "I'm going to bed."

At the doorway he stopped and turned. "Bad manners, of course, to leave so abruptly and without answering your questions, Mr. Gould," he said mockingly. "But what do manners signify if a man knows horses, is a fair mechanic and can, in fact, do a little of everything? And perhaps I also feel that knowing you gives me some special privileges. Though there's no *a* in the word privilege, Mr. Gould."

He closed the door, gently and definitely. Dodge, not having read Gould's letter to Coakley, stared at the former bewilderedly.

It just didn't make sense, what Mr. Dundas had said, so why should Gould's brown eyes suddenly look shiny with anger? He stood staring at the telephone for an instant before he finally jerked it closer to his mouth and snapped:

"Yes, I'm here! What—"

VIII

Valerie also found her reading matter uninteresting and, when she laid it aside, that even her capacity for sleep had been overstrained this afternoon. She kicked the covers off, beat up her pillow, turned it several times, hauled the blanket up from the foot of the bed as she grew chilly and finally switched the bedside lamp on again.

"Aspirin?" she muttered fretfully. "I don't believe it will help but I can try it."

She went into the bathroom and, glancing at its locked door, wondered if Bernard Gould was asleep on the other side of it. Still, there were plenty of rooms on the second floor available now, so probably this one wasn't occupied at all.

But it was. Bed springs creaked suddenly, as if someone's weight had been flung heavily across them, and someone began crying, not hysterically but with the dreary persistance of winter rain.

Valerie stood listening, with a bottle of aspirin in one hand and a glass in the other. At last she put them both back into the drug cabinet, returned to the bedroom and found her robe.

"If Michael won't come to bed so I can go to sleep he shouldn't expect me to mind my own business," she thought. "The worst he can do is to suggest that I do mind it."

She stepped out into the hall and knocked on the door beyond their bathroom. The bed springs creaked again; there was a sound of running water and then Bettina Lawton's voice asking:

"Is it—? Who is it?"

"Mrs. Dundas. I knew you were awake and I wondered if you have any aspirin."

Bettina opened the door quickly. "I didn't know you were awake. I'm sorry if I woke you but— Do you really want some aspirin?"

"No," Valerie said, smiling. "I wondered—"

"Yes, I was crying," Bettina admitted. "I'm afraid it was as much temper as anything else. Won't you come in, please?"

"That's what I meant to do if you wanted any-one to talk to. But why are you in this room if you do? And I can't imagine you even crying from temper."

Bettina closed the door, went over to the wash-stand and dashed cold water over her eyes again.

"Crying is all I ever manage to do when I'm angry. And I do want someone to talk to—though it all depends whom I have to talk to. I insisted on coming up here instead of staying even in a room adjoining Stella's. They were driving me frantic!"

Valerie sat down on the bed. "Too much solici-tude?" she suggested.

"Yes. Geoffrey is as sweet as he can be, but you know how men tiptoe about sickrooms. And the point is that I wasn't ill! They all told me I was— or should be—"

"Well, why didn't you tell them to get the hell out?" Valerie said deliberately.

She expected Bettina would look at her disapprovingly. No one had asked her opinion of Miss Lawton, but if they had she would have said: "A little too mealymouthed for my taste." But Bettina gazed at her almost admiringly.

"If I could! You aren't—aren't inhibited at all, are you?"

Valerie grinned. "Not to speak of. Being married to Michael two and a half years has destroyed all my inhibitions. I suppose what you really mean is I have no manners. I did have the habit of them once—"

"That's it—habit. I remember my grandmother slapping my hands when I was only five whenever I wasn't a little lady. I did love her, but she was— Well, she never stepped out of the house without gloves. And she never discussed any personal matters at dinner tables."

"I'm beginning to get the picture. 'A lady never shows annoyance'—or any other real feeling."

Bettina nodded. "That was part of her training—and mine. It was remarkable how she could keep a conversation going about nothing at all."

"I suppose that's an art in itself but I think it's pretty deadly. I've heard the English excel at that sort of thing. She wasn't English?"

"Oh no, though she'd been abroad and admired the English very much. She wasn't army. She could never understand why Mother was happy, married to my father."

"So often mothers can't."

"She thought Father wasn't polite enough to Mother and didn't appreciate her but just took her for granted. Well, I hardly knew my parents or any of my family. Stella's eleven years older than I am, and there are three boys in between. Grandmother didn't care for boys or think very highly of men and she thought Stella was badly brought up."

"I should think, with four children younger than herself, Stella must have done more bringing up than being brought up," Valerie remarked.

"I suppose she did. Mother wasn't well before I was born, and she and Stella went out to Santa Barbara where I was born. I suppose that's one reason Grandmother was fond of me. And I was a sickly baby. That's why I was sent to live with her. But I'm perfectly strong now and I wish people would stop treating me as if I were too fragile to—to stand a few blows and—and mentally fragile too."

"Do you really want to be treated like just a good pal—by men?" Valerie asked bluntly.

"Of course not." Bettina smiled reflectively. "Do you know why so many girls have to light

their own cigarettes and get out of cars unassist-
ed?"

"N-no. While Michael doesn't really believe
able-bodied females should be pampered with
those little attentions, he also is the victim of
habit and early training. What's your method?"

"No method—just observation. Most girls wish
men would do all those things but they don't really
expect they will and they don't wait long enough
for them to. No, I don't want to be treated like a
pal by men in—in ordinary social intercourse. But
it makes me mad when something like—like this
happens and everyone treats me like a child."

"I don't blame you, but they're just protecting
you, dear."

"I know. But I was irritated when Bernard acted
as if I was moving up to this room so I could talk
to Peter on the sly. I haven't made up my mind if
I want to talk to Peter at all. But—"

"Your brother-in-law irritates me, too, now and
then. Being part of his household must be quite a
change from life with Grandmother."

"In more ways than one," Bettina agreed.
"Grandmother practiced elegant economy like the
ladies in Cranford. And, while she wasn't well for
several years before she died, as she used to say,
she knew some of 'the very best people' in Santa
Barbara. But Barney's money couldn't buy Stella

and me even companionship for a while, and we still don't know anyone who is anyone. . . .

"Oh, I know that sounds horrid," she said as Valerie raised her eyebrows. "But, you see, Barney doesn't like that. But he does have his good points. He can be very generous when— Well, he has been to me. And he took Stella away from—"

"Yes?" Valerie said.

"Oh, an army officer's pay isn't too large. Our brothers are all in the army, in Hawaii and the East. We never see them, so, really, Stella and I are the only family either of us has and—well, Barney is generous to us."

"Um-m," Valerie said noncommittally. "Was it in San Antonio that Mr. Gould met your sister?"

"Yes, Father was stationed at Fort Sam Houston and— Oh, who is that? No, don't go," Bettina said, lowering her voice as someone wrapped imperatively on the door again. "Stay, just in case . . . Who is it?"

"It's me—Stella."

"Oh." Bettina slipped out of her chair and went to open the door.

Valerie could not see into the hall and if the voice there had not been identified for her by its owner she would not have recognized it immediately. It was now neither low nor fashionably husky, and the accent was that of an untutored schoolgirl.

"Gee, kid, this is a pretty kettle of fish," said the beautiful Mrs. Gould. "Barney just told me they're going to search the whole shebang tomorrow—and all our luggage besides. So can you think what's the best thing to do—?"

"But, Stella, there's—"

"I'm not kidding you," Stella said earnestly. "Barney's pretty sore about it, and you can bet your boots if he couldn't talk the sheriff out of it no one else can. So—"

"I don't care if they tear my room and my luggage apart!" Bettina said despairingly. "I've tried to tell you there's someone with me!"

"Then why didn't you speak up?" Stella stepped into the bedroom. She grimaced when she saw Valerie. "Oh gosh, I have blabbed off. Well, there's no use me trying to talk like Mrs. Astorbilt now, is there? And I'm sorry about your husband—"

"Sorry about— What do you mean?" Valerie said, springing up from the bed.

"Take it easy, kid. He's all right, and if he wasn't such a buttinsky it wouldn't have happened. I haven't got anything to hide, either, but I—"

"What," Valerie said through gritted teeth, "happened to my husband?"

"He just got hit on the head. He— Gosh, here he comes now. I— Well," Stella finished plaintively as Valerie swept past her, "you don't need to knock me over if you are in a hurry."

IX

The pain had wandered up the back of his neck to the top of his head and finally lodged stubbornly over his right eye. Michael buried that side of his face more deeply in the pillow and mumbled:

"When did you go in to console Miss Lawton?"

"Darling, if you'd just go to sleep—"

"Darling, how I would like to go to sleep!"

"I shouldn't have let you talk or talked to you."

"It wouldn't have made any difference," Michael said. "I'm suffering as much from a whisky-and-aspirin jag as anything else."

"Well, I don't know what time I went into Bettina's room," Valerie said. "But it was eleven-fifty when you came up, and I hadn't been with her more than fifteen minutes. Say I went in about eleven thirty-five. But the time was never mentioned, and I wouldn't have heard her in that room if I hadn't just happened to go into the bathroom. I'm sure she didn't hear me in there, because I hadn't even turned on the water."

"That is, you don't think she was trying to establish an alibi or even to impress you with her innocence? She couldn't have done the former. As nearly as I can figure it, I was knocked out at about eleven-twenty. Plenty of time for Miss Lawton to be back in her room, indulging in a quiet cry at eleven-thirty or thereabouts."

"Oh, of course. I suppose Mr. Gould will say he was with his wife at eleven-twenty, and she will back him up. But he hadn't gone to bed."

"I didn't ask where he came from when he appeared in the office."

"But you did give him something to think about," Valerie said approvingly.

"It was fun while it lasted, but the plain truth is that I lost my temper. Not too obviously, I hope. And I'm not certain it was wise to uncover an ace in the hole so soon. As to questioning people regarding their whereabouts at eleven-twenty, let the sheriff do it if he thinks he must. Six will get you ten, it's wasted effort."

"Probably. Michael, do you think Stella Gould could possibly be—well, as old as thirty-seven?"

"If she is thirty-two and can look twenty-five I should think that with a little more effort she could look twenty-five even if she were thirty-seven."

"Well, something Bettina said made me wonder if— No, it's too farfetched. But, Michael, if you had heard her! No wonder she talks so little. I suppose she speaks well enough when she tries to. She was excited and just let herself go. It wasn't just the difference in her voice but the expressions she used. 'Blabbed off . . .'"

"That's army slang."

"Is it? But no one says 'kidding' or 'bet your boots' any more."

"Probably her education has not progressed along some lines since she left high school."

"That's it—that slang of hers goes so far back I've never used any of those expressions myself," Valerie said. "Fifteen to twenty years back, I should think. Well, I suppose it isn't important, but it certainly was surprising. But, Michael, if they don't find your gun in the morning what are you going to *do?*"

"*Amor de mi vida,* Alling and decrepit as I am, if you ask me that once more I shall certainly rise from my bed and smite you!"

"Yes," Valerie said meekly, "but what *are—*"

Michael groaned. "Well, the reason Gould got upstairs to pass the news on to the fair Stella before I came up is that I stopped to talk to Briggs after I left Gould to argue with the sheriff. The argument, incidentally, was a very brief one.

"But I decided it might be as well to dictate a statement to Briggs that on such and such a day, at a certain hour, I reported to him and Dodge that my automatic, serial number so-and-so, was missing from my car. He's to have it typed and signed before we leave for home tomorrow.

"Because, so far as I know, what we're going to *do* is to go home as soon as we are allowed to," he concluded. "Go home, hand the aforesaid statement to James Sullivan and pray that the precaution will turn out to have been unnecessary."

PART THREE

"On your heels and on your toes,
Join your hands and around you
   go,
The other way back, you're going
   wrong. . . ."

Quadrille

I

"It's an interesting situation," James Sullivan said. He folded the statement typed by Briggs and signed by him, Dodge and Sheriff Payne. "Just in case anyone got shot with your gun and it was traced to you this would save you some grief. But do you expect anyone will use that gun to commit another murder?"

"I don't know," Michael said from where he was stretched out on the chesterfield in their own living room. "If I wasn't exhausted from a fruitless early-morning search for the gun, an inquest and a long drive home I might lie awake tonight wondering about that."

"Well, since they did make a thorough search of the hotel and everyone's luggage without finding the gun, it looks like it was never carried into the hotel. They may turn it up later around the grounds."

"The person who hit Michael probably wasn't certain he was really knocked out," Valerie said. "How could you tell in the dark? Your first thought would be to get back into the hotel at once. It would take less time to toss the gun into the shrubbery as you ran to the hotel than to put it back into the car."

"And, of course," Sullivan said, "there's always the possibility whoever took that gun didn't kill Logan but is someone who's scared of the murderer."

Michael nodded. "I thought of that later. Someone may know too much and won't or doesn't dare tell what he knows but knows also that he is in danger."

"Either way, I don't like it. We can't do a damned thing to protect anybody. We don't know who we need to protect. Officially we aren't interested in Logan's death. I can see that sheriff's problem. Offhand, there's just two lines to follow. One: trace a connection in the past between Logan and any one or several of your suspects—"

"And, as Payne pointed out, that will take a longer time than he could easily hold eight people at the hotel."

"I know. The other line would be to find out if anything happened at the hotel that would suggest a motive for Logan's death. That would leave out MacNair and his sister, since they were there such a short time before Logan was killed. Yet, from what you say, there's something fishy about them too."

Sullivan sighed and dug his knuckles into his forehead. "And, as to anything happening at the hotel, it's my experience servants don't miss much. If they'd seen anything—like Mrs. Gould or her sister carrying on with Logan—even Gould probably couldn't have kept them from telling it."

"If anything important happened at the hotel I don't think it was anything Logan did but something he may have seen," Michael said.

"Well, suppose Farnham is kind of smitten with Mrs. Gould or Miss Lawton—"

"Then why bring his wife and child to the hotel with him? And he was there only one night before Gould arrived. He went off fishing the afternoon he arrived at Summit House and rose before sunrise to go out again on Saturday. I can't see that he had any time for dalliance with anything but trout. If he was ever much attracted to Stella Gould I think it must have been some time ago."

"Yes, and if this Mrs. Farnham is the jealous type you say she is you can't put too much faith in what she says. If Gould has as much money as people think and he's so much older than his wife she might be glad to be rid of him even if there isn't another man," Sullivan said cynically. "From what you say about him, I'll bet he makes her walk the chalk line. But none of that is any of our business—now."

He got up and found his hat. "I'm going home and let you get some sleep. I appreciate you telling me all about this right away," he added rather maliciously. "You say you've told me everything, which is so unusual I have an idea you're expecting fireworks before long. And what are you going to be doing tomorrow?"

"That," Michael said candidly, "depends on whether our late bedfellows in adversity decide they want to know us better. Even in such a short time they may have come to love us. However, I won't wait around for the telephone to ring. I shall be at Gisele's as usual tomorrow morning."

II

Having skipped lunch, at two o'clock of the next—Tuesday—afternoon Michael was putting his desk in order, preparatory to going home. The telephone rang, and an efficient feminine voice, when its owner was convinced she was speaking to Mr. Dundas, said crisply:

"This is Mr. Gould's secretary. Mr. Gould would like to see you this afternoon. He is free at two-thirty. Will that be convenient? Two-thirty at his office? You know where it is."

"No," Michael said gently, "nor am I apt to, from personal observation. You may tell Mr. Gould I am not free at two-thirty and it would not be convenient for me to come to his office if I were."

He put down the telephone, got up and opened the door from his office into that of his manageress, Fanchon Weiss.

"I'm going home, Fanchon. If I work any longer that blasted headache will come back on me. And if a man named Gould calls we don't want any. If he persists you may graciously allot him a few minutes tomorrow morning if you think I can spare the time and he cares to come here."

"I get it," Fanchon said cheerfully. "I'll put the freeze on him. See you in the morning."

Mr. Dundas left the shop and drove home by the most direct route, to find Valerie talking to Mr. MacNair and the Honorable Maria.

"We're off for the farm in a few minutes," the latter announced briskly. "Geoff keeps an apartment in the city, and we slept there last night."

"Mrs. Alling wants us to come down to Esperanza de Oro over the weekend, Michael."

Valerie was all wide-eyed, girlish enthusiasm, a circumstance which caused her husband to view

her not only with distaste but also with faint sus-
picion. She might still be carrying out the instructions he had given her just after Logan's death—
but for reasons of her own.

"Barbecue and dancing," Mrs. Alling said. "It's
a costume affair."

Michael groaned. "I thought there was a catch
somewhere," he said, looking sternly at his wife.

"You men always take that attitude, but I suspect you really quite like to return to the day when
the male plumage was brighter than the female's,"
Mrs. Alling retorted. "I suppose nothing could
persuade you into Spanish regalia?"

"No! It takes a shoehorn to get into those trousers, and you daren't bend over after that."

"I wouldn't, being a trifle wide across the sit-
me-down, but you've no hips. And if Geoff will
wear kilts, with his spindle shanks," Mrs. Alling
said tactlessly, "you shouldn't complain so long as
you do have some kind of trousers."

"I fancy if your wife's wishes have any weight
you'll be there in some sort of costume," Geoffrey
remarked.

"Oh, of course we will be delighted to accept
your invitation," Michael said formally. "That is,
if it still stands when I've done asking questions."

"Questions? My word!" said the Honorable
Maria. "What questions do you—"

"Only three. Who sent Logan to you? When and why did you discharge him—if you did?"

Mrs. Alling looked at her brother and shrugged. "I told you so, my lad."

"He's only—"

"I'm not guessing," Michael said impatiently. "I know Gould sent Logan to Summit House. And Logan knew you. He referred to you as 'the Honorable Maria.'"

"Well, that tears it, rather," Geoffrey admitted. "Though it was only on Gould's account that we kept silent. Since you know so much, you must know that he didn't want to make the connection known—"

"No, the blithering ass," Mrs. Alling said. "He should have known he couldn't pull it off, though I'd give something to know how you know he sent Logan to Summit House, Mr. Dundas. Because we didn't."

"Logan must have known we were coming up there, though, and been prepared," Geoffrey said. "You saw that he looked us in the eye without giving any sign he recognized us. But he was a cheeky beggar."

"I saw how you looked him in the eye without giving any sign you recognized him," Michael said.

"I thought that if he wanted to brazen it out I'd play up to him. I fancy Maria's reaction was the same."

"Yes. Besides, I was surprised that Barney had found another job for him in spite of having sworn he wouldn't after our experience with him. And when Lilian Farnham questioned Barney about Logan Barney didn't admit to knowing the man, except as he had met him at the hotel. I had no chance to speak to Logan later, and Geoff wouldn't want to. Their last interview wasn't too pleasant."

"I tried to throw him out by the scruff of his neck—and," Geoffrey said, flushing, but with a very attractive smile, "found myself no match for him. He very nearly broke my jaw."

"Well, Barney asked if I could make use of Logan about the place," Mrs. Alling said abruptly. "That was September of last year, I think. Yes, war had only been declared a few days before, so it was early in September. Odd, to remember that. We didn't like it, but if anyone had told us that not quite a year later France would be conquered and Britain fighting alone—"

"Well, but I was about to say that I took Logan on and rather liked him, though he was apt to be impertinent. He was a good man with horses—"

"Did he ever say where he'd been just before he came to you, Mrs. Alling?" Michael asked.

"No. You'll have to ask Barney about that. Logan was with me six weeks and by that time he'd gotten one of our maids into trouble. Oh, of course the girl has no sense and was fair game for any man who came along. But I couldn't have that sort of thing going on, so I discharged Logan. Geoff took a rather sterner view of the affair and tried to discharge Logan more forcibly. He went off—he didn't say where. Perhaps Barney knows."

"And neither you nor the wronged maiden heard of Logan again until you ran into him at Summit House?"

"I had a letter from him about two weeks after he left us, postmarked Sacramento. He sent a money order for seventy-five dollars, made out to me, but there was a note saying it was 'for Rosie' —the maid I spoke of. Well, he knew I'd see her through it. As a matter of fact," Mrs. Alling said offhandedly, "I found her a husband."

"My sister," Geoffrey said, "is severely practical."

"Sentimentality does the Rosies no good," Mrs. Alling said. "I never learned a great deal about Logan's past life, any more than that he was a rolling stone. Others at the hotel were able to tell the sheriff that. If Logan had ever mentioned having any relatives I would have spoken out."

"Did any of the people who were at Summit House have an opportunity to become acquainted with Logan while he was working for you?"

"Not that I know of, Mr. Dundas. The Goulds and Bettina came down to the farm just once while he was there. Barney spoke to Logan, of course, when we were inspecting the stables. Stella was with us, but Bettina and Geoff had wandered off in another direction."

"Then the Farnhams or Peter Wallis didn't visit you while Logan was there?"

"Young Wallis has never been at Esperanza. And I only invited the Farnhams once, as a family. After we'd snatched the child from under horses' hoofs, hunted her for two hours and finally dragged her out of the barbecue pit, rescued her from a sow with a litter of pigs and been forced to listen to her sing in the evening—well! But no, the Farnhams weren't there at any time while Logan was with us. Not even Ray, who sometimes drops in alone."

"Then you've known him some time?"

"Really!" Geoffrey said stiffly. "Your first questions were more or less justified, since we should have admitted we'd known Logan, but—"

"What does it matter, Geoff? Ray Farnham introduced us to the Goulds. Geoff got to know Ray in the casual way men about town do get to know each other. Ray introduced him to Barney, and Barney seemed to take a fancy to Geoff at once. He invited Geoff to his home, and it wasn't long before Geoff was dragging me up here to meet them."

"Mr. Gould hasn't social ambitions, by any chance?" Michael said casually.

The Honorable Maria grinned. "Do I look as if I'd be any good at launching people socially? Besides, I don't and never have belonged to the upper crust of peninsula society. I live nearer Redwood City than Burlingame or Hillsborough.

"However, you can hardly blame the Goulds if they would like to meet some agreeable people. They knew no one when they came here to live. Barney's well known in financial circles, I suppose, but that didn't keep them from being well snubbed whenever he tried to capitalize socially upon any business connections he'd made. Naturally, I've introduced them to my friends, here and down the peninsula."

Michael considered asking if a Mr. Jones was among those friends but decided against it. Even if it meant getting into costume he wanted, now, to accept the Honorable Maria's invitation for the weekend, though you couldn't, he thought pessimistically, know how greatly the situation might have changed by that time. Still, he didn't want the invitation to be withdrawn and he was quite certain Mr. MacNair would resent having even carbon copies of telegrams sent to him read by Mr. Dundas.

"You have been very patient," he said. "But you must understand my being curious when I was certain Logan had known you. At least I didn't try to satisfy my curiosity until now."

Mrs. Alling grinned again. "You put it so nicely, Mr. Dundas. What you mean is that you didn't peach on us to the sheriff at Summit House. Why was that? Did you want to get home too?"

She got up, slung her purse over one arm and pushed a mistreated-looking felt hat to an even more unfashionable angle.

"This affair is for charity, by the by."

"Sweet charity! What crimes are committed in thy name! British War Relief?"

"Yes," Mrs. Alling said rather belligerently. "The people who come will get their money's worth, and I guarantee expenses won't eat up profits."

Geoffrey laughed. "She has several tough old steers she will sacrifice for the barbecue."

"No back chat, please. The barbecue will be good, as usual. It's on a very small scale, but, as a personal donation, several hundred dollars isn't— What is that very expressive phrase?"

"It ain't hay?" Michael suggested.

"Exactly. Of course you'll be my guests."

"But all donations will be gratefully received," Geoffrey said dryly.

"I'll write you a check."

"And I won't refuse to take it, Mr. Dundas. If we don't see you before I'll expect you two for luncheon on Saturday. Come along, Geoff. . . ."

"Well, that's two down," Valerie said, closing the door after them.

"It's three down. Gould had his secretary call and ask me to come to his office at two-thirty."

"Oh. Well, he'll learn. Three down, and Peter will undoubtedly make four before very long. I had probably better ask Patton if dinner will stretch to three people."

III

Peter said he hadn't realized that it was so near their dinnertime and that he wasn't hungry anyway. But he managed to eat a large meal and justified himself by the gloomy statement:

"I've hardly had a real meal or a wink of sleep since all this happened."

Michael looked at him unsympathetically. "It must be good to be so young, husky and full of vitamins that you find loss of sleep and appetite merely an interesting phenomenon."

"But I don't! I— Damn it, you're so cynical you don't even take love seriously."

"Not puppy love," Michael said coolly. "I do take marriage very seriously. *El día que te casas, ó te mates ó te sanas.*"

"'The day you marry you either kill yourself or save yourself,'" Valerie translated. "Of course, it is unkind of Michael to call yours puppy love."

"Well, I suppose I do make a fool of myself, talking—or shouting—too much. But it isn't in me to take things quietly. I—I can't sleep nights for thinking of Bettina." Peter reddened violently but went on quietly enough: "When she looks at me a certain way my knees feel weak, and just the idea that something might happen to her makes me go cold all over."

Before making a similar statement in the presence of witnesses Michael would have chosen a short session with thumbscrew and rack. He looked at Peter with a certain wonder and a good deal of compassion.

"You have all the symptoms," he said. "While from your viewpoint I am fast approaching senility, I haven't forgotten them. What you need is a drink. Come into the living room and get it. . . .

"And tell me," he added, handing Peter his drink, "why you were so anxious to meet Miss Lawton at that pool Saturday night—if you don't mind, and if there was any reason besides your reluctance to accept her engagement to MacNair as official."

"I hadn't anything new to say to her. I was just tight enough to think I had things to say that must convince her or that I could say them more convincingly a second time. I'd already talked to her before you reached Summit House. She said there are lots of reasons why she should marry MacNair but she couldn't say she was really happy about it. She said it was silly for me to think anyone could force her to marry MacNair but she admitted Gould wants her to."

"She insisted to me that Mr. Gould is really very generous to her," Valerie said. "And she said that she and Stella are the only family either of them has."

"And I think she's afraid if she doesn't do what he wants he'll take it out on Stella," Peter said. "I don't know just how he could, but even Bettina said he doesn't like to be thwarted or opposed. And she said that Stella is absolutely dependent on him, which I suppose is the truth."

"It sounds very Mid-Victorian," Michael said. "But girls do still marry primarily to oblige their families, and Gould does strike me as the sort who would go to almost any lengths to get his own way."

"And what's your opinion of MacNair?"

"A little too much the pukka sahib. 'Play up, play up and play the game!' Still, he isn't lacking humor. Perhaps when you'd known him ten years he might unbend and you'd find yourself liking him."

Even this faint praise displeased Peter. "If he wants to play the game why doesn't he go back to Canada and enlist in something?" he growled.

"Perhaps, since he is an American citizen, he believes that, having enjoyed the privileges of citizenship, he owes this country something."

"Oh. Well, he apparently has enough money to get along without working, if there's anything admirable about that. He was already hanging around when I met Bettina. That was a year ago at a cocktail party Farnham gave. I fell for Bettina like that!"

Peter snapped his fingers. "We started going around together when I could get a date. MacNair and I had plenty of competition, but most of the guys had even less to offer Bettina than I have."

"Don't say that. 'Modesty is a quality in a lover more praised by the women than liked,'" Michael said, grinning. "Did you say that Farnham or the Farnhams gave a cocktail party?"

"Farnham gave it. His sister was his hostess. That was about the last of August, and Lilian was still in Palm Springs. She was there over two months. When I first met the Goulds Farnham was with them a lot. Some woman told me the Farnhams and Goulds visited each other a lot or all went out places together. She said she wondered how long it would last because Lilian is the sort who gets very chummy with people and then gets her feelings hurt and quarrels with them and drops them."

"All that type wants is an audience," Valerie said. "When they have told you all about themselves they look about for a new audience."

"You're telling me! I mean, even a man can see Mrs. Farnham's jealous of any woman that's better looking or more popular than she is."

"That takes in a lot of territory," Michael said.

"Too much. Well, she came home about the middle of September, and several people told me that she went to Gould's office and made a hell of a scene. Said he'd better keep his eye on Stella and Bettina, that she wasn't going to have Ray at their beck and call. I suppose someone told her he'd been well looked after while she was away."

"What did Gould do?"

Peter shrugged. "No one knows. You'd think he'd have enough sense not to pay any attention to her. But even if he didn't believe her, I suppose, he didn't want to risk her throwing a scene in some more public place. All anyone knows is that Farnham is still Gould's lawyer and they see a lot of each other. But the two families don't visit back and forth like they did before."

"Weren't the Goulds in Texas last summer?"

"Yes. So was Farnham, for about a week. Gould and Stella and Bettina were there all of June. The heat got too much for the girls, so they came home, but Gould stayed on through July."

"Farnham and Gould seem to have known each other longer than anyone else in our little group," Michael said. "No—I'd forgotten. MacNair knew Farnham before Gould did."

"Well, if it comes to that, I've probably known Farnham longer than MacNair has."

"Have you? Of course, I never saw you two together except during the dance at Summit House."

"Oh, I don't know him well. He's a lot older than I am, but we're frat brothers. His father was a judge in Nevada, but he studied law at Cal. He used to drop in at the S.A.E. house when I was in college. I don't think he started practicing for several years after he graduated in law.

"He spent a couple of years somewhere in Arizona," Peter added vaguely. "I think he said he was threatened with t.b. I like him, but Lil— Mrs. Farnham—doesn't like me. You know, it's a wonder to me someone hasn't suggested MacNair might be attracted to Stella. Why pick on Farnham? I'd rather have him dropping in to see my wife if I was Gould than to have MacNair around

all the time. He's a lot nearer Stella's age than he
is Bettina's."

Michael and Valerie looked at each other, smiled
understandingly and let this pass.

"Well," Valerie said, "do you feel better now?"

"For having talked so much? I guess so. But I'd
feel even better if it had been MacNair who got
bumped off," Peter said with a casualness that was
far more impressive than his usual vehemence.

"If he had you'd be awaiting trial now,"
Michael said curtly. "The complete egoist!"

"I don't see why you say that. I—"

Patton appeared in the doorway, neat, trim and
as correct in every detail as she had been that night
of last November when Michael first met her in
the old Keith house on Union Street. One detail,
however, was not the same since the sight of cotton stockings whisking about the house depressed
Mr. Dundas. Though they did not even approach
sheerness, Patton now wore silk stockings.

"A Mr. Gould wishes to speak to you, sir," she
said. "I said I would see if you were disengaged."

"Oh—yes, I'll talk to him," Michael decided.
He left Peter glowering and went out to the telephone in the hall. "Gould?"

"I have to congratulate you on the way you've
trained the women that answer your telephones,"

Gould said. "The one in your shop gave me a polite run-around this afternoon. Well, I don't mind coming to your office. . . ."

"This squabble over precedence is a little childish," Michael said.

Gould chuckled. "Especially since you've got your way? Well, I just don't want to wait until tomorrow to see you. So can I drive over to your house now? That is, if we can talk privately."

"Just now that might be difficult. Mr. Wallis is here. If you must see me I'll be at your home in about fifteen minutes. . . ."

IV

What had been the "Appleton home" on Broadway near Buchanan was old and pretentious enough for the fact that Gould had bought it to be recorded in the newspapers two years ago. Since it had been designed for a large family and the only survivor of that family could no longer afford to live in it, Gould had gotten the house for a bargain-sale price.

Which, Michael thought, you would expect him to do, but he had shown shrewdness in his choice along other than financial lines. A certain prestige went with the possession of this house and a suggestion of stability and permanence, all valuable assets for newcomers to San Francisco.

It was an old red brick building with a small front lawn, shut off from the street by a low brick wall. The lower halves of the French windows on the ground floor were protected by ornamental iron bars, and long green shutters were folded back against the outside of the house. The walk from the street in to the front door was old brick, too, bordered with stunted trees in large round pots.

A small Filipino opened the door, but in an instant Gould appeared behind him. "Run along, Juan. You put whisky in my den? Then we can look after ourselves. This way, Dundas."

As they went down the hall Michael caught a glimpse of a living room impeccably furnished and as homelike as a hotel lobby. You felt it would always belong to the decorator and never to the Goulds. But, entering Gould's "den," it was equally evident the man had been his own decorator here.

There were deep leather chairs, a solid desk, a row of steins, a pipe rack, a respectable number of books, two bear rugs complete with heads that glared up at you from the floor. Instinctively one looked about for college banners, silver cups and trophies. How old, Michael wondered, had Gould been when he read of or saw a room like this and coveted it? At any rate, here it was: the masculine man's sanctuary, looking slightly disused.

"Well, I'll come right to the point," Gould said, sitting down behind the desk. "Help yourself to whisky while I tell you what I know about Tex Logan. You threw parts of my letter to Coakley at me Sunday night. Of course you won't admit that. Why should you? It's like Coakley to have looked through his desk for that letter—"

"On Saturday night when we were waiting for the sheriff to arrive?"

"—and not to have found it," Gould continued, ignoring Michael's question. "Then later he turns it up way back in his desk drawer. Well, Tex's father was an ace fire killer. He saved my life once. You know that when a gasser blows in, explodes and then craters all you can do is shoot her with nitro?

"I've done it myself. You take the stuff in to the edge of the crater, keep looking for the casing head, throw and run like hell. But the stuff goes off at three hundred and sixty degrees, and one day Bill Logan didn't throw quick enough. Well— exit Bill Logan."

"How old was his son then?" Michael asked.

"That was about ten years ago. Tex would have been at least twenty-five. His father got him plenty of jobs, and he was a good tool-dresser. But he never would stay anyplace long. Don't ask me what all he did or where he went. I only ran into him a dozen times in fifteen years. But after Bill died Tex would always hit me up for a job or a loan when he did see me."

"You must have been very generous. Logan had two hundred dollars on him when he died."

"I gave him twenty-five. But if he got into a card game before he went on up to Summit House he might have run that up to several hundred. His fast shuffle was something to watch. Well, Maria Alling called before she left town and told me she'd told you her experience with Logan. He blew in here one day last September, looked me up—"

"Here? At this house?"

"No, he telephoned first, and I told him to come to my office. Anybody in Texas could have told him I was living here now. He said he'd like to stay around here, so I sent him to Maria. When I asked him where he'd come from he just said: 'Oh, places.'

"Well, you know Maria had to fire him. I was pretty sore, but he kept out of my way. I didn't hear any more of him until he turned up about a month ago. And you probably know why I sent him to Summit House."

"But why not tell all this to the sheriff?"

"You didn't tell the sheriff too much yourself," Gould retorted. "You wanted to get home as soon as possible too. I wasn't telling Payne anything that might give him an excuse to hold me there. I don't know anything about Logan's possible relatives. His mother died when he was born, and an aunt looked after him—in Amarillo, that was. When he first turned up I did ask him how his folks there were. He said his aunt was dead and he hadn't been back there for years."

"This aunt had no children?"

Gould frowned. "I never met her, but she may have had. Her name was Anderson. But Tex did say he didn't really know anyone in Amarillo any more, which doesn't sound like he had any relatives living there. I don't care if Payne traces Tex back to Amarillo, as long as I don't have to hang around Summit House while he's doing it. I've got no connections there—I was born in Vermont. Of course, I know what's in your mind. You think Tex might have been blackmailing me. If he'd been able to do that he wouldn't have had to work. Besides, would you pick me out as a person to blackmail?"

"No. And have you picked me out as a person to bribe, Mr. Gould?"

Gould reddened angrily and then laughed. "I believe in plain speaking, and so do you—only the brand of language you use throws me off the track at times. But it's been my experience money is a great persuader—"

"And mine," Michael said. "What was your idea? Cash or a check?"

"No, just say I turned my wife loose in that shop of yours and promised to pay her bills, besides those for Bettina's trousseau, to come from your shop."

Michael grinned. "Now I must congratulate you, Mr. Gould. I've never been offered a more perfectly sugar-coated bribe."

"But I'm not offering it after making a few inquiries about you," Gould said. "From what people tell me about you, I decided it would be very bad policy. I'm just asking you to let this whole thing drop and warning you—no, advising you," Gould said hastily, catching the quick spark in Michael's blue eyes—"advising you to let it drop. Hell, haven't I told you what I do know as—uh—proof of good faith?"

"Is that what it was? However, what you've told me seems harmless, and you can't keep Payne from carrying on his inquiry—"

"You can help Payne by investigating down here. You already know more than I like. You've been talking to young Wallis tonight—"

"What do you think Mr. Wallis told me that you'd rather he hadn't?"

"God knows. But, to put it plainly, I don't want busybodies prying into my affairs or those of

people connected with me. They'll only dig up a
lot of facts that have nothing to do with Logan's
death."

"That's one of the hardships connected with
murder investigations," Michael said. "Most of us
have something to hide. But the police can usually be trusted to be discreet and they do need to
know all the facts before they can decide which
are irrelevant."

"That's what they say. I don't agree. I'm not so
sure they can be trusted to be discreet either. They
like to stand in with the newspapers. As far as my
own career is concerned, I've done my share of
dirty fighting—but I'm a success, so it don't matter. That," Gould said shrewdly, "is just pictur-
esque. I play it up instead of trying to soft-pedal
it. After all, I still have bunions."

He laid his square hands, calloused along the
palms, flat on the desk and closed them suggestively.

"But I won't have a hint of scandal touching my
wife."

"Caesar's wife?" Michael murmured. Gould
seemed not to have heard or not to have understood.

"My wife or Bettina," he said. "Or Geoff and
Maria. Not with Bettina and Geoff expecting to be
married soon. I intend to protect her and Stella—"

"A despot, but a benevolent one?" Michael said.

"Despot? Who have you been listening to? Goddammit," Gould protested, "why shouldn't my wishes be consulted? I've heard young Wallis call me a 'petty tyrant,' and no one looks at it from my viewpoint."

"I'll try if you'll tell me what it is."

"Why, if ever there were two pampered women it's my wife and Bettina. They aren't asked to do one damned thing but be agreeable. They've nothing to worry about or do but amuse themselves. But they get bored and want a change of scenery. That's why I left them at Summit House. Then they weren't enthusiastic about it, though they wanted to see the place because a lot of our friends had gone up there on my recommendation.

"And I'd hate to say what they cost me in a year. Yet if I want dinner at a time that don't quite suit them or make some plan that means one of them has to cancel an engagement—well, they're very polite and pleasant but they—they *look*."

"If it's that wounded-fawn look you refer to I do sympathize with you," Michael said.

"Shrinking, that's what it is. They manage to make everyone think I *am* a petty tyrant. Stella doesn't talk much but she has a way of saying: 'Barney wouldn't like it.' Well, grin!" Gould said, grinning briefly himself. "Bettina's worse. She'll say I'm generous to her and she's grateful, but all with the air of giving the devil his due. I could fight tantrums or temper but I can't fight that."

"Which is probably why they don't indulge in tantrums. You wouldn't put up with that, would you?"

"Why should I? I expect them to behave themselves in return for my looking after them in every way—and protecting them. I do expect them to do that."

"So I'd gathered," Michael said. "Is your interest in Bettina's marriage due to your protective instinct?"

"If I don't look after her who will? She has a good, level head but she's been sheltered all her life. She'll admit she wouldn't like to have to scramble after her own living. I'm only her brother-in-law and I'm not going to give her a dowry for just any young squirt to blow in. I have a hunch a lot of the young fellows that have hung around her have been attracted by my money."

"Perhaps I don't believe Peter Wallis is."

"That's where we differ," Gould said. "Young professional men like him get ahead quicker if they manage to marry a little money. Geoff not only has enough of his own, but Bettina will probably never have a chance to make a better match. But she don't have to marry him if she doesn't want to, and don't let Wallis tell you it's all my doing. And I don't know how we got started on this."

"You were telling me that your wife and sister-in-law don't appreciate you," Michael said blandly, "and defining your attitude toward your women-folk—which is very enlightening. But it's getting late, and I don't see any reason for prolonging this discussion."

"I think I've covered everything," Gould agreed. "And if Payne should ask you to help him—"

"I'll use my own judgment."

"Oh. Does that mean?"

"Surely you understand English, Mr. Gould. I know—this is none of my business. That is, it wasn't until someone took my gun."

"Oh, you don't think anyone got away from the hotel with that gun after the way they searched our luggage, do you?"

"I'll admit I now consider the incident mainly a personal affront." Michael touched the still-sensitive area over his ear. "But even if the gun is only lying in the brush somewhere near the hotel —that doesn't alter the fact that someone wanted a gun badly enough to risk stealing mine. Even if the thief couldn't risk keeping it when he had it, the situation that drove him to take the gun still exists. Does it matter whether Logan's murderer wanted a gun, having another killing in mind, or whether someone wanted a weapon as protection against the murderer? In either case someone is in danger."

"And your meddling won't help! It might scare someone into doing something he don't need to do. And the 'someone' who's in danger may be you!"

"Don't bellow," Michael said coldly. "I'll take the responsibility—and the risk. Shall I let myself out?"

V

A tan Packard was parked behind his own car when he reached the street, and Stella and Bettina were just getting out of it. The driver, a small man with a long, pointed nose, was standing to attention by the car door. His licorice-drop eyes met Michael's, and what jaw he had sagged. He recovered quickly and touched his cap when Bettina said:

"Mr. Gould said he wouldn't be wanting the car tonight, Bain. He didn't," she added to Michael, "say he expected you to come here, Mr. Dundas."

"He meant to come to us, but we had Mr. Wallis with dinner tonight and he's probably still talking to Valerie. Mr. Gould and I have been talking over old times."

"I'll bet!" said the elegant Mrs. Gould. "I'm going in, kid. It's getting cold out here. Good night."

"I suppose that's why Barney sent us to a movie," Bettina said. "Is—is Peter—?"

"He is not happy. Why don't you talk to him?"

"I'm going to, but he won't be any happier when I have. You might—it's not fair to ask you to—but you might tell him that Geoffrey and I are going to be married very soon."

"Oh?" Michael said. "When did you decide that?"

"When Geoffrey was here this afternoon with Maria. He and I talked alone after lunch and—well, we talked," Bettina said unsatisfactorily. "It was the first chance we've had to be alone since we were at Summit House."

"I wonder what you're trying to tell me."

"Nothing, except that— But I must talk to Peter myself. Good night, Mr. Dundas."

"Good night," Mr. Dundas said, and when she was in the house sauntered over to Gould's car which was parked before two tall brick pillars that supported an iron gate opening onto the driveway leading to the garage at the back of the house.

"Well, Squiffy," he said affably, addressing Gould's chauffeur.

"Nix—nix!" Mr. Bain protested. The tip of his nose, which had an independent life of its own, quivered agitatedly.

"Algernon, then?" Michael suggested.

"Call me Al. They call me Bain. That's my name, ain't it?"

"So," Michael remarked, "is Algernon. But those who know and love you must still call you Squiffy."

"I don't travel with the old mob no more," Mr. Bain said loftily. "I been on the level for t'ree years now. This ain't the only good job like this I've had. But it's the foist time I ever run into any of me old pals from— Say, how long has it been since me and you seen each other?"

"At least eleven years, I should think. I haven't seen you since I stopped driving taxis in the Mission. This does bring back memories. Do you remember when that fellow who stuck up a bank in Nevada was hiding out here? I never knew his hide-out until the police caught up with him, but you did, didn't?"

"Ni-ix!" said Mr. Bain in an anguished whisper.

Michael eyed him benevolently. "If it brings back painful memories, Squiffy, I won't go on. And I suppose you have references by now if you've been going straight for three years. And Mr. Gould probably doesn't know—"

"He don't know nothin'. But I get it. Whaddaya want?"

"Just to talk to you, Squiffy. I live at 75 Russian Hill Place. Could you manage to come up there tomorrow morning? I wouldn't tell Mr. Gould about it if I were you. And, if he should be watching us now, I am only asking you if you prefer a Packard to a Cadillac."

"I gotcha. I guess I can make it over to your place sometime tomorrow morning. The boss usually drives himself downtown, and the dames don't need me early. That O.K.?"

"I'll be expecting you," Michael said.

The house was dark when he reached home, and, though it was only ten-thirty, he decided to go to bed in case Squiffy Bain should appear at an early hour the next morning. When he put the light on in the bedroom Valerie lifted her head from her pillow, opened one eye, remarked, "Peter finally went home. You hurt his feelings. Why are other people's troubles so much less interesting than our own?" and went back to sleep.

Michael grinned and considered shaking her awake to tell her about his interview with Gould. But, while she would be perfectly amiable if he did and appear to be wide awake, it was possible that in the morning she would remember nothing that he'd said. He turned out the light instead and finally slept, to be awakened by what he at first thought must be the doorbell ringing—and in the middle of the night.

But Valerie was already out of bed and running to the telephone in the hall. That meant it must be past nine, since at that hour Patton regularly left the house to do the day's marketing. She did not "hold with buying a pig in a poke over the telephone," though she regretted that Mrs. Dundas must answer the telephone and doorbell for half an hour or so.

"Yes," Valerie was saying. "Yes, this is— Oh, Sheriff Payne. Just an instant. . . . Michael, plug in the extension in the bedroom. Mr. Payne wants to talk to you."

Michael groaned, dragged himself up on one elbow and managed to plug the telephone in without falling out of bed.

"What has happened that's important enough for you to call me at this hour of the morning?"

"What do you mean—this hour of the morning? I had breakfast two hours ago," Payne said. "Look—on those fingerprints—Logan did a hitch in the army from 'twenty-four to 'twenty-seven. He was born in 1903, so he was thirty-seven when he died. He joined up in San Antonio and was at this Fort Sam Houston a couple of years. He finished out his enlistment in Hawaii.

"He sure did get around," Payne added admiringly. "Well, he was born in Amarillo, and his father was his nearest relative when he enlisted. But the father's dead now, I learned when I got in touch with Amarillo."

"No other relatives?"

"An aunt named Anderson brought him up. He cleared out of Amarillo when he was about sixteen. This aunt had a daughter a little older 'n Logan, but she moved away, too, after her mother died. That was more than ten years ago, and no one has any idea where she is now."

"Anderson—Jones," Michael muttered. "I could do with some more unusual names. Well, that doesn't get you far, does it?"

"No," the sheriff said placidly. "But I thought you might like to know about it. You remember the barkeep up at the hotel?"

"The one with the wig?"

Payne chuckled. "That's Gus's own hair. Well, I been chewing the fat with him like I have with all the help. You know the Farnhams got in about noon on Friday? Logan took a fishin' party out that afternoon, and Farnham went along. Then Saturday mornin' a bunch went out for the day, startin' at sunrise. Logan didn't go because Coakley wanted him at the hotel."

"And what did Logan do that day?"

"Nothing unusual. Went for the mail, takin' the Farnham kid with him. Worked round the stables and so on. After lunch he took some women ridin' and got back fairly late. That is, a little before you 'n' Gould got in. But the fishin' party wasn't back then."

"No," Michael said. "I saw Farnham a few minutes after he got back to the hotel, and that was a good while after we arrived there."

"Yeah? Well, after Logan got back from ridin' he went in the bar and gave Gus an envelope to give to Farnham. He tells Gus he's goin' to be busy and that Farnham's due to go out again before sunrise Sunday mornin' with Gould, MacNair and some others. Logan says he don't intend goin' with them if he can get out of it."

"And it was the habit of the fishermen to go directly to the bar for a drink as soon as they returned to the hotel?" Michael said.

"How'd you know that?"

"Farnham told me. He'd come directly from the bar to what he thought was still his room. He was still in his fishing clothes."

"Well, that may explain it. He was late and knew his wife would be wanting him to get dressed and get dinner. Then he had to find out where their new rooms were, and probably when he did she kept jawing at him to hurry. So he never had a chance to look in the envelope and maybe never thought about it afterward because he didn't go fishin' again.

"Besides, Logan told Gus when he gave him the envelope that there was some trout flies for Farnham in it. Some he'd wrapped himself. He told

Gus Farnham had said he'd like to try some of them when they were fishing Friday and didn't have such good luck. He said since he was going to be busy Saturday evening he might forget to give 'em to Farnham then. And, as I said, he didn't mean to go out with the fishermen Sunday mornin'. So he told Gus to hand the envelope to Farnham when the fishing party came into the bar for a drink like they always did when they got in."

"And were there trout flies in the envelope?"

"Gus says he could feel 'em, that one of the hooks had worked itself through the envelope. But the envelope was sealed."

"Did you talk to Pruett?" Michael said.

"Yeah. I guess you did too. He said Logan did come to their room before he took them women ridin' and said he wanted to get some of his own trout flies."

"And then decided to change his shirt and took some time to do it—after Mr. Pruett had left the bedroom."

"Um-hum. Pruett says he got the idea Logan was waitin' for him to leave, but Logan may 've just been deviling him a little, because Pruett felt that room ought to be all his in the daytime. Well, that's Gus's story, and I'd like you to get in touch with Farnham and ask him about it."

"Why am I elected? Why don't you talk to him?" Michael objected.

"I could—over the phone. But that's not satisfactory. Then I'd have to wait for him to look for the envelope if he's still got it and call me back."

"Mr. Farnham may refuse to talk to me."

"Why would he if the thing's as harmless as it seems on the surface? You tell him I don't want to have to come down here myself right now and that you know a lot more about the case than the city police do. You seen any of that bunch since you been back?" Payne said casually.

"All of them except the Farnhams."

"How's MacNair and his sister?"

"Carrying on. Preparing to barbecue the fatted calf for British War Relief over the weekend. Why?"

"Oh, I seen that telegram—or the copy of it that Ben Coakley gave MacNair Saturday night. It come from San Francisco but it was handed in at a downtown Western Union office. The sender didn't give his own address, and, naturally, they can't remember at the office what he looked like. The name Jones don't get you nowhere."

"Mrs. Alling and MacNair were expected at Summit House, weren't they?"

"Yeah, but it was only Thursday night a wire came sayin' they'd be there Saturday. Gould wasn't expected at all. They didn't know till Saturday

that he'd be there," Payne said. "Pruett says ever'one was surprised that he was comin' up again.
Well, I know now that Gould sent Logan to Summit House."

"You and Mr. Coakley had your little talk?"

"Yes. I always suspected Gould sent Logan up
there. Ben's first story about how he happened to
hire Logan didn't hold water. But I'm not going to
tangle with Gould for a while yet. I don't suppose
I'd get any more from him than I've learned from
Amarillo. For instance, about Logan's dad being
an old friend of his. And if I'd known about that
wire MacNair got before he left the hotel do you
think he'd have explained it?"

"No. And I don't think he would explain to me
even if you told me what was in the wire."

Payne snorted rudely. "I guess you read that
wire when you used the phone in Coakley's office
Saturday night. And I should be pretty sore at
you, withholdin' information like that."

"But you didn't really want to be forced to detain us too long at Summit House, did you?"

"Well—no. For your own safety's sake, for one
thing. I ain't got enough men to have guarded that
hotel well enough if you was all cooped up in it.
Look what happened Sunday night. But this is
costin' the county money. You talk to Farnham
and let me know what he says. G'by."

VI

Valerie came back into the bedroom, closed the door and sat down on the bed.

"What," she said against her husband's right ear, "is that on our doorstep?—except that he is waiting in the living room now."

"Did the doorbell ring? I didn't realize it had. I suppose it was Squiffy. Do you mind?"

"Yes, it must be Squiffy. I never knew anyone called Squiffy, but anyone who is would have to look like the specimen in the living room. I've always wanted to meet one of these 'dese and dose' guys. Where did you get him? What is he?"

"By nature he is a pickpocket, but you know that pickpockets are very unpopular in San Francisco. If one comes in from out of town he leaves very hurriedly. But Squiffy can be happy only in San Francisco, so he curbs his natural talents."

"Oh. Then is it safe to leave him in?"

"It's safe to leave him alone in the living room. He won't steal our silver. He's harmless enough— the sort who runs errands for the higher-ups. Though, as Sullivan would tell you, we have no mobs or organized rackets in San Francisco. I suppose Squiffy has indulged in petty larceny in his time but until the last three years he would always claim he was a taxi driver."

"I see. What have you got on him?"

"Only Squiffy and I know. If I told you that would be three—and one too many. I believe everyone concerned, except Squiffy, is dead now. At least," Michael said, thinking of the Nevada bank robber Squiffy had, in a reckless moment, kept supplied with cigarettes and Prohibition liquor, "one of them came out shooting and died of six slugs in the belly."

"But where do you come in?"

"I wasn't involved in any way. Squiffy was so frightened afterward that he got roaring drunk and told me all about it when I put him to bed. You must already have guessed I knew him when I also was driving a wildcat taxi about the Mission. Squiffy has nothing to fear from me—but he doesn't know that."

"Whose car is he driving now? Mr. Gould's?"

"Yes." Michael got out of bed and looked about for a dressing gown. "We want to have an informal, pleasant chat with Squiffy. Tell Patton to bring me coffee in the living room when she gets back."

"She's here now, but I'll bring the coffee in," Valerie said, and when she had and prevailed upon Mr. Bain to accept a cup sat watching him drink it with an extraordinarily long little finger crooked to an equally extraordinary angle of refinement.

"Well," said Mr. Bain at last, putting his cup very carefully down on the nearest table and wiping his mouth with the back of his hand, "what's on your mind?"

"I only want to know if you're happy in your work, Squiffy."

"Ain't he a card?" Squiffy appealed to Valerie. "He always did talk like dat. You know, us guys used to call him 'the dook.'"

Valerie giggled. "Never mind," Michael said hastily. "How long have you worked for Gould?"

"He hired me last August, maybe because I ain't good lookin' and his wife and Miss Lawton is. A guy like Gould don't hire no good-lookin' shoffers if they got any sense. The goo-goo says his last one was a pretty old guy."

"How long has the Filipino been with them?"

"Ever since they foist moved here. He may just be dumb but he ain't talkin'. Me 'n' him's got a coupla rooms over the garage. The cook and maid don't sleep in. They're new too. Seems like the Goulds went to Texas in June last year. They wasn't satisfied with the cook or maid they had then, so they let 'em go.

"They put the goo-goo and shoffer on vacation wages and left them to look after the place, but the shoffer got himself another job. I un'erstand the dames come back in July, but Juan looked after them, an' dey can both drive, only Gould don't like 'em to. He's got a smaller car he drives himself an' sometimes he might let Miss Lawton use it, but not much. Mostly I take the women ever' place—"

"And report to Gould?" Michael said.

Squiffy shrugged. "I won't hold out on you, pal. Gould says when he hires me that he wants it un'erstood he pays my wages an' he can fire me an' dat I'm responsible to him and no one else. When I got a gander at his wife I t'ought I knew what he had in mind. But if she's cheated on him I don't know it."

"Has he asked you?"

"Well, after he was gone t'ree weeks this March he made out like he was checkin' up on the car, see? Gas and oil and repairs. But before he got t'rough I'd told him just about what his wife had did while he was gone. But it was all on the up-and-up."

"Suppose it hadn't been? Mightn't you be per-suaded to keep a lady's secret if she crossed your palm with folding money?"

"I won't say I wouldn't, though it's the truth I don't know nothin'. But Mrs. Gould ain't got no money to speak of. She can charge all she wants, but Gould checks up on the bills. I heard Mrs. Gould say so herself. It's funny how dames t'ink a guy can't hear nothin' just because he keeps his eyes straight ahead."

"That's true—but you also have very keen hearing, Squiffy."

"Dat's right," Mr. Bain said complacently. "Miss Lawton tries to shush her sister sometimes but she can't always, and I guess, from what she says, Gould never hands her out more 'n a fin."

"I'd slip him a fin," Valerie said indignantly. "A mickey finn."

"A fin—a mickey finn. Say, dat's good, ain't it?"

"I'd hoped," Michael said sadly, "that that quip would be received with the stony silence it deserves."

"Hunh? Well, I guess Mrs. Gould would like to slip Gould one sometimes. I hear her say to Miss Lawton once: 'You know Barney would fight it all the way to the Supreme Court before he'd give me a divorce—with alimony.' And she does complain about not havin' any cash and tries to borrow off her sister."

"And does Miss Lawton lend her money?"

"She buys her own clo'es and ain't got too much cash herself. I kind of gather sometimes Mrs. Gould buys things, charges 'em and hands 'em over to her sister for cash—at a discount. But I guess they don't even risk that often and not with high-priced things, except for one of them drippy long-haired fur jackets I seen Mrs. Gould wear once or twice, but now Miss Lawton wears it.

And maybe she just give it to her. I wouldn't call Gould tight in the ord'nary way."

"And I suppose he never forgets when he is riding with you that you may be listening?"

"I never heard him and the missus fight, if that's what you mean," Squiffy said.

"And, since Peter Wallis, Farnham and, I suppose, Geoffrey MacNair all have their own cars, you wouldn't have come in contact with them?"

"Oh, I see Wallis and MacNair around. Yeah, they got their own cars. This MacNair's sister, Mrs. Alling, she's got a Pierce-Arrow from way back. Not that it ain't still a good car, but, Jeez! the way she drives! I ain't seen this guy Farnham or his wife more than once or twice. Only, I hear 'em mention him—"

Squiffy hesitated, squirming reflectively about on the wing chair that was far too large for him.

"Well, I did hold out on Gould once," he said at last. "Dis was sometime last September. I was out in the garage one night about eleven o'clock, just t'inkin' I'd better get some shut-eye when she come kind of sneaking out like she hoped she could grab one of the cars. Gould was in, so far's I know. I had my orders not to let the cars out unless Gould says it's all right.

"Well, I guess she knows how it is when she sees me there, so she just tells me to drive her to

a hotel on Sutter Street. I got orders to take the
dames where they want to go if Gould don't say
diff'rent, so I take her there. It's one of these what
you call fam'ly hotels. She goes in and stays about
twenty minutes, and den I take her home. When
we get there she asked would I not say anyt'ing
about it to Gould if I don't have to."

"And you didn't?" Michael asked.

"Wait!" Squiffy said impressively. "It was—oh,
maybe six months after. I was taking Mrs. Gould
an' Miss Lawton an' this Mrs. Alling to the t'eay-
ter one afternoon an' I hear Mrs. Alling say she
hears the Farnhams is scrapping again and Ray's
livin' at the Trengrove Hotel again for a few days,
which means it's serious. Well, dat's the same
hotel I took Miss Lawton to—"

"Miss Lawton!" Valerie said. "But I thought—"

Squiffy grinned. "I never said it was Mrs.
Gould, did I? Gould never asked me nothin', and
I figured it wasn't his business. But it was Miss
Lawton, all right. And if you're thinkin' what I'm
thinkin'—" He grinned again, cynically.

VII

The clock striking ten and Patton's eyebrows as
she inquired if the "er—gentleman" would be
staying for breakfast brought Mr. Bain to his feet.
He left hurriedly, appearing not to notice that he

had acquired a ten-dollar bill and without asking questions.

It was not until Michael had finished describing his interview with Gould and telling her what he had learned from Payne that Valerie said what had been uppermost in her mind since Squiffy's departure.

"According to Peter, it was in September that Mrs. Farnham went to Mr. Gould's office and raised 'a hell of a scene.' If she did that I take it the situation was serious then. Serious enough—"

"For Farnham to have moved into the Trengrove Hotel, according to custom, for at least a few days," Michael said. "And you remind me that I must call him. . . ."

He went out to the telephone and returned in a few minutes, frowning.

"They say at his office that he's had to go to San Jose and won't be back before three—if then. And I'm afraid I can't very well go to his home, tell Mrs. Farnham what I want, stand over her while she looks for that envelope and if she finds it take it from her, unopened—if it can be found and is still sealed. I'd better deal directly with Farnham, and if I have to wait for him to call me it seems I'll get some work done today after all."

"I'm going to be downtown this afternoon. Is it all right if I drop in on you fairly late?"

"Of course. I'll leave word if I should have to meet Farnham before you get there," Michael said.

But he was still in his office, listening to what someone was saying over the telephone, when Valerie came in a little before five o'clock. He motioned to her to come closer until she could hear Farnham's voice clearly.

". . . remember the incident. The bartender did give me an envelope and said there were some of Logan's own trout flies in it that he thought I'd like to have Sunday morning. There were flies in the envelope. The point of a hook stuck through it in one place."

"But you didn't open the envelope?"

"No. It was so late that I knew Lilian would be wanting me to get dressed, and I hadn't even shaved yet that day. I put the envelope in my pocket, swallowed my drink in two gulps and went up to the third floor, as you know.

"Well, I never thought of those flies again, since we didn't go fishing on Sunday. When I finally found our new rooms after I talked to you I had to hurry to dress and didn't think of opening the envelope then. But it should still have been in the pocket of my fishing jacket—"

"'Should have'?" Michael repeated.

"It isn't now. I turned the pockets out this morning and put it away."

"Where was it before then?"

"When we got in from Summit House I simply dumped my things on the floor in my room. I told our maid not to touch anything. The jacket was in a suitcase that I carry reels, lines, leaders, flies and so on in. All the women, including my wife, know they aren't to meddle with that. But I think I can locate that envelope and I understand why the sheriff wants me to.

"Unfortunately, I have a very important appointment in a few minutes. I can't put this man off—I should have seen him this morning. I may not get home before six-thirty but I'll call you at your home as soon as I can. Will that do?"

"It will have to," Michael said. "Shall we say seven o'clock? My wife has just come in, and I don't know what her plans are. . . . What are they, my dear?" he asked, putting down the telephone.

"Oh, let's go up to the Mark. I don't want to go home so early."

"You only go to the Mark for the view," Michael said. "And it's foggy. But I don't mind. Let's sneak quietly out the back way before Fanchon finds anything more for me to do. The car is parked on the side street anyway."

Having successfully eluded Fanchon, he drove down Sutter to Mason, turned and shot up the hill to California. Here, where once lived the Western nabobs who, as a group, inspired the name Nob Hill, many of their names survive singly.

The dignified Fairmont looks over its square lawns toward the supercilious brown bulk of the Pacific Union Club. Next to this one-time home of his a small park bears Collis Huntington's name, and an apartment house across the street Leland Stanford's. And, with the singular inappropriateness that so often characterizes memorials, the Mark, a young hotel, a gay hotel, stands on the crest of the hill where Mark Hopkins, a man of simple tastes, reluctantly built a mansion to please his wife.

On the nineteenth floor Valerie and Michael sat at one of the coveted window tables and looked down at the city or out toward the Bay Bridge. The fog was an ever-moving, milky backdrop for tall buildings. Cable cars were ants sliding down California Street into Chinatown and away from it past the red solidity of Old St Mary's.

A waiter arrived, not too quickly and with an air of being quite willing to go away again if they were not ready for him. All the window tables were occupied now, but very few in the center of the room, under a ceiling like an overstuffed blue sky.

"If you can tear your eyes away from your beloved sky line," Mr. Dundas suggested.

"Oh, I want a zombie."

"You want a— I beg your pardon!"

"A zombie. It's a drink made with about six different kinds of rum. Dorothy, the girl who does my hair, told me about them. You never serve more than two to a customer, do you?"

"Well—it depends," the waiter said cautiously.

"You surprise me," Michael said. "Scotch and soda and one Coca-Cola. Good lord, Valerie! You've never drunk even one kind of rum. You must pick your drinks as you do your race horses —for their unusual or euphonious names."

"Only children who are brought up to see the view drink Coca-Cola. And you needn't be so—so dictatorial."

Michael whistled softly. "If you're going to make an issue of it I'll tell the waiter to bring you the legal limit: two zombies. It's your privilege to get tight if you want to."

"You're old-fashioned. It's all right for other women to drink zombies—but not your wife."

"My darling—will you shut your trap? If you're spoiling for a fight I'll be glad to oblige you when we get home. I've never asked you not to drink— only that you learn to handle your liquor before you drink in public. You don't like the taste of it, and a tablespoonful of whisky makes you dizzy. If it is old-fashioned to be glad I have never seen you swaying, slobbering and shouting at home or

in public, then I am old-fashioned. *¿Comprendes
tú?*"

"Yes." Valerie reached for his hand under the
table. "I don't want a zombie. I was just feeling
independent. You aren't angry?"

"Now you do sound downtrodden. If you will
hurry with this drink that's approaching I'll take
you in search of abalone, since Patton won't willingly cook the stuff. That is, if she will give us
leave to skip dinner at home."

He paid the waiter and when he had gone asked:
"Whom was that you spoke to?"

"Bettina and Peter. You can't see them—they
have a table over on the Golden Gate Bridge side—"

"I don't want to see them. ¡María santísima!
What places you women choose to assert your in-
dependence or to tell a man that from now on you
must meet only as friends!"

"Bettina knows that even Peter won't tear his
hair and shout up here. Shall we speak to them?"

"No, they are probably wondering if we will
and hoping that we won't. If you've finished let's
go down to Fisherman's Wharf. . . ."

"They've gone," Peter said. "What were you
asking me about Michael?"

"If he saw you again last night after he talked
to me in front of the house?"

"No. But I know what you told him to tell me." Peter might flare up again but just now he looked burned out. "There was a paragraph on one of the society pages today that said a little bird had whispered to the editor that you and MacNair would soon be middle-aisling it."

"Oh." Bettina flushed angrily. "Barney is responsible for that and he didn't consult me—"

"Does it matter? It's true, isn't it?"

"Yes, but Barney— No, it doesn't matter. But he does take too much on himself. You remember how he tried to—well, tried to keep me from talking to anyone at the hotel as long as we were there?"

"Why would I forget it?" Peter said grimly. "I didn't get a chance to talk to you, though I suppose if you had really wanted to talk to me—"

"With everyone watching us? If the sheriff could have thought of any reason why either of us would want to kill Mr. Logan he might have arrested one or both of us. Barney told me that, and I had to agree that he might be right. He said that the sheriff might think that you—that I—"

"That I killed Logan and you were protecting me? Well, we were outside and had to say we were. But we had agreed to meet at the pool, and Michael heard us. We told a straight story and the truth, but I suppose the sheriff might figure we had time to get together on our story."

"Yes," Bettina said. "And if we'd tried to talk together afterward he might have thought we wanted to agree what else we were to say if he kept questioning us. At least, that's what Barney said."

"Well, he may have been right. And I know I'd be in jail if it had been MacNair that was killed, or even Gould. What were you going to say about Mac-Nair? Or was it Gould you wanted to talk about?"

"I was—was angry with Barney," Bettina said slowly. "He seemed to be keeping watch over me. He saw to it that Stella was with me until late Sunday night. He—I don't know what he thought I might say, Peter!"

"He's too crooked himself to trust anyone."

"N-no. But does he think I know something that I don't know I know? Could I have seen or heard anything that night that I've forgotten? When I left the dance floor and started toward the pool I wasn't thinking of anything but getting there as quickly as possible. I don't remember even hearing any sounds in the trees or shrubbery. . . . But it's no use talking to Barney. He'd only put me off. I didn't talk to Geoffrey alone, either, until yesterday."

"You talked to him alone and now you're setting your wedding date," Peter said thoughtfully. "What does he know that he isn't going to tell—if you marry him?"

"I didn't say—"

"You don't need to. At the crucial time he was on the third floor looking for your wrap, wasn't he? And had a headache and stopped off to get some aspirin in his own room, and sister says she heard him. Yes, that's what sister says. The third floor—"

He smiled at her reassuringly. "Don't look so scared, honey. If this adds up to what I think it does it can be straightened out. Finish your drink. I suppose I have to get you home in time for dinner or Gould will jump down your throat, since you say MacNair's to be there tonight."

VIII

It was nearly fifteen minutes past seven before Valerie and Michael got back to Russian Hill Place, and Farnham, Patton reported, had telephoned at six forty-five.

"He said he had arrived home earlier than he'd hoped, sir, and then remembered he and Mrs. Farnham were to dine out. He was sorry he'd forgotten, but they must leave home by seven-fifteen. He didn't know when they would get home again—there might be cards after dinner and—"

"Is that all he said?"

"Oh no, sir. He said to tell you that he had found the object you and he discussed this afternoon and that it contained the other objects you supposed it did."

"Oh. Then I'll call Payne and—"

"But Mr. Farnham still wants to talk to you, sir. He wanted to know if ten-thirty would be too late to call again. I told him you are seldom in bed before midnight. I hope that was not presuming? He said he would call you by eleven at the latest."

"I'm glad you told him to call back but I don't see— Oh well." Michael walked over to the bookcases. "We'd better curl up with a good book and wait. . . ."

At ten-thirty he threw aside the last of half a dozen books he had dipped into during the evening.

"I think Farnham is giving us the run-around," he said abruptly.

"Why? He said he'd call you and that he wants to talk to you—"

"He doesn't have to talk to me if he doesn't want to, and why does he want to if that envelope contained only trout flies? If it contained something more important why wait until ten-thirty or eleven to tell me so, unless there's someone else he must talk to first? Five will get you ten, he invented that dinner engagement."

"He could have. And it is odd. . . ."

"I was inclined to agree with Payne this morning that the matter was hardly worth checking on.

Since he felt that way and wanted to handle it this way, we are forced to take Farnham's word for what was in that envelope. So I don't think I'll telephone him first. . . . You'd better come with me."

"To their home?"

"Yes. If necessary you can try to divert her. Perhaps we'd better say that we forgot to come home this evening and haven't received Farnham's message."

"But we were driving by their house and thought we would drop in? I'll look up their number in the telephone book and be ready in an instant."

The Farnhams lived on Marina Boulevard in a white stucco house whose front windows overlooked Yacht Harbor. As was usual in this district, the garage was under the house on one side, and a stairway with an iron railing led from a small tiled patio up to the front door.

The house was dark, and the garage doors locked. "Perhaps," Valerie whispered, standing in the patio and noting automatically that the plants in their hanging pots needed watering, "they did have a dinner engagement after all."

"We'll see." Michael started up the stairs. "If they're not home they should be very soon."

He rang the doorbell, and, as if that action released some force pent up in the dark house, a woman began to scream. Valerie stopped with the sound, halfway up the stairs. She clung to the iron railing, shivering. Yet the screams were not those of a person in terror but, rather, a protest against belief.

They broke off even before Michael began pounding on the door. Footsteps came toward them draggingly. For an instant Lilian Farnham stood staring at them foolishly before she screamed again. The sound seemed to surprise her. She sti-fled it with a hand against her mouth.

"Mustn't," she mumbled. "Mustn't—wake any-one. Can't—can't wake—the dead." In another instant she was shaking with laughter.

Michael slapped her face. She wilted under the blow, slipped slowly to her knees and lay there, whimpering, laughing, pounding her hands against the hall floor. Michael caught and held them and pulled her to her feet.

"This is the real thing," he said. "It may take a doctor to bring her out of it. Where— *¡Válgame Dios!* Valerie—"

A door down the hall had opened, and Patri-cia, wearing rumpled pink pajamas and still half asleep, stood blinking at them.

"I'm awful thirsty. And I heard a funny noise and— What's the matter with Mommy?"

"Get her back into her room," Michael said. "I can manage here. . . . Mrs. Farnham! Where is your bedroom?"

The woman stopped trying to twist away from him and fainted. Michael set his teeth and kicked open the nearest door off the hall. It led into a disorderly and deserted living room. He laid Lilian Farnham on a couch there and came back to the hall.

Valerie's voice, in Patricia's room, was only a soothing murmur, but the child's answer was distinct.

"Well, if Mommy is sick why didn't she call Daddy? She don't like me around when she's sick. I make her nervous. But why don't Daddy hear her? Maybe he couldn't sleep and went in his study and went to sleep there. Maybe he's there now. . . ."

Raymond Farnham was in his study across from the living room with two bullet holes in his back. He lay on one side, arms outflung, as if he had tried to raise himself. His head rested against one of them, and his peaked eyebrows still kept their look of rueful humor.

Michael backed out of the room, closed its door and found a telephone farther down the hall. Inspector Sullivan lived not four blocks from here. He was at home and, though it was "pretty irregular," he would be with them in five minutes. Yes, he would notify headquarters, and Michael would please not touch anything. He should know better by this time but—

"Don't worry," Michael said. "We have other things to think of, as you will see when you arrive."

He put down the telephone, glanced into the living room and then went in the direction of Patricia's voice, now asking: "Why can't I go look for Daddy? I won't bother Mommy, but she'll want Daddy."

She was very wide awake, sitting cross-legged on her bed in a small room papered in pale pink decorated with Teddy bears and wooden soldiers. Valerie stood between her and the door, already looking a trifle worn.

"I can't get her to go to sleep or stop asking questions."

"She doesn't have to go to sleep," Michael said. "Who is your mother's doctor, Patricia?"

"She has lots of doctors she goes to see in their offices, but Doctor Barker comes here when we're really sick."

"Suppose you call him, Valerie. I think Mrs. Farnham needs someone besides a police surgeon. She is still unconscious, and I'm not certain it's best to try to bring her to just now. Wrap your handkerchief around the telephone when you use it. . . . Was your father angry when he discovered you had gotten into the suitcase he carried his fishing tackle in?"

"Oh, he said he'd spank me next time I— How did you know?" Patricia said. "Did he tell you?"

"No. How did he know you'd been into his suitcase?"

"He just guessed I had just because he told me to keep out of it."

"And I 'just guessed' too."

"Oh. But I only took one fishline," Patricia said. "Just an old fishline isn't anything when he had lots, is it? But I might use it to catch fish when Pearl takes me walking 'long the water."

"But you need bait to catch fish," Michael objected. "Bait or flies. Your father is a fly fisherman, isn't he?"

"He wouldn't use bait for anything," Patricia said scornfully. "Well, so the envelope fell out of his fishing jacket, and I opened it. It was just an old envelope with no writing on it. But the flies were pretty, and Daddy has lots, so I took those."

"And he made you give them back to him?" Michael said sympathetically.

"Unh-uh. You want to see them?" Patricia scrambled off the bed and over to a diminutive bureau. "See? If I don't want to use them to fish I can put them on my doll's hat for a feather. Ladies are going to wear feathers this year, Mommy says."

"Yes, I believe they will. But I don't know what kind of flies these are, so how can I buy others like them? Trout flies do have names, don't they?"

"You don't know much about fishing, do you? There's black gnat, royal coachman, silver doctor— I should think you'd know *that!*"

"I'm afraid I didn't. If these flies have names why weren't they written on the envelope, Patricia? Or printed on it?"

"It was just an old, dirty envelope, and the flies weren't on the kind of card flies usually come on. They were just hooked through a piece of paper— gray paper like you write letters on. That's funny, isn't it?"

"Yes. And I suppose you threw the paper away?"

"That's what Daddy said. But I'd just put it in my little wastebasket over there, and Daddy got it out of that. He took it away and said I could keep the flies. He wasn't mad any longer. I mean, he looked awful funny but— That's the doorbell."

"I know." Michael looked out the door and down the hall. Sullivan was alone. His cohorts would not arrive for several minutes, and in the living room Lilian Farnham was calling for her husband.

Patricia was listening, too, tousled head cocked to one side. She eyed Michael with the puzzled, yet shrewdly speculative, glance children so often turn on grownups.

"Why does she keep calling Daddy like that? Your wife said maybe he just stepped out, but why doesn't he come back? I want to go—"

Michael stopped her at the door and then closed it. "*Ayúdame Dios,*" he muttered, picked the child up and sat down with her in the nearest chair. "Listen, Patricia . . ."

IX

"In the study—you think?" Sullivan said. "Well, where's Michael?"

"He has his hands full," Valerie said wearily. "There's a child in a bedroom back there."

"Oh. No, we don't want her around. Damn, it does seem like the boys should be here by now. Well, let's take a look at the wife."

Lilian Farnham stared at them vacantly but as soon as Sullivan began: "Mrs. Farnham, I'm Sullivan of the homicide detail—" she cowered down against the chesterfield, dangerously near hysteria again. Sullivan looked at her with an experienced eye.

"She isn't faking. I won't ask you any questions now, Mrs. Farnham, but I'm going to take you to your bedroom where people won't bother you. See if you can locate it for me, Valerie. No-ow, I'm not going to hurt you. Put your arms around my neck. That's right. Why, you aren't even a good armful. . . ."

He carried Mrs. Farnham down the hall and laid her on the bed in what was obviously a woman's room, untidy, crowded with possessions, stuffy with the scent of powder, cigarette smoke and perfumes.

"You just lie quiet for a while, and we'll send a doctor in to you."

"Are you always so chivalrous?" Valerie murmured as Sullivan backed away from the bed.

He shrugged. "Why not? It's a mistake to ask a woman in her condition any questions. They can claim later that you took advantage of 'em. There's the boys now. Look—you'd better stay with her—"

"I thought so."

"Well, I'll send a doctor in but I want him to look at Farnham first. So you stay here. . . . I'm coming! Don't bang the door down!"

He left the bedroom and Valerie standing irresolutely in the middle of it. She winced as she realized that a child was crying now in the little room at the end of the hall. Only Michael and Patricia would ever know what he'd said to her—except that anyone who knew him could be certain he'd told her as much of the truth as she could understand.

So she shouldn't mind staying here, Valerie thought—if Mrs. Farnham needed or wanted her. But she knew why Sullivan had asked her to stay and when the woman on the bed suddenly put out a groping, blue-veined hand she took it reluctantly.

"Something to hold on to," Mrs. Farnham muttered. "Nothing left at all— So funny—I said so many times I wanted a divorce from Ray if I could have Patricia. . . . But I didn't really want Patricia. I just wanted to hurt Ray. I never did want her. I only had her because I thought then he would really love me and be grateful to me."

"But he—he must have loved you," Valerie said inadequately. "He married you—"

"Yes, he was in love with me then. But he wouldn't love me enough. He liked other people. He wouldn't give up his old friends. Even if they were men they took him away from me. He liked other women too. He wanted to see other people—he wouldn't be satisfied just with me. Why wouldn't he?"

"I—I don't know," Valerie said helplessly.

"I don't either. I couldn't even make him jealous. I tried. I used to be very pretty, and men liked me, but Ray liked to have them like me— then. Later on I wouldn't risk even a harmless flirtation. It might have given him a chance to get rid of me. I wouldn't ever have let him be the one to leave me.

"But why couldn't he understand? I hated every woman he even liked to talk to—anyone that took him away from he. I wanted to claw their eyes out. But he wouldn't understand, and that made me nervous and sick and—"

"You're ill now. You shouldn't talk. . . ."

"But I have to tell someone," Lilian Farnham said. "People don't understand. Of course, when I was ill and bad tempered he didn't love me. But it was his fault I was like that. I'd have done anything to hurt him. I'd lie awake nights thinking of ways to make him come crawling to me—"

Valerie shivered. "And from love like this, good Lord, deliver me," she thought.

"Of course, I'd have forgiven him—but not until he'd been hurt like I have. Then he would always have been grateful. But it didn't happen like that."

"How did it happen?" Valerie said.

She risked the question, feeling hysteria was dignified when compared with the admission Lilian Farnham had just made. But she received the question calmly and when she finally spoke Valerie felt for the first time that she might be striving for effect—an effect of childish and bewildered submission.

"If I tell you perhaps they won't bother me. Something woke me. It must have been the—the shots. But I'd taken two sleeping tablets, so I couldn't think what the noise was. I called out to

Ray, but he didn't answer. I got up and looked in his room, but he wasn't there. I thought he was working late in his study— too late. I went in to tell him to go to bed and—and he was there. He was—he was— And while I was standing there you rang the doorbell. I—"

"Don't try to talk about it," Valerie said, feeling the complete hypocrite. She pulled her hand away from Mrs. Farnham's and opened the door to a redheaded police surgeon she'd met before and a short, thick-set man with a formidable jaw. The latter identified himself as Dr Barker, shouldered the police surgeon aside and tramped over to the bed.

"I'm sorry, Lilian," he said briefly. "Can't say more than that. Let's have a look at you."

Mrs. Farnham turned her face into the pillow and began crying weakly. Valerie slipped out of the room and leaned back against the door for an instant, eyes closed. When she opened them Sullivan was coming out of the study. . . .

Detective inspectors, like patrolmen along the water front, usually hunt in pairs. But, oddly enough, since he was the type usually labeled "genial," James Sullivan had never pulled well in double harness.

A certain Inspector Hunt once remarked acidly that "Sullivan would rather pick Michael Dundas' brains when he's on a tough case than work with anyone on the force." In moments of exasperation Sullivan would tell Michael: "I'm the only guy on the force that would put up with you." Which statement was true—but so was Inspector Hunt's.

As Sullivan had ability and seniority and was politically well connected, the higher-ups were inclined to let him work alone when he wanted to. So tonight he was unhampered by the presence of another inspector.

Sergeant Cooley, who had known Sullivan since they were boys South-of-the-Slot, also knew his ways and was an admirable Watson. In the study he stood patiently, notebook in hand, awaiting Sullivan's orders, but equally prepared to be merely an attentive audience of one.

"Well, the room doesn't tell us much," Sullivan said finally. "Everything in order, though it could do with some dusting. Looks like he was working—or tried to work. Lawbooks on the desk, papers—"

"Some law case he had in hand," Cooley ventured, looking down at the papers from his station at the end of the mahogany kneehole desk.

"Yes. He doesn't seem to have done any writing or made any notes. Doesn't look like anything's disturbed or anybody looked for anything. We can tell better about that later. Look, Tim. See if

there's some stairs down to the garage and basement. There are in our house, and it's pretty much
like this one. Well, Doc?"

"Oh, he hasn't been dead long." The police surgeon rose from his knees. "All right, you can photograph him. I'd say he wasn't killed any earlier
than ten-thirty. Bullets still in him."

"Ten-thirty? That's fixing it pretty close, because it was about five of eleven when Michael
called me. He said they got here about ten forty-
five, and Farnham was dead then."

"Dundas up to his old tricks?" the doctor inquired. "Why ten minutes before he notified you?"

"He had a woman in hysterics and a youngster
on his hands. I want you to take a look at this
Mrs. Farnham. She was shot to pieces when I saw
her."

"Worst case of hysteria I ever saw with a woman
who emptied an automatic into her husband," the
surgeon said thoughtfully. "You know -the gun
just went off and shot him, and then she wished it
hadn't? Well, where is Mrs. Farnham?"

"Bedroom down the hall. Don't be rough with
her. But I'd like to talk to her if you think—"

Cooley came back into the study with a stranger whom he introduced as "Doctor Barker. He
says he's Mrs. Farnham's doctor and Mrs. Dundas
phoned him."

"You known the Farnhams long?"

"Since before the child was born. If Ray had been making the money then that he was now undoubtedly Lilian would have had a specialist who'd have charged her three prices. I'm one of these old-fashioned family physicians who still makes night calls," Barker said rather absently. He looked down at Raymond Farnham and added: "Pity."

"You don't seem much surprised," Sullivan remarked.

"Death doesn't surprise a doctor," Barker said sententiously. "I see he didn't kill himself."

"Did you think he might? Did he have a gun?"

"He kept a gun in one of those desk drawers, but don't ask me what kind. I fish, not hunt, when I manage to get a vacation. There were some burglaries in this neighborhood, and Lilian was nervous. He said he'd had the gun for years and took it out and loaded it. And he obviously didn't shoot himself in the back—and he wasn't the kind of weakling who kills himself anyway."

"Looks to me like he may 've been going toward the door when he was shot," Sullivan said. "That seem reasonable to you?" The police surgeon nodded. Barker merely grunted. "Well, maybe you can tell us about the servants, Doctor Barker?"

"They don't sleep in. They have a cook—that is, they have a new one about every three months—

and a bone-lazy colored girl who's good to the youngster. They pay her extra to stay here with Patricia when they're going out. And where is Patricia? Has anyone thought of her or—?"

"Wouldn't her mother?" Sullivan said. Barker shrugged. "Well, she's well taken care of. You gentlemen better go see Mrs. Farnham. I want to talk to her if I can. . . . Well, Tim?"

"Sure, there's some stairs down to the basement and garage," Cooley said. "There's a door down the hall that opens onto them. It ain't locked. Then there's a back door in the basement that opens out onto the back yard and it ain't locked either."

"Easy for anyone to get out without being seen leaving by the front door then. Well, I'll leave you in charge here." While Sullivan had been talking to the doctors the photographers and fingerprint men had been going on with their work. "Take a look at Farnham's bedroom too. I want to talk to Dundas."

He stepped into the hall and saw Valerie leaning against the closed door of Mrs. Farnham's bedroom. "Better not ask her any questions right now," he thought. She looked pretty tense, so Mrs. Farnham had probably talked. Give Valerie time to think it over, and she'd tell him all about it.

"Want to come with me?" he said. "I want to see what Michael's up to."

"'Up to'? He's done a very unpleasant job for you—"

"I know," Sullivan said placatingly. "I've broken bad news like this to a lot of people but I don't like telling a youngster one of her parents has been killed. Maybe you'd better tell me how you and Michael happened to come here. He didn't take time to and he may not be able to talk before the kid."

"Perhaps not. Well, it began with a telephone call from the sheriff, Mr. Payne, this morning," Valerie said. "He had been talking to the bartender at Summit House, and the bartender told him . . ."

X

"This is Inspector Sullivan, Patricia," Michael said. "He's the man I told you about—"

"The one that has to ask questions when people get killed?" Patricia said, sitting up and wiping her nose on the sleeve of her pajamas.

"Yes, that one. I suppose, Sullivan, you don't know why we happened to come here?"

"Yes, I do. Valerie brought me up to date."

"Then suppose you tell the inspector what you've told me, Patricia, beginning with when you reached home on Monday night."

"Well, we got home. So yesterday Pearl—that's our colored girl—was making up Daddy's bed. So I looked in his fishing suitcase. I took a fishline out of it—and his fishing jacket, because it was on top of things. And an envelope fell out, so I opened the envelope."

Patricia had begun apathetically, but her sense of the dramatic reasserted itself, until now she began illustrating her statements with appropriate gestures.

"There was a long piece of paper inside, with three fishing flies stuck through it. The paper was just an old piece of paper but it had pictures and letters on it—"

"Hunh?" said Inspector Sullivan. "It did!"

"Yes." Patricia nodded importantly. "First there was a picture of a hat—"

"A hat? Oh, now, look here—"

"It was a hat! A big hat with a dent in the crown. And then there was a cute little house."

"Hat—house," Sullivan muttered. "It doesn't make sense. Are you sure—?"

"She is," Michael said. "Obviously I didn't suggest to her that she saw pictures of a hat and a house on that slip of paper. It's very natural that she should remember them and as natural that she can't remember what followed the picture of the house—which, she says, was 'just a little house with a door and a window.'"

"I do remember there were a whole lot of letters after the house," Patricia said. "The letters were printed the way people print them—"

"Can you read?" Sullivan asked.

"Of course I can! Well, I can read pretty good, even if I am delicate and miss school sometimes. The letters were written like two words—a long word and a short one. But they didn't spell any words I know, and there was a whole lot of Xs in one of them—the long one."

"Enter: the mysterious X," Michael said.

"It doesn't make sense," Sullivan repeated.

"No, but it is fairly certain Logan must have decorated that strip of paper in the fashion Patricia's described when he was in his room last Saturday afternoon. Then he stuck three of his own trout flies through the paper, put them in an envelope and gave them to Gus, the bartender."

"And Gus gave it to Farnham, who never got around to opening the envelope," Sullivan said. "I understand that. Patricia opened it—"

"And put it and the paper in my wastebasket over there," Patricia said, "till this evening Daddy came asking me about the flies and had I been in his suitcase. So I told him—about the pictures on the paper too. And he took it out of the wastebasket and then after a minute he looked awfully funny."

"Yes?" Sullivan said encouragingly.

"He stood there for a minute—like this." Patricia drew her soft brows down into a scowl. "Then he said to keep the flies and he walked out."

"Where was your mother when this was happening?"

"Why, Mommy had a late 'ppointment for her hair. She called before Daddy came home and told Pearl she had to wait because some other woman was late and they were late taking her, so she would just take a taxi and go straight to the Martins'—"

"What d'you mean?" Sullivan said sharply. "Didn't she come home at all?"

"She woudn't be here now if she hadn't, would she?" Patricia said sensibly. "She and Daddy were going to the Martins' for dinner. She told Pearl to tell Daddy she'd meet him there. But she didn't, because Daddy didn't go. Pearl was supposed to stay with me, but he told her to go on home, and she did."

Sullivan looked at Michael. "Well! That does make a difference, doesn't it?"

"I suppose so. But we don't know whether Farnham decided not to meet Mrs. Farnham at the Martin home because he didn't want to see her until he could speak to her privately or whether he stayed here because he had other arrangements to make. He did tell Patton he probably wouldn't be home before ten-thirty, probably to keep me from telephoning or calling on him here before then."

"But he was home," Patricia said uncomprehendingly. "And, anyway, Mommy had told Pearl she was sure they'd be home by ten because the Martins are deadly bores and people always leave early."

"Lord, little pitchers do have long ears," Sullivan said. "I suppose Farnham knew what time Mrs. Farnham would be apt to get home then. Did your father do any telephoning, Patricia?"

"He called the Martins and told them an important case had come up and he was sorry but he couldn't make it and please to explain to Mommy. When I woke up and heard her in the hall I thought she was mad at Daddy about that."

"Uh—you mean, you thought they were quarreling?"

"Yes," Patricia said calmly, "and that she was very mad and starting to stamp her feet and scream."

"Oh. Good lord! No wonder you're so— Well, then, you hadn't heard your mother come in?"

"No. Daddy put me to bed at nine, and I went to sleep. Some funny noise woke me up. Was—was it the gun, Mr. Dundas?"

"Probably," Michael said matter-of-factly. "They do make a noise."

"As to no one else hearing the shots, it's the same old story," Sullivan remarked. "So many cars go along Marina Boulevard people would put the shots down to backfire from some car. I suppose you don't know these Martins you speak of, Patricia?"

"They're old and have lots of money, and Daddy is Mr. Martin's lawyer. Mommy don't like them but she has to be polite because Mr. Martin is important to Daddy," Patricia said glibly.

"But Farnham risked offending Martin," Michael said. "I was wrong when I guessed he had invented a dinner engagement. But it doesn't matter whether he had forgotten it or simply didn't mention it to me this afternoon. It's what he did about it that's important."

"Yes, but—uh—should we—uh?" Sullivan said, glancing meaningly at Patricia.

"Talk before Patricia? I suppose not, though what she can't understand won't hurt her, and she might as well know what is within her comprehension. Haven't you an aunt, Patricia?"

"Daddy's sister? Aunt Evelyn? I like her, but Mommy doesn't. But she's in New York."

"We'll have to find her address and notify her," Sullivan said. "But that makes it bad, unless there are some other relatives—"

"Not here," Patricia said. "I just have a grandfather—Mommy's father—and he lives in Boston now. They don't get along."

"Hm-m. Michael, do you suppose you could—?"

"I'm afraid we can," Michael said. "Would you like to go home with us, Patricia?"

"Yes, I would. I like you."

"Then you may if you'll stay here quietly until we're ready to leave," Michael said, putting her on her feet. "'Quietly' means that you aren't to bombard Valerie with questions. She's tired."

"Amen!" Valerie said fervently as the two men left the room. In the hall Sullivan shook his head.

"Is she really as hardhearted a brat as she seems?"

"Hardhearted? She has already learned to accept things as they are. She has learned that she 'gets on Mommy's nerves.' I suppose she knows instinctively that Mrs. Farnham hasn't asked for her now. I doubt if she's ever run to her mother for comfort. She did love her father, but children are easily diverted."

"Well, a noticing child like that is a help if you're sure you can depend on— Something?"

"We found Farnham's gun," Cooley reported. "It was under the desk—not the kneehole part, but like someone had thrown it down so it slid under the drawer that comes down closer to the floor."

"Like someone grabbed the gun out of the desk, shot Farnham, standing there while he walked away, and then threw the gun down?"

"Could be," Cooley said cautiously. "Two shots fired from it. No fingerprints. It only takes a minute to wipe 'em off, but a gun's an inconvenient kind of thing to have in your possession. Well, we'll have the usual reports for you, Inspector, but they're all what you might call negative. Farnham hadn't slept in his bed. There's nothing that seems important in his room either."

"And you didn't turn up a piece of paper about— say, six to eight inches long? There would be pictures of a hat and a house on it and some letters."

"A hat? No, we didn't find anything like that. But I'll look again," Cooley promised. "I'll swear there was nothing like that in the living room, so if you want to set down in there go ahead."

XI

Sullivan sat down on the chesterfield and lighted a cigarette. "Well, the question is: Did Logan intend to blackmail Farnham, and if he did why was Logan killed? Because, from the evidence, Farnham never got Logan's message until this evening. It evidently meant something to Farnham, and I can see that Farnham could have been blackmailed, though I can't guess where Logan could get any information for blackmail. But if he did have some why go about putting the bee on him that way?"

"Blackmailers do have to exercise some discretion," Michael said. "I'd be very careful how I approached a clever lawyer like Farnham. Perhaps Logan would have preferred to speak to him privately but couldn't make an opportunity to do so. Farnham left the hotel before sunrise on Saturday and returned very late. I imagine Logan wanted to make certain Farnham would seek him out Sunday.

"If he had to commit himself on paper it was certainly only common sense to think out some cryptic message that would mean something to Farnham and no one else. He could claim that he left only three trout flies at the bar for Farnham and leave it up to Farnham to say why anything written on that slip of paper constituted blackmail."

"Y-yes," Sullivan said. "But—"

"I know. The message doesn't make sense. It doesn't call to mind any of the usual material for blackmail. And, as you say, if Farnham didn't get the message and no one intercepted it—"

"That's not likely, do you think?"

"No. Well, if the message was an attempt at blackmail and Farnham didn't see it until tonight why was Logan killed? You might say, because Logan's information concerned not only Farnham but another person that Logan couldn't blackmail—"

"Couldn't?"

"You can't get money from people who haven't it. Logan couldn't collect any real money from Stella Gould, Bettina, Peter or Mrs. Farnham. But he could have whispered a word in this second person's ear. From what I was told about him, he might have found that amusing. But it would have been bad business."

"Yes," Sullivan agreed. "People pay blackmail for secrecy. And there's another thing. If that was a blackmail message why did Farnham want to talk to you tonight? All he had to do was to tell you there were only trout flies in that envelope. He didn't have to tell you that Logan had intended to blackmail him."

"If I had known Farnham better I'd try to guess whether or not be would have admitted that under certain circumstances."

"What circumstances?"

"If Logan's little love letter made him suspect who had killed Logan. It seems Farnham must have wanted to talk to someone else before discussing the matter with me. Was he going to warn someone or ask for an explanation?"

"As he meant to talk to you later, I'd incline toward the last idea," Sullivan said.

"The difficulty is that there's another possibility. Logan might not have been blackmailing Farnham.

He may have had information to sell, not merely information he would promise to forget for a price."

Sullivan nodded. "I was thinking that. That would account for Farnham meaning to talk to you when he'd checked up a little. From what you say, he'd have been glad to get a divorce from his wife on his own terms. Suppose—"

"But would he turn his wife over to the police even if he suspected she had murdered Logan?"

"I don't know," Sullivan said gloomily. "I suppose not. Still, could any man go on living with a woman he suspected was a murderess?—and let her have a hand in raising his daughter?"

"That last consideration might turn the scales against her. Even if he only convinced her that he could, and was going to, divorce her and obtain complete custody of the child—"

"That would be enough to make her see red. But that still begs the question of what he meant to tell you. If he suddenly divorced his wife you and all the others might wonder why she let him. He might have thought up some story he was going to tell you to try to cover up for her and throw you off the track—after he had warned her. Suppose he said he'd let her get the divorce as long as she kept her mouth shut and let him have the child?"

"That isn't bad. But it's all guesswork."

"Well, here's some more. Suppose Logan had it in for Gould, and Farnham did too? Or Logan had something on Gould he thought Farnham might like to know? Oh hell! That's enough of that. Wait a minute. I'm going to try to talk to Mrs. Farnham."

He returned in five minutes, frowning discontentedly. "Barker claims she isn't fit to be questioned. He's given her an opiate and telephoned for a nurse. I did get her to tell me she got home at ten. She was sore because Farnham hadn't showed up at the Martins' house. They had words, and she got a headache, and Farnham gave her some sleeping tablets and insisted on her going to bed. When the shots woke her she didn't realize at first what they were but she went into his study and found him there.

"But sleeping tablets don't usually take full effect in such a short time," Sullivan added. "We've only her word for it that she and Farnham didn't keep on quarreling—until he was killed. Her bed was mussed up like it had been slept in, but that's a detail she could have tended to. Anyway, it looks like your gun wasn't used to kill Farnham."

"I suppose the theft of that gun served its purpose," Michael said wearily. "It drew me into this. And it warned us there might be another murder. And I've gone through some futile gestures trying to prevent it."

"How could we when we didn't have any idea who might be killed? But now Logan's death is our business too. We'll start checking back on him ourselves and on all of these people. I'll be seeing all of them tomorrow and I'd better not take any more time talking to you. Of course, Cooley will cover the other houses on this block when he gets round to it but—"

"But I'm afraid you'll have to listen to me for a while longer," Michael said. "Though, God knows, I'd rather go home. I've some information you should have before you approach the various suspects. It came to me from talking to Peter Wallis, Gould and Gould's chauffeur, Squiffy Bain."

"Squiffy? Is he still around?"

"He's walked the straight and narrow for three years—he says. So don't let Gould know the source of your information. I'll begin with Peter and end with Squiffy, and then we are going home. . . ."

PART FOUR

"Let's vary piracee
With a little burglaree."
Pirates of Penzance

I

At a little before eleven o'clock of Thursday morning Michael stopped his car in front of the Gould home. He slammed the door so that the window rattled reproachfully and then admitted that nothing but his own curiosity had forced him to come here. Stella Gould had been persistent but placid when she telephoned at ten o'clock to ask him to "please drop by and see me before noon. Barney's out, and I want to talk to you."

When he told her curtly that he was still only half awake and in no mood for conversation she said tranquilly:

"This wouldn't be exactly conversation. I could come over to your house, but Barney wouldn't like it."

And Barney wouldn't like this, Michael thought, ringing the doorbell. The Filipino opened the door, regarding him impassively. He said: "This way, please," and conducted him upstairs.

He stopped before a door that had a brass knocker in the shape of a cat's head, raised his hand to it and then stopped. On the other side of the door Stella was speaking, slowly and most earnestly.

"In*ex*plicable," she said. "In*ex*tricable, *ap*plicable, *hos*pitable, con*tem*plative, quin*tup*— Darn it! *Quin*tuplet, *des*picable, in*cog*nito—"

The Filipino turned and looked at Michael blankly. "I think she is alone," Michael said, grinning. "You might knock anyway."

"In*ex*plicable, in*ex*tricable— Oh! Come in," Stella said, and opened the door. "I didn't think you'd get here so quick. Sit down. Did you hear me?"

"Distinctly. Am I mistaken in supposing that somewhere you've found a list of words most commonly mispronounced and their correct pronunciations?"

Stella nodded and sighed. "Why, if it's pro*noun*ced, shouldn't it be pro*noun*ciation?" she said. "But you've got the swellest voice. Just like Ronald Colman's."

"Thank you," Michael said, not too gratefully. "I'm afraid I don't share your passion and my wife's for Mr. Colman. But, my dear girl, when you have learned to pronounce inexplicable and inextricable correctly what use will you have for the words?"

"I know what they mean," Stella said good-naturedly. "And at least people do talk a lot about the quin—quintuplets. I get awful tired having to watch myself when we're with people that matters. They expect my voice and English to match my looks, and they don't. I get by unless I get excited or have to do a lot of talking, so mostly I just don't talk much."

"Why not go to a good teacher? He will train you to say: 'The rains in Spain are mainly on the plains' or 'The duke laughed, "Ha, ha, ha!" as the hounds came r-running.'"

"Gosh! I know the first one—I've seen *Pygmalion* four times. I just love Leslie Howard. But what's the last one for?"

"Pear-shaped vowels, I've been told. Didn't you go to high school, Mrs. Gould?"

"Sure, till I was sixteen. But I was more interested in beaux than books. And there was too much to do at home for me to study much there. Aren't you going to sit down?"

She gathered up the full skirt of her padded house coat and settled herself on a chaise longue. For the first time Michael really looked at the room. He closed his eyes involuntarily, opened them and looked again.

Whatever was not glass was completely covered with silk, satin or lace, either black or white. The rug was white velvet, the wallpaper white with a black stripe, the drapes white satin with what appeared to be black orchids woven into them.

"What do you think of it?" Stella said, watching him with an unexpected twinkle in her eyes.

Michael discarded several comments as being, if nothing more, mildly indelicate. He said at last, thoughtfully: "It has been some years since I have been in a bedroom like this," got up and opened the door. "In case your husband should return unexpectedly."

Stella chuckled. "I know what you're thinking. It's what Barney said when he first saw the room. Especially the bed."

The bed somewhat resembled a thin slab of devil'sfood cake generously frosted with white and further decorated with a thick froth of whipped cream.

"What, no cherry?" Michael murmured. "I don't see how any man could manage to— Oh well, never mind."

"I know it's vulgar," Stella said cheerfully. "But I never could have too much silk and lace around me, though I'd like it better if it was all pink. I just love pink. But after a painter told me I oughtn't to wear anything but black and white I don't. I guess some of my clothes were pretty loud once. But when I was a kid I wanted a pink silk party dress more than anything."

"Didn't you get it?"

"No. Any more than I got the pink silk evening dress I wanted later on. Gosh, Mr. Dundas, army brats aren't exactly smothered in clover. Momma was a poor manager and, with one baby after another, she didn't have time to look after me. When people say to me how glamorous army life must be I want to give them the horselaugh."

Michael winced. "Eliminating expressions like that one from your vocabulary would benefit it more than learning how to pronounce quintuplet."

Stella flushed. "I know. But I can't seem to get the hang of the slang that's fashionable now. And if you're going to be like that I can't talk!

"I was going to say I was born in the Philippines, and between then and the time I was sixteen we were at about three different army posts, all over the United States. Then Poppa was transferred to Fort Sam. That's where I first saw Tex Logan. You don't seem surprised."

"The sheriff already knows that Logan joined the army in 'twenty-four in San Antonio."

"I told Barney they'd find that out. Not that he ever knew I'd ever seen Logan before till I told him the night we got back from Summit House.

He'd mentioned Tex Logan and Tex's father to me, but it just happened I was never around when Barney ran into Tex before we moved here."

"Mr. Gould told me that Logan was never in this house."

"Of course he wasn't. And the name didn't mean anything to me. Just his face was familiar the time I saw him at the stables at Maria Alling's place. I got just a glance at him but I did try to think where I'd seen him before and then just forgot it."

"That's natural enough, since you didn't see him again—then."

"I didn't. But when we got to Summit House and he was around naturally I kept trying to place him till I finally connected him with Fort Sam."

"Weren't you surprised that your paths should cross again?"

"They'd never really crossed before. Poppa may have been a mustang, but, mustang or not, no officer's daughter mixes with enlisted men. But trails do cross. Take a Prairie Jack like Logan—or like Barney was—and every place they go they run into some other rolling stone they met somewhere else. It's like that in the service, too, especially with these barracks-bag soldiers. I'm so used to people being here today and gone tomorrow I just expect to run into them again some other tomorrow."

"Did Logan recognize you?" Michael asked.

"I don't know. I've changed a lot since I married Barney. I was always pretty," Stella said matter-of-factly. "But I didn't always dress or do my hair like I do now. Logan stared at me a lot, but I'm used to being rubbered at."

"But you didn't think it was necessary to tell him you were Lieutenant Lawton's daughter?"

"Why would I? Barney wouldn't have like it. I was all set to say to him how funny it was that his Tex Logan should turn out to be someone who'd been in Poppa's regiment. But when Logan was killed I didn't. Barney said he didn't want to admit he'd known Logan because the sheriff might keep us there. He said it would be simpler to tell him after we'd gotten back here. So I just kept my trap shut too."

"But you're opening it now."

Stella shrugged. "It 'll all come out in the end. The city police aren't going to be like a hick sheriff, though I don't think he's such a boob as Barney did. And after what's happened to poor Ray Farnham the police will get busy, and Barney's money isn't going to cut any ice with them. He hasn't lived here long enough to have any pull."

"Does he realize that?"

"He used to know who he could bulldoze and who he couldn't. But he's changed a lot too. He

VIRGINIA RATH

was a swell fellow when I married him, even if he didn't have the dough he has now. Oh, he wasn't broke then," Stella said. "He had what seemed plenty to me, but before he really struck it rich there were times when the bank roll was pretty flat.

"Like the time he drilled three wildcats, and they were all dusters. I've lived in shacks in more than one town on a boom. I kind of got a kick out of it then. It 'd kill me now. It's been so long since I had to stand reveille or K.P. that I've gotten soft."

"And Mr. Gould?"

"He thinks he ought to have his own way about everything. Kind of like Napoleon."

"Napoleon?" Michael repeated, thinking of Logan's caricature of Bernard Gould.

"I know about Napoleon—him and Josephine both. I do read. I've seen pictures of him that sort of remind me of Barney when he's laying down the law. But don't make any mistake about me being grateful to him. He married me, and no questions asked—though neither did I ask him how many times he shacked in with some pretty Mex before he married me. He's a lot older than I am, but I never thought much about that till he began turning into a stuffed shirt.

"Maybe that isn't the right word," Stella added. "But this society stuff gives me a pain. I suppose since Barney has everything else he wants that too. But you can't buy it with money. I know all about cliques and inner circles."

"Because Papa came up from the ranks?"

"Yeah—yes. I guess you've heard how snooty they are in the service. Besides," Stella admitted, "I was too pretty and flirted too much for any of the old cats at Fort Sam to give me the benefit of a doubt. But, honest, formal parties bore me stiff. Bettina don't mind them. Gramma brought her up on that kind of thing.

"Barney's always gotten what he's gone after, so he thinks it's just a matter of time till we'll be in society. Not the inner circle here—even he isn't jeepy enough to expect that. I wouldn't even be surprised if he decided to go in for politics. I'm willing to play ball, the best I can, but I don't like him using Bettina to get ahead."

"Oh?" Michael said. "But, while your sister is very attractive and obviously well bred, is that enough to make her the steppingstone into a more select puddle?"

Stella giggled. "You mean Barney's a big frog in a small puddle now? He does want to get in a bigger one. He's as bad as Gramma used to be, talking about Bettina making a good match. And Geoff is what they call an eligible bachelor. He knows lots of people here. Though, as I tell Bettina, a bachelor's something hostesses can't have too many of, but when one marries that's something else again.

"Bettina don't like being snubbed any better than I do but she hides it better. And Maria would be behind them—and us. She knows people here that get their names in the papers—the right way. That's one thing that's eating Barney—he don't want ours in the papers the wrong way. And Maria knows a whole raft of people down where she lives. A lot of them are pretty horsy." Stella sighed. "I hate horses. I haven't ridden since one threw me off in a patch of cactus."

"Nor I, since one tried affectionately to remove my left ear," Michael said sympathetically. "Is Mrs. Alling well-to-do?"

"Well, I— Oh well, she says herself she has a lot of land and, though she raises enough on the place to feed herself and all the bums that hang round that hacienda, she don't have any cash. She had to give up racing, you know. Geoff would help her out if she'd let him. He's got a lot more dough than people would think from the way he lives. His wife—"

"His—what?" Michael asked.

"Oh gosh, I guess I've blabbed off again. It don't really matter, but you just don't mention her."

"Does your sister know?"

"She knows he was married and his wife's been dead about ten years. He told Barney and then he told Bettina—that."

"That much and no more, you mean?"

"I didn't say that—and I don't know. I'd better not talk about it. And I wanted to ask you about Ray Farnham."

"You've read the morning papers, haven't you?"

"Yes, but— Did Lilian do it?"

"You think she might have?" Michael said.

"In one of those tantrums of hers. She wouldn't ever have let him go of her own accord, you know."

"No," Michael said, recalling Valerie's account of her ten minutes with Mrs. Farnham, "I'm afraid she wouldn't have."

"If she had a chance to make it look like she was the one who'd had enough she is just stinkin' mean enough that she wouldn't think about his career or anyone else's reputation, just so she could have the upper hand."

"You seem to know her quite well."

"I did," Stella said. "We were almost chummy for a while. Any woman needs another woman to talk to sometimes. But it didn't last. I've never had any real women friends. I suppose it's because they think I'm too good looking. You don't know what a strain it is to be called beautiful and have to live up to it. And that's all I've got. There's probably only two ways I could earn my own living, and one of them is hashing. I've done that—I skipped out of San Anton' for a while when I was eighteen. But if I had to do it now— Well, look at this!"

Her gesture embraced the room and all its furnishings. "I'm used to this kind of thing now. I'm soft. I'm not really important to Barney. It's enough for me just to look well. He likes me to depend on him and let him take the lead. I'm lazy —I admit it. I won't put up a scrap unless it's really worth the effort."

"In which way you differ from Mrs. Farnham?"

"I'll say so! I suppose you heard how she made it impossible for us to go on being friends with her and Ray like we were once? I liked Ray real well too. He seemed to like me, though we never had much to talk about. He liked Barney too. He said he admired his energy, though he did have the nerve to laugh at him sometimes."

"Does that take so much courage?" Mr. Dundas inquired.

"I guess it wouldn't worry you that Barney don't like to be laughed at. Well, Lilian not only practically accused me of having an affair with Ray but she said some nasty things about Bettina too. I guess it's possible Bettina could have had a case on Ray when we first met him, though she never acted like it. Gosh, she's had plenty of beaux, and he was almost old enough to be her father. Not that he seemed old—and I guess she did admire him. Who told you about the row Lilian raised?"

"Peter Wallis. Is it true that now and then Mr. Farnham used to clear out and stay at the Trengrove Hotel for several days?"

"T-the Trengrove? Oh—yes, I guess that was where he'd go when things got too hot at home. Like the fellows in the movies who move to their clubs. . . ."

"Yes, except that Farnham chose the hotel instead. A very wise choice, I think. One runs into inquisitive friends at clubs. But was he forced to go to the Trengrove at the time we've been speaking of? Last September, that is, when Mrs. Farnham threw that now-historic scene in Mr. Gould's office?"

"Y-yes, I guess he cleared out for a few days till Lilian got over it. But if Peter told you all that he's got a nerve, shooting off his bazoon that way. Because when he was just out of college he was very friendly with the Farnhams. Did he tell you that?"

"No, he did not."

"Well, probably Peter's ashamed of it now but he had a case on Lilian— Oh, she isn't over four years older than he is and she'd be attractive if she'd get that chip off her shoulder. Even two years ago she was a lot better looking than she is now. She hasn't been well, though part of the time she's just goldbricking, and even when she's really sick it's mainly that rotten disposition of hers that makes her that way. She wasn't so bad even two years ago, and it was three when Peter saw so much of her."

"Just what did Mrs. Farnham say about Peter?"

"Oh, that he was a 'sweet boy' but she had to tell him she mustn't see so much of him when Ray began to get jealous. She'd never admit it if it was Peter who got tired first. She didn't like it when she saw he'd fallen for Bettina. She began calling him a fortune hunter and a gigolo. I guess she never stopped to think what she was if he was a gigolo."

"I can see how he may have drifted into it," Michael said. "Many young professional men earning very small salaries are encouraged to amuse bored wives."

"They don't always need encouragement, so long as they can get free meals. Oh, I don't blame Peter. Only, it's funny he didn't tell you about him and Lilian when he told you so much else. Or maybe it's not."

"His not being entirely frank is less peculiar than the fact that you apparently have been," Michael said bluntly. "You didn't have to talk to me like this. Why have you?"

"I didn't intend to gab so much, but one thing seemed to lead to another. I guess I was just aching to talk anyway."

"Then why not talk to your sister?"

"Bettina and I don't talk as much as you'd think. She don't know what Barney might worm out of me and she might talk too much to Peter—or Geoff. But Geoff don't shoot his mouth off, and Peter might. I don't want Bettina to worry about my affairs, though I'm afraid she does. And I've got the idea lately she thinks I'm hand in glove with Barney to make sure she marries Geoff.

"But I won't try to kid you. I did want to make a deal. I thought if I talked to you, then maybe you'd put in a good word for us with this Inspector Sullivan. Maria Alling was talking about you and she said you'd helped Sullivan on several cases, so you must know him pretty well."

"I can't keep him from questioning you, Mrs. Gould," Michael said.

"I know. And I'll answer him, very prim and proper, which means I won't say much or only what Barney will let me. But don't it depend a lot on the cop in charge how much the newspaper reporters get to know?"

"To some extent, though reporters often discover facts for themselves. What is it you want to hide? And can't you leave it to your husband to try to corrupt or intimidate our public servants?"

"That," Stella said, "is what I'm afraid he'll try to do. Do you know where Inspector Sullivan is this morning?"

"He telephoned and said he was going to the Farnham home. He wanted to talk to Valerie and was doing so when I left to come over here."

"Why? Though it's none of my business—"

"Valerie was alone with Mrs. Farnham for about ten minutes last night. I wouldn't let him question her about it then. I suppose he is at the Farnham house now. Is that where Mr. Gould has gone?"

Stella nodded. "I'm scared he'll make Sullivan sore, though he said he was just going over as a friend of the family. And Barney isn't going to like me butting in— My gosh! What's that?"

The first crash was followed by another, and that by the sound of shattering glass.

"It sounds as if someone is moving furniture downstairs," Michael said. "Who is here besides the Filipino?"

"Bettina—and Geoff phoned and said he'd come over this morning—"

"A lovers' quarrel perhaps. Oops! Another redskin bit the dust!"

"If that was that big Chinese jardiniere— Why do you just sit here!" Stella reefed in her skirt and hurried into the hall. Michael took a final, still-incredulous look at the black-and-white bedroom and followed her out to the stairway.

II

In the hall below Mr. Wallis was earnestly endeavoring to knock Mr. MacNair's head loose from his shoulders. So far only the furniture had suffered. A table and chair had been overturned, a small vase and a large one broken.

Geoffrey had assumed the correct attitude for boxing, but Peter was obviously in favor of a toe-to-toe slugging match. He urged Mr. MacNair to stand still and fight, trying to pin him into a corner where he would have to.

Wisely, considering Peter's formidable shoulders, Geoffrey stayed on his bicycle. Now and then he landed a blow of the powder-puff variety while ducking Peter's tremendous haymakers. The Filipino circled about them like a small dog keeping an eye out for the bone two larger dogs had laid claim to.

He saw Stella, shrugged helplessly and then sprang back against the wall. Geoffrey had slipped on some rose leaves from one of the shattered vases and, in doing so, obligingly brought his chin into contact with one of Peter's agitated fists.

He reclined briefly among the scattered flowers and rose, with his pale eyes hard and cold. "If you will be a bloody fool!" he said, and smote Mr. Wallis forcefully on the nose.

Bettina, standing in the doorway of the living room, hastily turned her eyes from Peter's gory nose and appealed to Michael.

"Why don't you stop them? Peter—please! Mr. Dundas, why don't you—? Oh, Peter!"

"Call again!—in a voice that he will know," Michael advised. "Boys! Boys! You see, Miss Lawton? They don't stop."

"I think you're p-perfectly hateful," Bettina wailed as Mr. Wallis managed to belt Mr. MacNair ungently in the middle. "If you'd *do* something—"

"I'm not a man of action," Michael said, looking at his fine, slim hands. "Though it is tempting. Either of them would be a sucker for a straight left."

"Just what I was thinking," Stella said. "You might get between them—"

"You should live so long. I might catch one of Peter's haymakers while I was— Ah! The marines have landed."

The Honorable Maria paused for one instant in the front doorway, grasped the situation and marched forward. One large hand settled on Peter's coat collar. She yanked him toward her, planted an elbow against his chest and pushed her brother away with her other arm.

"Of all the asses! What are you rowing about?"

Geoffrey's pale hair was hanging limply over his eyes, and a corner of his mouth was bleeding, but he was still dignified.

"Wallis was apparently waiting here until I arrived. He pushed his way in and began accusing me of something—I'm not quite certain what."

"That's a lie," Peter said. "You and your convenient headache and that fifteen minutes you spent on the third floor Saturday night! The floor Logan's room was on. But no! you won't tell what you saw or heard there so long as Bettina—"

"Peter!"

"You know what I said at the Mark yesterday. I'm not going to see you sacrifice yourself just so MacNair will keep his mouth shut!"

Bettina turned her back on him. Michael glanced from her to Stella and thought that Stella had gone back into her picture frame again. He started down the stairway as Bettina said unsteadily:

"I—I wish you'd go away, Peter. You have things—twisted. And I can't bear any more scenes like this. Barney might have been here and— Please just go away. I'm very sorry, Geoffrey."

"It's quite all right, my dear."

"Sure it is—when you can hide behind Sister's skirts," Peter said nastily. "I can't hit you without pushing her around. If you'd like to come outside for a while

"I would be delighted," Geoffrey said. "Please don't interfere, Maria. This isn't your affair—"

"Rot! I've been at the Farnhams'. That detective inspector is on his way over here now."

"I don't give a damn if he is or who sees us," Peter said. "What difference does it make to me if— Hunh?"

"Let me see your hand," Michael repeated. "Your knuckles are beginning to swell. . . ."

His own two hands closed over Peter's wrist. He twisted it swiftly up behind his back. "Hammer lock," he said pleasantly. "Don't squirm—you'll hurt yourself. Strength doesn't count in this case."

Peter tried once to free himself, set his teeth and decided not to try again. "I'll pay you back for this," he promised.

"Don't be theatrical. I want to talk to you—outside. Will you come quietly?"

"I won't!" Peter looked from Stella to Mrs. Alling and Geoffrey, then at Bettina's slim shoulders. He shook his red head—an angry and impotent gesture. "All right. I know when I'm unpopular. . . ."

"Now," Michael said, closing the front door, "what is it all about?"

"Why should I tell you? You'd knife your own mother in the back. I've a good mind to—"

"Don't. I don't intend to break my hands on that iron jaw of yours. But I took a course in jujitsu once to help me deal with large, hotheaded fools like you—when necessary. MacNair was on the third floor Saturday night. Your idea is that he saw something there, something perhaps connected with Logan's room which was on that floor?"

"Bettina didn't say so in so many words. She let it slip out when she told me that after she and MacNair had a chance to talk privately they're setting their wedding date. Well, what does that look like? He's got some kind of hold over her—or she thinks he has. Because maybe he never even went up to the third floor but just down the stairway from the second and outside the back way—"

"Well, make up your mind," Michael said. "And, meanwhile, be considering what you're going to tell me about your—shall we say—'friendship' with Lilian Farnham three years or so ago."

"My—my what? Oh, my God! Has someone resurrected that? Look—I'm not proud of it. I wouldn't want Bettina to know about it. But there wasn't—"

"I know. You never said a word to Mrs. Farnham you would not have said to your sister if you had a sister. If I were you I'd run along to my job."

"The hell with my job!"

"Just as you say. But Sullivan is parking across the street, and Gould just behind him. I think your presence here while Sullivan is interviewing suspects is an unnecessary complication. I'll make your excuses to him, and he'll contact you eventually."

"Maybe you're right," Peter said. He departed hurriedly, turning a corner as Sullivan shouted: "Hey! You there! Who was that, Michael?"

"Mr. Wallis. He has to get back to his office."

"Why did he ever leave it?" Gould snapped. "And what are you doing here?"

"I didn't detain him." Michael pointedly addressed Sullivan. "He must have tried to see Mac-Nair at his apartment and when he couldn't decided to try here. Have you come from talking to Mrs. Farnham?"

Sullivan grunted. "If you want to call it that. She's a wreck but she's faking half her hysterics now. She hasn't changed her story any though. She did say"—he glanced rather maliciously toward Gould—"that all their friends knew where Farnham kept that gun. Well, let's get at it."

"I've already told you, Inspector—"

"I know." Sullivan cut Gould short. "You, your wife, Miss Lawton and MacNair had dinner here last night. MacNair left at ten, and the rest of you went to your rooms. But I want to hear them repeat it to me."

They did repeat Gould's statement, sitting in a stiff circle in the living room. Sullivan made a few notes in a small loose-leaf binder that, as Michael knew, was only one of his stage properties.

"That's just fine," he said affably. "But how about you, Mrs. Alling? I know you dropped in at the Farnham place to see how she was getting along, but weren't you here for dinner, too, last night?"

"My good man, I wasn't in the city last night. Geoff drove up yesterday and stayed at his apartment. He meant to drive back to Esperanza de Oro this morning. So he was up early and when he read the newspapers he called me, and I drove up at once."

"The Farnhams were that good friends of yours?"

"I quite liked Ray. And there's the youngster, poor little beggar. I guessed that Lilian would be in no condition to think of her. I was prepared to take her home with me, but they tell me you're looking after her, Mr. Dundas."

Michael sighed. "She was awake before eight this morning. My wife remarked with unusual sarcasm: 'What is a home without the patter of little footsteps?' Our maid assured me she could 'cope' with Miss Farnham. But I won't be greatly surprised if Patton delivers an ultimatum when I reach home—'Either Patricia goes or I go.'"

"Well, I'll take her if necessary," the Honorable Maria said. "And I'll tell you before you begin your investigation, Inspector, that I could have left Esperanza last night, driven here and home again without anyone knowing it. Space is one thing we don't lack there, either in the house or outside. My rooms are to themselves, and the garage is, for example, some distance from the men's bunkhouse."

"It's nice of you to warn me. Anyway, if Farnham telephoned you he didn't do it from his home," Sullivan said. "There 'd be a record of it if he had. Maybe you people would be interested to know Farnham was killed with his own gun."

"And I fail to see why you insist on trying to connect Farnham's death with Tex Logan's," Gould said impatiently. "We all know what the— uh—unfortunate situation was between Ray and Lilian. We know her—uh—unfortunate temper and—uh—"

"Clear your throat, Barney," Mrs. Alling advised. Gould's tanned face took on a brick-dust hue.

"Well, to put it plainly, she often worked her-self up to almost insane fits of temper. I've won-dered what would happen if she ever had a weapon handy when she was that way. . . ."

"Then, I take it, she invaded your office un-armed last September?" Michael said. Sullivan broke in before Gould could answer.

"I'm coming to that. But we have evidence that Farnham's death is connected with Logan's. He wasn't killed until he turned up a—a message Logan had tried to get to him. I've been in touch with Sheriff Payne, and now we're trying to find out a few things about Logan too. Now—isn't it true that about the middle of last September Mrs. Farnham came back from spending two months at Palm Springs?"

"Do you want an answer to that?" Mrs. Alling said as Sullivan paused.

"No. We know that and we know that Mrs. Farn-ham got—ideas that led her to go to Mr. Gould's office and tell him Farnham was too friendly with Mrs. Gould and Miss Lawton here—"

"Can't you see that's the kind of thing she would do? I paid no attention to her," Gould said loftily. "Ray and I continued to be friends. The only thing was that we couldn't all four go on meeting on our old footing after that."

"I can understand that. But she did make things so unpleasant for him that he moved out for a night or two to the Trengrove Hotel on Sutter. We've checked on that. Well, Miss Lawton, why did you go there to see him kind of late one night while he was staying there?"

III

"Nonsense!" the Honorable Maria said forcefully.

"Whatever gave you that idea?" She turned to Bettina and when the girl refused to look at her added aggressively: "And if she did go there to see Ray—what of it?"

"Exactly." Gould was suddenly suave and paternal. "Don't let them frighten you, my dear."

"I'm not trying to." Sullivan also eyed Bettina paternally. "But she did go there pretty late and, if my information's correct, didn't want anyone to know about it."

Bettina looked up from the hands that were twisted together in her lap. "If it wasn't correct you wouldn't mention it, would you?"

"Of course, it's none of his business," Gould said. "But why not explain?"

"It had nothing to do with—with this. I wanted to see Ray and I did. I'm of age and my own mistress—theoretically. I wasn't even engaged—"

"My dear, I haven't asked you to explain," Geoffrey said. "I'm sure there was some good reason for what you did."

"There was—but it wasn't the reason that's in everyone's mind. I—Ray wasn't my lover. And I can—can prove I've never had one!" Even Bettina's small ears turned crimson, but she went on, steadily enough: "That is, to be quite specific, any doctor you'd like to name would say—"

Geoffrey's distressed "Bettina, my dear!" was drowned out by Gould's strenuous "My dear child! Don't speak so recklessly!"

"Mr. Gould believes in plain speaking—but only so long as it's exclusively a masculine privilege," Michael drawled. "I'd say Miss Lawton has been both specific and practical—admirably so."

Bettina flashed him a grateful look and then burst into tears. "Oh—you men!" said the Honorable Maria. "I hope you're satisfied." She pulled Bettina from her chair and led her toward the door. "Never mind, Geoff. Anything you have to say can be said later. By your leave, Inspector?"

"Can—may I go too?" Stella said. "Unless there's something more you want to ask me?"

"That's all—now. Unless— What is it, Michael?" Sullivan said.

"I only wanted to ask Miss Lawton if she has a fur jacket—silver fox perhaps?"

Bettina dabbed at her eyes with a crumpled handkerchief, standing, with Mrs. Alling's large tweed arm about her shoulders.

"I have a silver-fox jacket," she said apathetically. "But why?"

"How long have you had it?"

"Since—" Bettina stopped abruptly and went through the motions of drying her eyes again. "Since Barney gave it to me last Christmas," she said then. "It is a silver fox, isn't it, Barney?"

"Oh yes. Yes, certainly. I gave it to her last Christmas," Gould agreed. "And what the hell is it to you?"

"Merely professional curiosity," Michael said. "I was mentally constructing an evening gown for Miss Lawton and wondered what her wrap would be."

Sullivan grinned, looked at Michael questioningly and, getting no response, turned to Geoffrey.

"You seem to have run into a little hard luck," he said. "What has this Peter Wallis got against you—besides wanting to marry your girl?"

Geoffrey's pale eyebrows rose rebukingly. "I fancy it's evident that we had a slight altercation but I really would prefer not to discuss it."

"Oh yeah?" Sullivan said combatively. "And I'd prefer you did. Why was he so anxious to see you?"

"Wallis is a man of action," Geoffrey said with a faint smile. "That is, he acts first and thinks afterward. He is rather like a child squalling for the moon and thinking he might get it if he cries loudly enough. I fancy Mr. Dundas agrees with me?"

"Yes. And I think Sullivan had better talk to Peter personally. I must be going, at any rate. Are you through here or—?"

"No—yes, I suppose I am. I'll talk to you all again later. . . . What's the big idea of walking out on me and handling MacNair with gloves?"

"I don't want to offend him just now," Michael said, getting into his car. "Do you remember that the Honorable Maria is giving a benefit dance day after tomorrow?"

"Saturday? She hasn't spoken to me about it—"

"She will. I'm certain she won't postpone the affair. Perhaps the Farnhams were asked to it, but so have a great many other people been— her friends down the peninsula. You can't force her to change her plans unless you arrest her or MacNair."

"And I can't keep the Goulds and Miss Lawton from going unless I turn up some very strong evidence against them before then? I doubt if I will by that time, since no one in the neighborhood saw or heard anything around the Farnham

house last night. I'm afraid it will take a lot of
digging to get anywhere. Well, you and Valerie are
invited to this shindig, is that it?"

"Yes. I won't attempt to justify myself," Michael said with a rueful smile. "You know I won't
bow out now. And if Mrs. Alling insists on carrying on I want to be there."

"I'd as leave you were. I don't like the idea of a
big dance like that."

"And a costume dance, which makes the setup
even less desirable. Well, you've seen the notes
Valerie made of the conversation between Mrs.
Alling and MacNair not long after Logan was
killed. You remember that when MacNair said he
had stopped in his own room to get some aspirin
she said she hadn't heard him, though her room
was next to his. . . ."

"She may not have been in her room to hear
him."

"That's true. But you wanted to know what
Peter had to say to MacNair this morning. Well . . ."

He told Sullivan what Peter had said, both to
Geoffrey and himself.

"You see? Peter may have something there, but
if you questioned MacNair along those lines he
has only to deny Peter's accusations. He might
talk if you let him know that we know Mrs. Alling
wasn't satisfied with his account of his movements

at the hotel that night. But just now I'd prefer not to let them know that I do know that."

"I see. No, you couldn't very well back me up if you want to stay on visiting terms with them. I'll talk to young Wallis—"

"And ask him to tell you all about his beautiful friendship with Mrs. Farnham several years ago."

"Hunh?"

"Yes. It surprised me but it shouldn't have, now that I recall some of Peter's remarks about the Farnhams. But I've been rather ignoring Mr. Wallis, except as an innocent bystander."

"Wait!" Sullivan said as Michael put his foot on the starter. "Where are you going?"

"To the shop. I must do a few hours' work there, though I feel as if I'd been put through a clothes wringer," Michael complained. "Heaven knows what time it was before we settled that child in bed and fell into our own. And she was awake before eight—"

"I know. But why did you want to know what kind of fur jacket Bettina Lawton wears?"

"It didn't matter what kind it was, so long as it might be called 'drippy' and 'long-haired.' I wanted to know when she acquired such a jacket. Think over Squiffy Bain's deposition, Inspector. I'll probably be home at three o'clock if you want to get in touch with me. . . ."

It was, however, nearer five o'clock when he drove back to Russian Hill Place. The sound of the car brought Patton hurrying to the front door before he could ring its bell or let himself in.

"Miss Patricia is asleep, sir," she whispered. "We tried to get her to take a nap, but she wouldn't—"

"You've had a hard day, haven't you?"

"Well, Miss Patricia is rather—strenuous, sir. Not what I would call a quiet child. We allowed her to 'play theater.'"

"You must have been rather desperate. I know Valerie, at least, loathes child stars."

"I must own I don't like to see a child put herself forward. But it occupied her mind, singing and dancing for us. Madam had an appointment with the hairdresser at three. Miss Patricia got crying after she had gone. It was rather distressing but, no doubt, the best thing for her. She really cried herself to sleep. So—"

"So you're anxious she shouldn't be awakened," Michael said. "So am I. And I'm sorry we had to bring her here. I don't like to add to your work."

"Work? I haven't too much work to do, sir. I have everything to do with, and, if I may say so, neither you nor madam is at all demanding, besides dining out so often. No, I'd rather— But you want a scotch and soda, sir? One moment. . . ."

She returned presently with a glass containing precisely the correct amounts of whisky, soda and ice.

"I was going to say I'd rather be occupied all the time, sir," she went on. "If I'm a bit tired I sleep better. I find myself waking early, expecting the postman long before he's due."

"Have you had any more letters from England? I've been too busy to think of asking you."

"The letters aren't satisfactory when they do arrive, besides being so slow. I had one while you were away—from my married sister. And very cheerful it was. Now the French are beaten—not that I ever really trusted the French, sir—there's no more grousing as there was in the early days of the war."

"Your people don't live in London?"

"No, thank God. They live near Shrewsbury—my married sister, my uncle and a cousin or two. She writes very calmly, Harriet does, about blackouts and gas masks and coping with any parachute troops that might drop down amongst them. And Harriet would be more than a match for any bloody Nazi— Oh sir! I do beg your pardon!"

Michael grinned. "Please don't. I'm sure you'd also be a match for an entire fleet of Nazi parachutists. Has your sister any small children?"

"No, I'm thankful to say. She's older than I am, and her one boy was killed in the last war. I always thought it a pity he was the one to go and not this uncle I speak of. He was what we called 'a conscientious objector.' Went to jail rather than fight. He calls himself a pacifist."

Patton again so far forgot herself as to sniff scornfully. "No doubt he quite liked it there. He was never one to hold a situation long, but a great talker, he was."

"What did he talk about?" Michael said. "The day when the British lion should lie down with the German lamb?"

"Yes, though he didn't put it quite like that. Any of us would be glad to see the day come when there's no more war, sir. And it might if women had the ruling of the world, though I'm not certain there wouldn't be women willing to lead a nation into war. Give them enough power, and they might be as bad as the men. As I always said to Uncle Samuel, human nature doesn't change."

"No, it doesn't appear to. It— What did you say?" Michael demanded, sitting erect.

"Why, you heard me, sir. Didn't you agree that human nature doesn't change? I mean, unless we all come to be perfect there will always be wars. And when you get a maniac like this Hitler who makes up his mind he— What is it, Mr. Dundas? Have I said something that—?"

"You've only been very helpful. It is possible," Michael said, half to himself. "And I should have thought of it before. I've been so engrossed with this little problem that I've ignored world events."

He put his highball glass down and rose quickly. "I'm going down to the public library. I'll be back before very long. . . ."

IV

The old grandfather clock in the hall struck eleven. Michael threw down his book and looked at Valerie in silent exasperation. She had been yawning since ten o'clock but she had gotten out her knitting and was working, if in a very desultory fashion, on a sweater she hoped to finish in another year. Which meant she was determined to sit here until he was ready to go to bed.

"Aren't you sleepy?" Michael said finally, with what she at once recognized to be suspicious solicitude. "Why don't you go to bed?"

"Why do you want me to?"

"What makes you think I want you to?"

"You've been watching the clock since ten," Valerie said with an irritating smile. "And you talked too much at dinner, so I wouldn't ask what you were thinking of. Also, your little fib about going to the library to consult an encyclopedia wasn't as plausible as your lies usually are." She gestured toward the bookcases. "Remember how we stumped the experts on 'Information Please'?"

"I should never have told Patton that I was going to the library," Michael said regretfully. "Well, we can't go on sitting here like the gingham dog and the calico cat. ''Twas half-past twelve, and (what do you think!) Nor one nor t'other had slept a wink. . . .'"

"I am prepared to sit here until twelve-thirty if necessary," Valerie said placidly. "And I know that poem myself. 'While the old Dutch clock in the chimney place, Up with its hands before its face, For it always dreaded a family row!'"

"Fair warning? Well . . ." Michael got up and separated her from her knitting. "Do you know that there are times when I could wring your neck?"

"You might as well wring it as break it—or my ribs," Valerie murmured. "I'll go with you on your own terms—but I'm going."

"I suppose it's not a bad idea to take you with me," Michael admitted, kissing her more gently this time. "We could always say—afterward—that we wanted fresh air and decided to take a short ride. But my terms are that you stay in the car and that you won't ask questions."

"If I may ask just one now? Whose house are you going to burgle?"

"How did you know?"

"Oh, you'll never see a murder case through without breaking into someone's house. Geoffrey MacNair's apartment, I suppose. Even you wouldn't try to risk getting into the Gould home—I hope. Where is Geoffrey's apartment? And are you sure he isn't in it?"

"When Sullivan called after dinner to report no real progress he said the Honorable Maria had gone back to Esperanza de Oro and MacNair had asked if he could follow her after dinner. His apartment is on Bush and, I am glad to say, in a quiet block. When you're ready . . ."

He drove down Leavenworth and parked the car just off Bush. "The chances that anyone we know will see you should be about a hundred to one," he said. "But if anyone should—"

"I'll say you've gone down the street to that grocery at Jones that's open until midnight," Valerie said. "How long?"

"My dear, I don't know. If MacNair keeps his personal papers at his sister's home I'll be back at once. If he keeps them in his apartment I may be gone some time. And you keep your fingers crossed."

He walked quickly around the corner into Bush Street. He had driven past Geoffrey's apartment house on his way home from the library and been pleased to discover it was one he knew rather well.

The apartments were the completely furnished two- and three-room species preferred by the unmarried and by families whose personal possessions could be packed into three suitcases. A bachelor friend of Michael's had lived here once, and he had visited him frequently in his own more or less unregenerate bachelor days.

That was why he knew there were fire escapes at the back of the building as well as in the front, fire escapes outside very convenient French windows. He remembered helping Tom Jordan shove a feminine visitor down one when her irate husband arrived very unexpectedly.

He recalled also that the place was the typical downtown apartment house where the tenants speak only to the manager and the manager speaks only of rent overdue. He was not likely to be challenged by another tenant even if he was seen entering Geoffrey's apartment. That is, so long as he seemed to be opening the door with a latchkey and acted as if he had every right to do so.

Still, he was glad to know it would be possible to leave Geoffrey's apartment by another exit than the front door. And pleased, too, that Geoffrey lived in a back apartment and on the second floor.

He rang the bells of all the apartments on the top floor and was finally rewarded by the clicking of the front door's latch. He slipped into the small lobby and back against its wall. Perhaps five minutes passed before a woman's voice floated down to him.

"No, I don't hear the elevator. It's another of those fresh peddlers ringing our bell to get in the house," she said, and slammed a door.

Michael grinned, walked boldly up the stairway to the second floor and on to Geoffrey's apartment. No one came out into the halls or passed by while he was opening the door.

Which, he thought, was probably just as well. The picklocks he was using had been given him in gratitude by a man who styled himself, and rightly, an expert locksmith. What Inspector Sullivan called old Hymie Rose has nothing to do with the case.

Michael had never found a lock he could not open with Hymie's keys, and they did not fail him now, but the trial-and-error method took time. Another five minutes passed before he stepped into Geoffrey's bachelor *pied-à-terre*.

The place was so completely quiet that he hesitated only an instant before turning on the lights. A long hall ran from front to living-room door, with bathroom, kitchenette and a small dining room opening off it.

In the living room the blinds were already pulled down over the French windows. Michael set one a little ajar over the fire escape before he looked about him. The living room was any living room in any not too moderately priced furnished apartment.

There was the usual chesterfield with matching chair, the inevitable bargain-basement tile-top table and magazine end table, two stiff-backed occasional chairs, one reproduction of Maxfield Parrish's "Daybreak" and one of "The End of the Trail." At first glance Michael thought that two framed photographs, one of the Honorable Maria, one of Bettina, were the only things about the place that in any way identified it with Geoffrey.

Then, looking into the dining room, he saw a very expensive combination record player and radio that certainly had never been provided by the management. Neither was it likely that they had furnished the old mahogany secretary that stood in another corner of the room.

Michael approached this eagerly, found it unlocked and its contents orderly and uninteresting—until in a bottom drawer he discovered a small steel letter file. This was locked, but the lock was the type that, as Mr. Dundas muttered to himself, "could be picked with a hairpin." In another two minutes he was reading Mr. MacNair's personal letters.

There were not as many of them as he had hoped, but what there were, including one from a lawyer in Toronto, dated June twenty-fourth, were enlightening. There were two more letters from this gentleman who signed himself Donald Menzies.

Michael had reached the final sentence of the third—"You may be certain we are exercising the utmost discretion and will continue to do so as long as . . ."— when the opening and closing of a door and the sound of voices down the hall brought him quickly to his feet.

He turned out the dining-room lights, thrust the letter he had not quite finished reading back into the file and returned it to the desk. His only cause for self-congratulation was the fact that he had switched off the hall and living-room lights. Generally speaking, he had been a plain, damned fool. He had been so certain Geoffrey was out of the city by now that what precautions he had taken had been purely instinctive.

One of the voices was certainly Geoffrey's. "And here am I," Michael thought, "nicely trapped in the dining room. If he learns what I've been doing—well, as he would say, 'that tears it.'"

He shrank into a corner that could not be seen from the living room and considered whether he should try to hide in the kitchen or make a dash for the fire escape. He could have taken the latter course of action when he first heard the men at the front door, for there was another man with Geoffrey, a man with a deep, yet peculiarly soft voice. The plain truth was that he wanted to see this man, wanted, if possible, to hear what Geoffrey was saying to him.

At the moment they seemed to have paused somewhere along the hall. ". . . forgotten there's no scotch," Geoffrey said. "If you don't mind waiting while I go down to the nearest grocery . . . Well, if sherry will do it's in the kitchen. This way. . . ."

That Geoffrey should go into the kitchen first, taking his guest with him, was a bit of sheer luck he didn't deserve, Michael thought. He waited until he heard cupboard doors being opened on the kitchen side of the swinging doors. By the time Geoffrey came through the dining room Michael was on the fire escape.

He caught one glimpse of Geoffrey's visitor as he crossed the room to the chesterfield: a short, compact man in the fifties, with a large head, very heavy black brows and a thick mat of black hair streaked with white. His dark suit was not merely conservative—it was reactionary. With it he wore a stiff white collar and small black bow tie, besides a black derby he was carrying in one hand.

The man disappeared from his range of vision, and he didn't dare push the window farther open. He must be content with hearing what the two men said without seeing their faces, while hoping that Geoffrey would not notice the windows were not latched.

Apparently they were drinking their sherry slowly and obviously they were drinking it silently. Michael looked uneasily toward the back windows of the apartment above Geoffrey's. Light streamed from them, which meant there was not only someone in that apartment but that its tenants hadn't drawn the blinds.

On a sudden impulse he pulled his hat low over his eyes, fished a handkerchief from his pocket and tied it over the lower half of his face. If he should be seen he had better look like a highwayman. . . .

He pressed closer to the window as Geoffrey spoke. "As I was saying, just now I don't know with any certainty when I'll be here and when with Maria. I can always contact you easily and I can depend on your being discreet, Mr. Jones. I don't want messages coming through the Redwood City exchange or to risk any message you might have to give being taken down by a servant."

"That wouldn't be wise," Mr. Jones agreed. "You'll be going down to Mrs. Alling's tomorrow?"

"Yes. I'd intended driving down tonight until you said you wanted to talk to me. Well, I feel I must see Maria through this affair she's giving. We've really no excuse for canceling it. She says our friends down there would wonder why we did."

"I agree with her. But we've been uncommonly lucky so far, and our luck may run out. The situation is—regrettable. However, you believe you can depend on the lady. I would say, from what you have told me, that— Eh! What's that?"

Michael dodged back from the window, looked up and into the face of an apparition in chin bandage, wave-preserving net and a Chinese kimono. The eyes under the net grew round and rounder until finally— "E-e-eek! Help!" shrieked the lady on the fire escape above. "Help-help-help! Burglars! There's a man on the fire escape!"

Michael took the drop from the last rung of the fire escape to the garden below recklessly, stumbled and went to his knees. He hobbled across the yard, found escape blocked by a high wooden fence and hesitated.

There was always the service entrance which should lead him back to Bush Street, but someone

might be quick witted enough to be waiting for
him there. He backed away, testing his ankle gin-
gerly, drew a deep breath and put himself at the
fence.

Though he always insists he is hopelessly un-
athletic he is, if nothing more, as agile as a cat.
Somehow he scrambled to the top of the fence and
dropped down its other side with a jar that made
him grit his teeth.

He was in another back yard, but one blessedly
dark. The windows overlooking it remained un-
lighted while he searched for a service entrance.

He found it after an unpleasant five minutes of
fumbling and stumbling about in the dark, felt his
way along the narrow concrete passage and came
safely out onto Sutter Street. . . .

During the last fifteen minutes Valerie had re-
verted to a childhood habit of biting her finger-
nails. She greeted her husband with a wan smile.

"In case you'd be interested, a radio car went
into Bush Street hell-bent about five minutes before you got back to our car," she said when they
were halfway home.

"That woman must have called the cops. Well,
she can't describe me, and I took nothing from
MacNair's apartment, so don't worry, darling. But
I will admit it was an unpleasantly close shave."

"As Stella Gould would say, don't try to 'kid'
me. You enjoyed it. Since you did get away, you're

fairly strutting. Well, tell me about it. Was it worth it?"

"Decidedly. But I'm not going to tell you anything except that MacNair is still in town and he . . ."

V

Michael unlocked the front door without having noticed, until they stepped into it, that the living room was dimly lighted. Patricia Farnham was sitting on the chesterfield in her favorite cross-legged position. She eyed them interestedly and with a most discouraging alertness.

"I woke up. I'm not a bit sleepy. But I came in here quiet, just like a mouse, and didn't wake poor Patton. I only turned on one little light too. I thought maybe you'd be home soon."

Valerie groaned softly. "Go to bed. I'm not sleepy," Michael said. "I mean it, my dear."

"You're tired."

"I still won't be able to go to sleep for some time. I give you my word I won't leave the house again tonight. I'll get this to bed. . . . You're a nuisance, Patricia."

Patricia giggled. "I can't help it if I'm not sleepy. Didn't you just say you aren't sleepy? Well, then! Did you hurt your foot?"

"I twisted my ankle." Michael limped over to a chair and sat down. Patricia promptly left the chesterfield to climb onto his knees.

"I might go to sleep if you tell me a story."

"I don't know any stories you're old enough to hear. If you must sit here, *por Dios,* sit still!"

"Well, if you don't know any stories, you can sing. Valerie said you might. This afternoon she said it—that if I'd be good maybe you'd sing me a cowboy song like Tex Logan did."

"She must have been at wit's end. Well, close your eyes. Heaven knows the average cowboy ballad, properly droned through the nose, should induce sleep," Michael said, and began at random:

> *"Cowboys, come and hear the story*
> *Of Roy Bean in all his glory. . . ."*

Patricia obediently closed her eyes but when, after several verses, Michael paused hopefully she shook her head. "I'm awake. Go on—I like it."

Michael sighed and continued:

> *"Though the story isn't funny, there was*
> *   once Roy had no money,*
> *Which for him was not so very strange or*
> *   rare;*

> *So he went to help Pop Wyndid, but he*
> *got so absentminded*
> *That he put his RB brand on old Pop's*
> *steer.*
> *As old Pop got right smart angry, Roy*
> *Bean went down to Langtry. . . ."*

"I'm not asleep," Patricia said plaintively. Receiving no answer, she opened her eyes. "My, you look funny. Aren't you going to sing any more?"

"I've sung—enough. Association of idea is a remarkable phenomenon, isn't it? Mr. Logan mentioned lifeguards, dude wranglers and hotel musicians to Valerie and— Well, it's worth considering, at any rate. Will you bring me a pencil and paper from that desk over there, Patricia? Thank you. You remember the strip of paper the trout flies were stuck into? Well . . ."

Michael printed a capital *M* and then drew a curved line directly under it so that the legs of the *M* rested on the line.

"Did what you called a picture of a hat on the strip of paper look like that?"

"Of course," Patricia said. "That is a hat—a big hat with a big dent in its crown."

"It does resemble one—at first glance."

"It's a hat," Patricia insisted. "Though I see how you made it and I never thought of drawing a hat that way." She closed her eyes again. "Yes, it looked just like this," she decided. "I can see it. But I just remembered something, Mr. Dundas."

Michael looked at her apprehensively. "Oh, I'm still sure about what was on the paper. This is just something I didn't remember last night. It was hard to think then. But when I close my eyes now I see the big hat and the little house after it, and the house has a little number on it."

"Oh. Where?"

Patricia frowned. "Right over the door, I think. And just a tiny little number."

"Small in size, you mean?"

"Yes, written or printed awfully small. I don't remember what number it was, only I think it was at least ten and not twenty. I know numbers up to a thousand," Patricia said proudly. "And then after the house were the capital letters—"

"That were written like two words—a short word and a long one—but didn't spell any word you recognized," Michael said thoughtfully. "And there were several *X*s among those letters—"

Patricia laughed. "Yes, like love and kisses. You know—*X X X* for kisses?"

"Yes, I know. Do you think—?"

Michael paused, thinking how he might put his question. Patricia was not particularly suggestible; in fact, she was less so than many adults. But he didn't want her to take the line of least resistance now, to agree that what he advanced as a possibility was so, simply because he thought it might be.

That was why, after all, he didn't ask: "Might there have been an *M* and as many as four *I*s in that series of letters?" He got to his feet instead.

"Aren't you going to finish about Roy Bean?" Patricia asked.

"No," Michael said, "I am going to stoop to bribery. If you will go to bed now tomorrow I will sing cowboy songs until you howl for mercy. I will even, so help me, let you sing to me. . . ."

VI

Valerie woke suddenly at eight o'clock the next morning because she finally realized that she had the bed to herself. Considering Michael's dislike of rising before ten and what had happened last night, this was enough to make her spring hastily out of bed and start for the hall, pulling on a robe as she went.

However, she discovered at once that Michael hadn't slipped away to engage in extralegal activities again. He was at the telephone in the hall, with his back to her.

"Yes, that's right," he said. "Try that number first. . . ."

Valerie crept closer until she was near enough to the telephone to hear both sides of the conversation. She stopped quickly as Michael said:

"Hello? Rocky, how long have you been in and around your present hunting grounds?"

"Oh, about thirteen years," Mr. Allan said as casually as if Michael had asked the question sitting in the same room with him. "What's that got to do with what's on your mind?"

"How do you know what's on my mind, *amigo?*"

"Fred Payne called me up and asked could you be trusted. I told him you've never double-crossed me—yet," Rocky drawled. "I also suggested you can be coaxed but you can't be driven. I told Fred he'd probably get some help from you if he let you do things your own way. Fred said he'd kind of figured that out for himself. His head is cut in, even if some of those people at Summit House must 've thought he was pretty dumb."

"I am not one of those people. And it's your fault that we ever became involved in this affair. It was you who suggested to Valerie that we come home by the Yuba Pass. But, to get back to my original question, you do know Reno quite well?"

"Oh, sure. You know it's the only town of any size anywheres near us."

"Then did you ever know a Judge Farnham?"

"Not pers'nally. I got the wife I started out
with. Though, even if he did have to preside over
a lot of divorce cases, he was pretty well thought
of as a jurist. He's been dead seven or eight years.
Raymond Farnham's death has made the Reno
papers, him bein' a native son. Nobody seemed
much int'rested in Logan's. I never heard of
Logan or any of the others that are connected with
Texas. I— Look, fella! Do you want to have your
ears pinned back? Well, keep on and you will!"

Michael grinned. "Is the son and heir distract-
ing your attention?"

"I don't mind him climbin' up my back but I
do object to him holdin' on by my hair," Rocky
said mildly. "Scram! You heard me. Eleanor! Will
you remove your son? Tell me why he minds you
so much better 'n he does me."

"Probably because he doesn't see me so often.
You were going to say?"

"Oh, I reckon Farnham must have a lot of old
friends aroun' Reno but I wouldn't know who they
are."

"Sullivan will check on that, I suppose. The
trouble is that there's too much delving into past
histories to be done."

"And, as I know, that usually takes a hell of a long
time. Well, do you think you know a short cut?"

"I hope so. Because otherwise I'm afraid of what might happen Saturday night. After two murders what's another? And, given a large estate, soft lights and a hundred or so people in costume—"

Valerie sneezed. Michael turned and looked at her forbiddingly.

"My love, I don't want to be unkind, but will you go far, far away from here—out of listening distance?"

"But why—?"

"You know damned well why. It isn't necessary or advisable that both of us should know too much. And if you hadn't suspected I'd say just what I have you'd have made your presence known before now."

Valerie heard Rocky chuckle. She said "Damn!" emphatically but she, as well as Michael, recognized an ultimatum when she met one. She went off to the bathroom and turned the water on full force. But she lingered long enough on the order of going to hear Michael say:

"If you saw a capital *M* written over a curved line what would that suggest to you? . . . Yes, I suppose you could call it that. . . . Yes . . . I remembered that. . . . You do? Well, I did think of Arizona. . . . Oh. You don't know who— No, the name I had in mind was Anderson but—"

At that point Valerie was forced by her own scruples to close the bathroom door. She was deliberately slow with her bathing and dressing, but when she finally stepped into the hall again Michael was still at the telephone. He grinned when she cleared her throat ostentatiously.

"I've finished. . . . Yes, I'll tell Sullivan what I've told you, Mr. Payne. I didn't want to waste any time getting in touch with you. But you'll consult with him regarding any arrangements that have to be made? Thank you, and good luck to you, too, Sheriff."

"Are you going to call Inspector Sullivan now?" Valerie asked as Michael put down the telephone. "That is, when will you be ready for breakfast?"

"In ten minutes. Sullivan will have left home by now, and I don't know where he may be. I'd rather have some coffee before I attempt to locate him."

But Sullivan appeared, himself demanding coffee, before they had left the breakfast table. Mr. Sullivan was in a bad humor.

"That guy Wallis has skipped out," he announced.

"Peter? But why?—and when?" Valerie said.

"Early this morning apparently. I didn't get around to him yesterday. Other things seemed more important. He asked for the weekend off, and that's all they know at his office. He seems to have slept in his bed last night but he's not at his rooming house now. He wasn't invited to this Mrs. Alling's blowout, was he?"

"No, I'm quite certain he wasn't," Michael said. "Have you sent out orders to pick him up?"

"I thought I'd talk to you about him first. He wasn't told not to leave town. We haven't," Sullivan said gloomily, "enough against anybody to forbid 'em to leave town."

"So they intend to tomorrow night?"

"Yes. Of course, the San Mateo County authorities are going to co-operate with us." Sullivan looked at Patricia who was eating marmalade with toast. "See here, kiddie, do you remember Peter Wallis?"

"Was he the redheaded one? I haven't seen him for a long time till we were in the mountains. I was just a baby when he used to come see Mommy and Daddy so much. Why, I had to take a nap every afternoon and go to bed early at night then."

"Yes, I figured you must still have been pretty young," Sullivan said gravely. "Er—" He glanced from her to Michael and cleared his throat suggestively.

"Patricia, the inspector is about to divulge official secrets. He'd rather you weren't here to hear them. Run along to the kitchen and brighten Patton's existence, will you? . . . Well?"

"Oh, I spent hours talking to that colored girl of the Farnhams'. She's the sort that giggles and lies and bawls when you lose patience with her. She didn't do anything but corroborate what we already know about the Farnhams' relations with each other. She remembered Wallis was around a lot for a while, but either this Pearl wasn't curious, like most servants are, or she's too dumb to remember anything. She's the only servant that's been with them long. I haven't located the cook they had at the time Wallis was seeing so much of the Farnhams.

"And Mrs. Farnham is still in bed with a nurse. She hasn't even asked to see Patricia. I don't like the way she's acting. She seems to be brooding now. Wouldn't you expect she'd be flinging accusations right and left?"

"Yes, I would," Michael said.

"Well, she hasn't. She just lies there with her eyes closed, but when you do get a look at 'em you get the idea she's doing a lot of thinking."

"Very likely she is. Have you talked to the Gould servants?"

Sullivan frowned. "Yes, but I can't get anything from the Filipino. I have a notion Gould's made it worth his while to hold his tongue. Of course Squiffy Bain came clean with me. But he says

MacNair did leave the house about ten o'clock the night that Farnham was killed."

"But no one knows whether he went straight from the Gould home to his apartment here?"

"No. No one in that apartment house knows when he got in—if at all. Funny thing, though— someone tried to break into that place last night. A dame in the apartment above MacNair's saw a masked man on his fire escape. Funny, isn't it?"

"Very," Michael said. "Was anything missing from MacNair's apartment?"

"No. He said he didn't think anyone was trying to break into his place any more than any other in the house. Well, he has no alibi. Squiffy swears that no one in the Gould house used a car after ten. He and the Filipino were in their rooms over the garage by that time. But no servants sleep in the house.

"As to Mrs. Alling, that place of hers is just like she described it. She could have driven away from there and back with no one knowing it, and if she did none of her servants do know it or will admit it. But in that connection— Got a cigarette?"

Michael pushed a pack of cigarettes toward him. "Well," Sullivan continued, "Farnham did leave his house after he'd put the kid to bed. He dropped in at a cigar stand on Chestnut for some cigarettes. There's a pay phone there, but the place was crowded, and the fellow behind the counter can't say if Farnham used the telephone. If he made a call from there we haven't been able to trace it. But if he made an out-of-town call it's certain he didn't make it from his own home."

"No, of course he wouldn't," Michael said rather inattentively. "If you've nothing more to report—"

"I happen to know a guy that used to live in Toronto and I talked to him. It seems old Mac-Nair had some gold mines and was fairly well off. I suppose Mrs. Alling got half what he left—and, incidentally, Alling didn't amount to much."

"She certainly doesn't speak of him very often," Valerie said. "She did say he was tubercular—"

"*And* a boozer. He died down in Arizona. He didn't leave much but that ranch which is expensive to keep going. But MacNair has plenty of dough. He married a rich man's daughter. The father died soon after that and left it all to her.

"Then she up and ran off with another man. No one knows what happened between them, but finally she came back to MacNair—and he took her back. About six months later she took an overdose of sleeping medicine, and all her money went to MacNair."

"Convenient—for Mr. MacNair," Michael said.

"That's what I thought. Well, were you going to say you've got something to tell me?"

"Yes. And if you'll drive me to the shop I'll talk to you as we go. I'll get my coat. . . ."

Valerie followed him into the bedroom. "Are you going to tell the inspector that you were the man on Mr. MacNair's fire escape? I ask because I think we'd better get together on our stories."

"No, I'm not going to tell him. I didn't tell Payne that. He and Sullivan can get along very well without knowing what facts I gathered during that little excursion. I told Payne and I will tell Sullivan my interpretation of Logan's message to Farnham. It will take them some time to discover whether or not I'm right. And more time, if I am, for the—proof—to reach here. Meanwhile, I don't want Sullivan asking questions that might expose our hand too soon. Is that clear?"

"As mud. Aren't you going to kiss me good-by?"

"You have been so devastatingly polite for the last hour that I hesitated to risk it. . . . Don't strangle me, *querida*. Though it's a pleasant way to die. . . ."

He pulled her closer into an embrace that was sufficiently devastating if not at all polite. "Though it is in the nature of an anticlimax to mention it, I really am going to the shop," he said finally. "You may call for me there around five if you like, since I won't have the car."

"And after that?"

Michael shrugged. "Oh, we will spend a quiet evening at home. You'd better call the Honorable Maria and tell her we can't make it for lunch."

"I will—but why?"

"I want to keep in touch with Payne and Sullivan until late tomorrow afternoon. That would be hard to do if we went down the peninsula too early."

"Well, I'll tell Mrs. Alling you must work at least until noon. And I'll stop by for you at five," Valerie promised. "But," she thought, "six will get you ten, he won't be at Gisele's then or will just have come in."

Therefore she was agreeably surprised when Fanchon Weiss remarked that she imagined "the maestro is about ready to go home because, thank God! he's done a real day's work." And Michael's quiet evening at home also unwound its slow length according to schedule.

That is, it was at least as quiet as an evening could be when Patricia was one's house guest. After dinner Michael redeemed the pledge he had made the night before, even to allowing her to sing "On the Good Ship Lollipop."

Midway of this ordeal Valerie slipped quietly away into the bedroom. Michael was probably right when he said that he was "afraid Patricia will be an actress in time, with or without encouragement, because she has not only talent but backbone and a thick skin." "Perhaps I'm wrong," Valerie thought, putting their overnight bags on the bed. "At least, so many people think it's 'simply darling' to see a child shouting out songs and being just too cute that I must be."

She got her own costume from the closet, a Spanish gown and the creamy lace mantilla that had belonged to Michael's Argentinean mother. By the time she had fitted them into the case Patricia's song was finished.

"What will it be?" Valerie inquired, looking into the living room. "Your favorite Gaucho costume? You've never complained those trousers are not comfortable."

"No, those are. . . ." Michael sat for an instant regarding her thoughtfully. At last he smiled, as he might have when admitting that the joke was on him but still a good one.

"You needn't bother to pack my bag. You have a lamentable habit of forgetting to put my toothbrush into it. I'll pack it tomorrow if you don't mind?"

"I'm not that fond of packing," Valerie said. "Or very good at it. And I think I'd better get Patton to repack my dress."

Patton had just finished this task when a series of loud thumps beneath the bedroom made the two women look at each other questioningly.

"Whatever on earth—" Patton began.

"It's only Mr. Dundas in the basement, moving trunks," Valerie said resignedly. "He must want something from one of his, but I have no idea what it could be. Thank you, Patton. And if you think you can coax Patricia into her bed I'll get into my own."

PART FIVE

"Oh, do you bring me silver, poor boy,
 Or do you bring me gold?"
"I bring you neither," said the man.
"I bring you a hangman's fold."
Bow Down Your Head and Cry

I

As soon as they had driven through Esperanza de Oro's iron gates it was evident that when Mrs. Alling had said, "Space is one thing we don't lack," she was, if anything, guilty of understatement.

The house was half a mile from the gates that separated the estate from an oiled dirt road, the large red stables nearly that distance from the house. Valerie could not guess which of a dozen or so buildings behind the house might be the garage.

They were all low, long wooden buildings that seemed to have been flung down carelessly and allowed to stay where they fell. Most of them were partially hidden by palm trees, acacias, lemon, orange and olive trees. Smoke curled over several roofs beyond the treetops, and the air was heavy with the smell of burning oak logs and roasting meat.

Michael stopped the car beside the house which must at one time have been true Spanish but now rather resembled a swastika. Its core was brown, its various wings deep yellow. Obviously no two had been added at the same time. They were like patches stitched at lengthy intervals onto an old but cherished garment.

There were large lawns in front of the house, thick, deep lawns that badly needed cutting. Wisteria and bougainvillaea sprawled over the house and clung there. Flowers bloomed diligently in huge beds, unweeded and unpruned. Wherever you looked the effect was that of luxuriance accepted carelessly and, at the same time, of property deteriorating slowly for lack of efficient caretakers.

The Honorable Maria appeared at the front door, shouting a welcome to them and the command to "look alive and drive this car into the garage" to some unseen "Hank." Hank materialized: a nondescript man in blue jeans, with a large cud of tobacco in one cheek. At the door an elderly Chinese houseboy took their bags.

"This is Wong," Mrs. Alling said. "I couldn't get on without him and his cousin who cooks for me. The west wing, Wong. I hope," she added, leading the way along a narrow, tiled corridor, "that you two can sleep in the same bed."

"We always have," Michael said.

"Good. I could give you separate rooms but not twin beds. We aren't modern at Esperanza." Mrs. Alling turned a corner at the end of the corridor. "Here you are—private suite with hot and cold running water, though I'll warn you the water is more apt to run cold than hot."

This "private suite," Valerie learned later, jutted lonesomely out from the house, as did two more at other corners of it. She was never quite certain how you reached those.

She carried away from Esperanza de Oro a confused impression of many corridors that made abrupt turns and came to equally abrupt endings, of trees and shrubbery brushing the sides of the house and flowering vines framing its windows, of an excess of small rooms like monks' cells and, in contrast, at least two that were as spacious as public dance halls and almost as sparsely furnished.

In the quarters assigned to them the bedroom was dominated by a vast carved-oak bed. A worn wicker table and chairs were unworthy attendants for this museum piece, while in the smaller adjoining room a rosewood escritoire shuddered away from a cheap pine dressing table. As Valerie was to learn, everything at Esperanza had either attained the pricelessness of age or had come from mail-order catalogues and the hands of whatever amateur carpenters were about the place.

"I hope you'll be comfortable. People who can't make themselves so aren't asked to come again," Mrs. Alling said cheerfully. "You'd better dress at once. That's what everyone else is doing now. There will be food in the dining room when you're ready—and I was beginning to think we'd have eaten it before you arrived."

"We are rather late. But," Michael said glibly, "I had an important order that had to be gotten out today. There were so many last-minute alterations that I had to work later than I expected."

"What he means is that he had to wait later than he expected for the second of two telephone calls," Valerie thought. "Or three, if you counted all communications from Inspector Sullivan since ten-thirty last night."

From what she had heard of Michael's side of the conversation then, she believed his interpretation of Tex Logan's message to Farnham had proved to be the correct one. Sitting down on the bed to take off her stockings, she recalled stray sentences:

"That fits in nicely," Michael had said. "But merely a description won't do. . . . I know he hasn't. But if they are willing to come here . . . Oh, I see. That explains several points that weren't clear in my mind. . . . I agree with you. The evidence should be conclusive before you act. . . . Yes, call me here before ten tomorrow or after one. I'll be at the shop in between."

Valerie had no way of knowing whether or not Sullivan had called Michael at Gisele's, but they had talked over the telephone again at two o'clock and finally at six-thirty. She had heard nothing of the first conversation but at half-past six she was putting on her hat and coat in the bedroom, and Michael did not ask her to close the door into the hall.

After listening to Sullivan for perhaps two minutes he said: "Well, it was your idea to send him there. . . . I know you did but I'm as well pleased that it's turned out this way. . . . As long as it's gone this far, isn't it easier to bring the kettle to the teapot? . . . Nothing so drastic as that. I might throw out a few hints to undermine morale before the blitzkrieg. Of course, that's disgustingly theatrical, but the psychological effect might be excellent. . . . If I were you and still had doubts I wouldn't risk it. . . . Yes, we'll start at once."

He put down the telephone, looked into the bedroom and said briefly: "If you're ready let's be on our way."

And, Valerie recalled, sitting down before the pine dressing table to comb her hair, it was while they were on their way here that Michael had remarked that there would be officers of the law present tonight even if they might not be easily recognizable as such.

"I'm not certain just what etiquette prescribes in a situation like this," he said. "I know Sullivan has been in touch with the sheriff's office in Redwood City. But he is still in San Francisco."

"And what about Peter? He wasn't listed as wanted for questioning in today's papers."

"His description has been circulated—discreetly," Michael said. "He'll turn up. . . ."

Valerie was ready for her dress now, but Michael still sat by the window in the fading light, finishing his third cigarette.

"Even if you do dress like lightning you'd better be getting at it," Valerie said. "I'll get your things out and— Good heavens! What is this?"

Michael glanced morosely at the short plaid garment she held up. "That," he said with uneasy dignity, "is a kilt. The Maclean of Duart tartan—"

Valerie sat down on the bed and laughed heartlessly. "Now I will have seen everything when I see you voluntarily expose your knees in public beneath a loud plaid skirt."

"The entire knee is not exposed. The kilt," Michael said in a lecture-room voice, "should reach the center of the kneecap. And don't cast aspersions on your own tartan."

"It looks awfully red to me," Valerie said—
"what part of it isn't green squares and blue lines.
Where on earth did you get it?"

"I dug it out of my trunk and found that it's
resisted moths nobly. As you've heard me say,
my grandfather Maclean is still conscientiously
Scotch, though he's lived in Wisconsin for fifty
years. On his birthday the entire clan used to turn
out in kilts. He even managed to produce a piper
or two to march about the table."

"If you haven't worn it since you left Wisconsin
thirteen years ago why wear it now?"

"You'll find out." Michael slid out of his trousers and cast them onto the bed with a final
deeply regretful look. "Good lord, Valerie! I know
this is funny, but will you stop watching me?"

"Sh-h! A question that has often troubled me is
about to be answered. . . . Oh, you *are* going to
wear something underneath?"

"Don't be an idiot." Michael grinned reluctantly.
"Though there was a time when your Highlander
did not. The sporran"—he took his from the suitcase—"helps to hold the kilt down. And this, my
love, is a dinner jacket, Highland cut. Observe
that it is almost a swallow tail, but with the tails
cut short. I am sorry not to entertain you further by appearing in shoulder plaid, bonnet and

claymore, but there are limits to what I will do to further justice. Now, will you kindly finish dressing yourself?"

II

The front half of the central part of the house was one huge room that had been stripped for dancing. Behind it was a dining room, large enough in its own right, with double doors now hooked back against the walls. A long refectory table was spread with a buffet supper, and Wong was carrying around drinks when Valerie and Michael came into the room.

The Honorable Maria's other house guests were already there, including a couple of the sort Stella would probably call "horsy," though Mr. Doty wore a domino, and his wife a gingham Mother Hubbard and a sunbonnet. Except on the twin subjects of horse racing and breeding, they had little to say, but their presence did impose certain desirable restrictions upon the conversation.

Mrs. Alling had donned an ancient dress of yellow-white silk that might have been her wedding gown and had obviously been let out in several places. Bettina wore a simple First Empire gown of pale green, but Stella was attired in bright pink silk, preposterously high-heeled shoes and a stringy feather boa. She smiled as she caught Michael's eye.

"This is really pink, isn't it?" she said in her company voice. "'N— pink,' some people call it. And that's what it's meant to be. I'm blacking up later."

"Women beat me," Gould said. "Why, with all the costumes in the world to choose from—"

"I thought this would be—fun," Stella murmured. "Rather a—change, for me. You don't have to black up, Bernard, though the grease paint I have is really only a mulatto shade and not disagreeable to use."

"There's no point to my outfit if I'm not at least a high yaller," Gould said. He was wearing a violently checked suit, white spats and an ornamental vest. He looked from Geoffrey to Michael and grinned. "Well, I never thought I'd see two of you."

Geoffrey's legs were, as his sister had said, "spindleshanks" and hairy as well, but he appeared perfectly at ease in his kilt, shoulder plaid and bonnet. He eyed Michael's kilt interestedly.

"Isn't that the Maclean of Duart tartan?" he asked. "Did you only happen to pick it up or—?"

"I'm entitled to wear it," Michael said. "I was born a Maclean. You seem to be quite an authority.

I can't tell one tartan from another." He gave Valerie the plate he had filled for her and sat down. "However, I do know that you are wearing the MacFarlane tartan."

He did not even glance at Geoffrey's kilt, which to Valerie's untutored eye looked much like his own. For an instant no one spoke. Then Bernard Gould asked:

"Why MacFarlane and not MacNair?"

"So far as I know, the MacNairs have no tartan. They are septs or dependents of the clans MacFarlane or MacNaughton. Mr. MacNair happens to be a MacNair of Clan MacFarlane."

Michael ate half an enchilada before he added casually: "I do always recognize the Black Watch tartan. Some of my forebears have worn it—as I imagine some of yours have."

"Y-yes. Yes, certainly," Geoffrey said. His eyes sought his sister's, and she answered with an almost imperceptible shake of the head.

"The—the Black Watch?" Bettina said hesitantly. "Isn't that a regiment?"

"Formerly forty-third regiment, later forty-second, now first battalion Royal Highlanders—other-wise the Black Watch," Michael said precisely. "Famed in song and story. There are others, of course. The Royal Scots Fusiliers—the 'Fusilier Jocks,' for instance, though they are a Lowland

regiment. I believe the rank and file wear dou-
blet and trews and not kilts, but their tartan is
the Black Watch tartan. You'll correct me if I'm
wrong, Mr. MacNair?"

"I think your—information is quite correct,"
Geoffrey said impassively.

He walked over to the table and poured himself a cup of coffee as one of several frowsy, bux-
om Mexican girls who kept rushing through the
large rooms without, apparently, ever accomplish-
ing anything came in to announce that "a Mr.
Dundas is wanted on the phone." She added: "I'll
show you where it is," and finally, catching Mrs.
Alling's eye: "sir."

Michael was out of the room for not more than
five minutes. He was frowning when he returned to
it, and after looking thoughtfully at Mrs. Alling:

"I think I'd better tell you that Sullivan just
called to tell me that Mrs. Farnham has managed
to slip away from her nurse and out of the house,"
he said.

"Out of the house? Do you mean to tell me
those blasted incompetents on the police force
weren't watching the house?" Gould demanded.

"They were. But there came a time when the
man at the back doors was forced to go into
the house. The nurse was in the kitchen, and
Mrs. Farnham went down the stairway into the

basement. They haven't picked her up yet, and she might possibly head this way."

"And I fancy she is hardly responsible for her actions," Mrs. Alling said. "But we'll do our best to guard against unpleasantness. Admission is by card, but once the dancing is well started I can't watch the doors to see that no gate crashers enter. There will be a man at the gate on the highway, and we'll speak to him. Barney, suppose you see that this room is cleared. We'll need it for dancing too. I want to run out to the barbecue pit while I can. You and Geoff come along with me, Bettina. . . ."

"I'll finish dressing," Stella said. She rose languidly, her feather boa slipping from her shoulders to the floor, almost at Michael's feet. She bent to pick it up as he did, murmuring:

"You two say you're going to walk around outside. I'll meet you there pretty soon. . . ."

Gould was already so busily engaged in superintending the removal of chairs and table from the room that no excuse for quitting it was necessary. Valerie and Michael strolled through the enormous living room and out onto the walk between the lawns. In a few minutes Stella came around one of the building's far-flung corners.

"Just like a rabbit out of a hat," Valerie said. "I still don't know my way around this place."

"It takes time. Come back here." Stella motioned toward a group of olive and orange trees to one side of the lawns. "You stay, kid," she told Valerie. "It 'd look better if someone happened along. Well—"

"Yes?" Michael said encouragingly.

"Well, you probably guessed Bettina went to see Ray at the Trengrove Hotel for me last September. That was the day Lilian threw a scene in Barney's office. Well, he told her politely to go to the chaplain and get a crying towel—"

"What?" Valerie said.

"Hunh? Oh, he told her to shut up. He said he knew I or Bettina didn't care anything about Ray except as a friend. He sent her off with her tail feathers dragging but he came home and raised hell. He said Ray should have more sense than to see so much of us when Barney was in Texas and Lilian in Palm Springs—when Ray knew what Lilian was like.

"Well, Ray didn't know she'd gone to Barney. He'd already been at the Trengrove one night. So I thought Ray had a right to be warned before he saw Barney. I couldn't slip out or even telephone, with his eagle eye on me, so I coaxed Bettina to go and tell Ray what had happened."

"Coaxed? You mean you bribed her, don't you?"

"You can't blame her for not wanting to go. But she needed a fur jacket, and I offered her that one if she would, so she did. And I still think it was a good thing, because Ray went home and put the fear of God in Lilian for a while. She called Barney and said she hadn't realized what she was saying and just to forget it. And that," Stella said with some satisfaction, "took the wind out of Barney's sails."

"Does he know all this now?" Michael asked.

"Oh, sure. We went it hot and heavy after you and Sullivan left Thursday morning. Ten years ago he would have hit me. Of course, I should have spoke up when Sullivan began bothering Bettina Thursday. But if I'd told him the truth Barney probably would have blacked my eye. I knew he'd caught on right away and I could square things with him and Geoff—for Bettina—afterward. You can use your own judgment about telling Sullivan, but I can't have him getting ideas about Bettina—if he tries to go any farther with that one."

"And is that all you have to tell us?"

"If you're thinking about what Peter said—I can't help you there. I've got an idea Geoff thinks he saw me on the third floor of the hotel the night Logan was killed."

"Did he?"

"Of course not. But I can't get anything out of Geoff. Say, do you expect Peter to turn up here?"

"Honey draws flies," Michael said. "But did you know that Mr. Wallis is temporarily missing?"

"Barney saw him Thursday afternoon. Don't ask me what about. He wanted to see him again yesterday and couldn't locate him. Well, I'd better get my blackface on. You know, I expect to have a good time, acting my part and not having to be on my dignity."

She turned to go and then stopped. "About Lilian Farnham—I was at a costume party with her once, and she wore a kind of Turkish outfit—with a veil. I thought I'd just mention it. . . ."

III

It was ten-thirty when a man wearing an old Rough-rider's uniform sidled up to Michael as he and Valerie left the dance floor and stepped outside.

"I'm Morris—deputy sheriff," he said. "You're Dundas, aren't you? Well, Sullivan's on his way now. He should be here in less than an hour. Maybe you'll be glad to know that," Mr. Morris said glumly. "We're all in a fog."

"Are there many of you?" Michael asked.

"Enough," Morris said indefinitely. "But, hell! everybody's scattered around, not to mention there being such a crowd here. We're doing our best."

"Have you, yourself, seen or heard anything interesting?"

"No-o. Well, MacNair was called to the phone a while ago. I heard a little when the music stopped for an instant. He was talking to a guy he called Jones. He said something about somebody knowing something by tomorrow. Or maybe it was that he—MacNair—would know something by tomorrow. I couldn't risk getting close enough to make sure. Look—have you seen a redheaded n— anywhere around?"

"A redheaded— No, I haven't. There are at least half a dozen here in blackface—"

"Gould and his wife and three Al Jolsons and this other guy. I ran into him over by the barbecue pit. It looked like he was wearing a wig, but it was on a little crooked. I thought I saw red hair underneath, but the lights weren't so good, and, while we were told to keep an eye out for this Wallis, we had orders not to scare him off."

"I know. However, I think I'll see if I can catch up with him," Michael said.

"I've got no orders to stop you."

Morris strolled into the house and joined the circle that had formed in the front room: a circle like a thick doughnut with a very small hole. Within this one of the Honorable Maria's young friends who fancied herself as a torch singer was getting ready to declare that she would never smile again.

"I must say Mrs. Alling gives good value," Valerie remarked. "We've had tap dancers that weren't half bad, and I believe there is an accordionist and a baritone to follow. And, as she promised, the barbecue is good, and there is enough of it, with all the trimmings, to feed an army. But how can you find anyone here if he doesn't want to be found?"

"I'm hoping that perhaps by now he will want to be found." Michael drew her arm through his. "Let's walk about for a while, anyway. . . ."

Since nine-thirty the dancing floors had been packed. It made no difference that there was always a line of people leaving the house to go over to the barbecue pit and another returning from it.

The parking space available about the garage, stables and bunkhouses had been exhausted some time ago. Cars were now parked in a double row before the house and down the road toward the entrance gates. Their owners had cheerfully alighted in thick dust and come laughing into the house: pierrot and pierrette, courtiers, soldier, sailor and clowns, ballet girl and forty-niner, black dominos and elaborate Louis costumes, cowboy and cowgirl, pirate and nun.

There were other couples wandering about the grounds as Valerie and Michael walked along the driveway that ended at the garage. The barbecue pit was to their left, with long tables lighted by lanterns hanging on wire strung from tree to tree. As they walked farther along the driveway those lights were hidden by other trees and clumps of shrubbery. From one of these a voice spoke suddenly.

"Ps-sst! It's only me. Is it safe to come out?"

"Why wouldn't it be?" Michael stopped and lighted a cigarette. "Aren't you well disguised?"

"I was, but my blacking's getting a little moist." Peter emerged from his hiding place. "And how do I know you won't yell for the cops?"

"How do you know there are any about?"

"I saw a guy in a Roughrider's outfit giving me the once-over. I've been trying to keep away from anybody who might recognize me, but it's getting late, and I'm not getting anywhere."

"Where do you want to go?"

"You know I want to talk to Bettina," Peter said impatiently. "I haven't had more than a glimpse of her. You tell her I'm here and bring her to me and then you can do as you damn please about handing me over to the police."

"Nobly spoken," Michael drawled. "The world well lost for love. Couldn't you have managed to see her without going to all the trouble of fleeing the city to turn up here in blackface?"

"Never mind about that. I want to see her, and what are you going to do about it?"

"Try to persuade her to talk to you," Michael said pleasantly. "But it might be difficult for her to make an excuse to come outside by herself."

"She can always powder her nose," Valerie said. "But I don't know where her room is."

"Neither do I. Perhaps you'd better meet in our quarters," Michael said. "They're on this side of the house, Peter, at its back and jutting out from it. You should be able to find your way there or near enough to see the light when I put it on. I'll raise a window for you, and you'll be able to climb in easily enough. Then we'll try to find Bettina. Don't be impatient—it may take us some time to locate her."

"Are you playing Cupid?" Valerie said as they started back toward the house. "Otherwise, why so helpful?"

"I shall turn on the lights, raise a window and conceal myself in a closet," Michael said. "You will lure Bettina to the rendezvous."

"Well, if you think it's necessary—"

"I don't like to skulk in closets. It's undignified and it would be very embarrassing to be caught there. But I want to know what Peter's plans are. You do your part of the job, and I'll do mine. . . ."

IV

He heard Peter scramble over the window sill only
a few minutes after he had slipped into the closet
and locked it on the inside. But he was beginning
to be very weary of his almost unventilated hiding
place and repressing an inclination to gasp, open-
mouthed, like a fish out of water, before he heard
a door open and Valerie saying:

"No, I won't go too far away and I'll warn you
if anyone that matters comes this way."

The door closed. There was a moment of
silence before Bettina said:

"Peter, you shouldn't have come here."

"How else was I to talk to you—alone? I couldn't
ask you to meet me downtown yesterday—"

"I wasn't thinking of myself. I heard Barney
tell Stella that he thought you'd 'skipped out.' He
said he supposed the police were looking for you.
Peter, you didn't run away because—"

"Well? Because why?"

"Barney—Barney hinted that you might not
want the police to—to question you."

"My pal!" Peter said grimly. "The dirty double-
crosser. Well, I cleared out because I had something to think over. I didn't want to be told to
stay in the city when you were coming down here.
Well, I finally made up my mind. I'm going away,
Bettina."

"Going— You don't mean—"

"Not running away, no. I can have a job in L.A. if I want it. Don't worry about me. I won't have to look around for a Foreign Legion to join if they pass the conscription bill— Oh, I know that's not funny, but it's the best I can do on short notice. And don't you think I'd better go away?"

"I know you should. I—I've made a bargain and I— Well, what can I say, Peter? Anything I can think of sounds trite and foolish—"

"And I can't even kiss you! Though maybe it's just as well. If I could— Sweetheart, did I hurt you? I didn't mean to—"

"No," Bettina said softly. "You didn't hurt me."

"But I got some of my blacking on your hair. Let me wipe it off. . . . There's just one thing more. I don't know if Gould will be satisfied to let well enough alone and I want to tell you I was never in love with Lilian Farnham.

"If I did see too much of her at one time, it was just one of those things you drift into, living in a boardinghouse room with a small salary. Some couple tells you to drop in any time. The man even tells you to play escort to his wife when he's busy—"

"Peter, you don't suppose we'd known Lilian any time before she mentioned you, do you? But, once I'd met you, and after the first time I saw you together—saw her try to take a possessive attitude toward you and how angry she was when you were very formal with her—I could guess a great deal she hadn't told. I don't care what Barney might say—I wouldn't believe it."

"All right. And just remember I'll never love anyone but you until I die. I'm going now. . . ."

It was insufferably warm and close in the closet. Michael passed his sleeve over his forehead and waited. When he heard nothing but a sudden creaking of bed springs he risked turning the key and easing the closet door open a trifle.

Bettina had flung herself, face down, onto the bed. Michael considered trying to slip past her, but she was crying very quietly, and he would have to skirt the bed to get out of the room. He had had a word with the deputy, Morris, before he came in here. Morris would have been waiting outside when Peter went out the window and could be depended on not to lose sight of him.

Bettina sat up, drying her eyes. Her back was toward Michael, and she saw the door into the adjoining dressing room swing slowly open at the same minute that he did. She shrank farther back on the bed, telling herself she must not scream, that there was no reason for screaming. It would only be one of Maria's numerous maids, caught in the other room and afraid to make her presence known while two people were talking in here.

Eyes like coals almost, but not quite dead, looked at her over a black veil. Lilian Farnham came slowly toward the bed in her costume of sheer Turkish trousers, sash and embroidered jacket. She stopped before she reached it, one arm extended in a sleepwalker's gesture.

"I'm very tired," she said. "I went into that room to hide. I sat down and I must have gone to sleep."

Bettina slid slowly toward the foot of the bed, trying to distract Mrs. Farnham's attention from the movement with a soothing:

"You must be tired, Lilian. Have you seen Maria? I'm s-sure she would like to— Lilian! What—"

Mrs. Farnham glanced down toward her right hand, resting on the handle of a dagger thrust through her belt.

"That?" She giggled. "It's part of the costume. But it's very sharp. I was very glad when I found it with the costume. It makes me feel safe. I can't find Stella. I haven't seen her anywhere. . . ."

She nodded her head slowly and thoughtfully. "That's what I was going to do—find Stella. I'll look again. She must be here. . . ."

Bettina's feet touched the floor now. She sprang up, ran desperately toward the door. Lilian

Farnham slid around her, quickly and silently as a snake, and was at the door before her.

"I don't want you to run away," she said softly. "You might get to Stella first. Maybe I'd better—"

"Mrs. Farnham!" Michael touched her shoulder, and she whirled about to face him.

Bettina, an instant before rigid to resist attack, leaned back against the door, trembling violently. It did not occur to her then to ask where Michael had come from. She thought: "Lilian's gone mad. Surely they must see that," and listened to Michael saying:

"If you'll dance with me, Mrs. Farnham, I'll find Mrs. Gould for you. That's why you haven't seen her—because you haven't been dancing. But you must be quiet and not talk."

"I know," Mrs. Farnham said wisely. "And I can dance, because no one will know me."

"You'd better straighten your veil, don't you think? There's a mirror in the next room."

"I know. I will," Mrs. Farnham said docilely and moved toward the dressing room. Michael turned quickly to Bettina.

"Find Mrs. Alling and tell her about this. Tell her to humor Mrs. Farnham when I bring her out there, and we'll try to get her away quietly."

Bettina ran out into the hall, turned the corner into the main corridor and just escaped colliding with Valerie, hurrying toward her.

"I'm sorry. I wanted to warn you that Inspector Sullivan has arrived—"

"Your husband is in there with Lilian Farnham," Bettina said. "And he told me to find Maria. . . ."

She went on toward the front of the house without realizing, until she had almost reached the dance floor, that the orchestra was playing "Irish Washerwoman" while the Honorable Maria's guests danced the Virginia reel.

V

The reel had come to a breathless finish when Valerie and Michael, with Lilian Farnham between them, pushed their way toward Mrs. Alling. Bettina and Geoffrey were standing beside her, and a girl in a brief romper suit was assuring her that "It was keen, Maria. It may be corny but it makes people loosen up. Let's have a Paul Jones too."

"I daresay it can be managed. If you'll pardon me an instant?" Mrs. Alling took Lilian Farnham's cold hand. "I haven't seen you yet this evening," she said matter-of-factly. "Suppose we go to my room and—"

"No. I want to see Stella. Where is Stella?"

"I said I'd find her for you if you danced with me," Michael broke in. "Mrs. Alling, since the young lady over there likes the old dances, even if they are corny, why don't we demonstrate one?"

He added, so low that Valerie had difficulty in hearing him: "I'd agree if I were you. It's either Ring, Ring or let Sullivan order all but a very few guests off the dance floor."

"Ring—" The Honorable Maria looked suddenly very old. "Sullivan's here then? I daresay my guests will be leaving very soon, in any case, but do it your own way." She addressed the orchestra and then her guests. "Play something else suitable for an old-fashioned dance. We're going to show you one. Clear a space, please!"

"We want Mr. and Mrs. Gould," Michael said. "Mr. Gould as a dancer, not as prompter, this time. And Mr. MacNair can surely manage to walk through this. Miss Lawton—and, if Mrs. Farnham will excuse me, I'll provide her with a worthy partner. If we could have another dancer in black-face—Mr. Morris?"

Morris propelled Peter Wallis through the crowd and into the limelight. Peter, his blackface badly smudged and running over his collar, scowled at Michael, started to wipe off his forehead and thought better of it. Mrs. Farnham merely glanced at him and went on staring at Stella as if trying to satisfy herself that the mulatto in bright pink could possibly be the beautiful Mrs. Gould.

Valerie found herself wanting to laugh—and not just hysterically. This was pure theater, and

Michael, who detested the theatrical, had for the moment lost that alert sense of the ridiculous that was his nearest approach to self-consciousness. He was as sure of himself as any veteran actor and commanded his audience as easily.

"That's six, and we need two more," he said, looking toward the door. "Two guests who have been unavoidably detained have arrived just in time to help out."

A man and woman came forward, the man in his forties, with small, rounded ears standing straight out from his head. He wore wrinkled and dusty riding trousers, a soiled shirt and broad-brimmed Stetson. The woman with him was tall and muscular, heavily tanned, her eyes black and rather prominent.

She wore a fringed buckskin jacket and divided skirt, leather boots trimmed with silver and a Stetson only slightly smaller than her companion's. Both skirt and jacket were marked with an *M* touching a quarter circle.

"This is Mrs. Walker," Michael said. "And some of you here know Mr. Alfred Payne. If you're ready?"

"No," Geoffrey said flatly. "I'm fed up with this nonsense. No doubt, it amuses you to pull the strings and see the puppets dance, but I—"

"You won't dance, Mr. MacNair? Or should I say, 'Lord Tarbet'—now?"

"Then you—" Geoffrey made Michael a stiff, formal bow. "If you wish. I hadn't intended to—"

"I know. You hadn't intended that anyone should know so soon. But I've known since Thursday night that you—"

"You don't need to give me any more time, if that's what y'all are talkin' for," drawled the woman named Walker. "I spotted her in two minutes in spite of the way she's dressed. It was the one over that-away who came to the Rocking M last year with the man y'all say was Mr. Farnham."

She raised a tanned forefinger. "The little one in the green dress," she said.

Bettina screamed once, turned and ran at the crowd between her and the door. When Payne and Sullivan caught her she was sobbing, clawing and kicking at those who surrounded her. She began to scream again as Sullivan's hands closed over her wrists. . . .

PART SIX

"Lady to the center and seven
around,
Swing your corners, everyone,
Leave her alone and swing your
own. . . ."

Quadrille

Michael Dundas to Rocky Allan

Amigo mío:
As you complain that the newspaper accounts of "the tragedy" are unsatisfactory and that you have reason to be curious regarding this case, I suppose I must give you the explanation you demand, even if it will take me hours to do so.

When I was trying to decide where to begin Valerie said: "With Bettina, of course." I suppose she is right, that you must understand Bettina to understand why she killed two men. She killed Logan because she was determined to marry Geoffrey MacNair and she was afraid Logan stood in the way of her doing so. And she wanted to marry Geoffrey because he is a wealthy man and the chances were nearly ten to one that he would be the Earl of Tarbet.

But, as Sullivan objected, "Why, even before she'd killed Logan and wanted to hide everything that might suggest she had a motive for killing him, did she give the impression she didn't really want to marry MacNair but was being persuaded into it?"

Valerie said, as she is saying now—and I might get on more rapidly if she didn't insist on reading this over my shoulder—

"If any of you had asked me I could have told you what sort of person Bettina really was. I understood her perfectly when I had talked to her that Sunday night at Summit House, when she tried to enlist my sympathies and talked too much about her upbringing and the grandmother who was responsible for it.

"I'm sure that Grandmamma considered man a base animal. Of course, a wife must 'do her duty,' but her husband must also be mentally on his knees to her, admitting she was pure and holy and far too good for him. And Bettina couldn't have been uninfluenced by that viewpoint.

"Anyway, she certainly meant, as many women do, to have the upper hand always. She would never have married a man who didn't 'adore' her. She meant Geoffrey should be grateful to her all their lives together and always a little doubtful that she really loved him. Well! If even before she killed Logan she had said: 'Yes, I want very much to marry Geoffrey,' she wouldn't have had the upper hand."

"And where," I ask, "does Peter come in?"

"She could play him off against Geoffrey. Besides, Peter worshiped her too. She would never have let him go either," says the oracle. "She'd have married Geoffrey and whenever she met Peter smiled a brave, sad smile and declared with a choke in her voice that she was happy but 'if—if only things had been different!'"

And, from what I overheard between Bettina and Peter not twenty minutes before she was arrested, I must agree with Valerie. But she isn't finished.

"Besides, she wasn't entirely proof against physical attraction, which Peter has plenty of. From his accounts of their various interviews, she played her part beautifully. It was an exciting game to her. And it's so often the soft-spoken, wistful, helpless-appearing women like Bettina who get a real strangle hold on a man. But do I have to tell you all this? Surely it wasn't too long before you guessed a good many of the things I've been saying about Bettina?"

(You will realize this is a question I don't care to answer. If I say "Yes" I am a conceited ass. If I say I was completely fooled by a slip of a girl I don't rank highly as a judge of character. I will only admit that I have come across Bettina's type before. I am, in fact, constantly exposed to it during business hours.)

"And"—Valerie speaking again—"she was wild for social position and money. Of course, it's no fun being a poor relation to a man like Mr. Gould. But she admitted her grandmother had trained her to be a shining light of society and she resented not knowing 'anyone who was anyone' when she came here with the Goulds.

"Stella admitted they'd been snubbed, and Bettina didn't like it. But she could have hidden her feelings and climbed. I think a number of things Stella said to you showed she realized that, in her quiet, ladylike way, Bettina was a climber. There are lots like her, but, good heavens! who'd want to be an English countess—in these days?"

And who would want to be one—in England? But Geoffrey would certainly never take Bettina to England in wartime. I doubt if she ever asked herself what this war, even if the British win out, may do to their aristocracy. Also, Geoffrey MacNair was wealthy, whatever Lord Tarbet might be. And if you don't think Americans are still impressed by titles—well, read your local newspapers.

Very well—Bettina wanted to climb, and I think that brings us to Farnham. None of the men she met in San Francisco were what she would consider a "good match"—with the exception of Farnham. He was well off, rising steadily in his profession and already rather well connected socially. With a different sort of wife he might climb to respectable social heights.

As to his wife, a quiet divorce could be arranged, giving Mrs. Farnham custody of the child. And everyone's sympathies would be with the second wife, so sweet and gentle and unlike the first. That, at any rate, is what Bettina not unnaturally believed.

Undoubtedly they were also strongly attracted to each other. I imagine Farnham was pretty well bowled over, or he wouldn't have taken the risk he did take. I fancy also that he was clever enough to realize finally that Bettina wasn't quite the person he'd thought her.

She said—amateur killers do talk when the world first falls to pieces about them—that she "was certain she really loved Ray and thought he wanted to marry her." What she will say now that she has a lawyer to advise her is another matter. But, since she must admit to having gone off with Farnham, that's as good a line as any.

Well, by what steps the affair progressed to its climax we will probably never know. But they must have been very discreet—until they decided to be completely indiscreet.

That was in July of last year, when Stella and Bettina and Farnham were here, Gould in Texas, and Mrs. Farnham at Palm Springs. Farnham went to Reno "on business." Bettina went to visit friends at Lake Tahoe. The Blodgetts are a happy-go-lucky family that Gould hardly knew but did not approve of, which fact gave Bettina an excuse to caution Stella not to tell Gould where she had been. When Mrs. Farnham had raised that scene in Gould's office in September Stella did not care to tell him she had been alone at any time during his absence.

Bettina asked, on Saturday the fifteenth, to be driven to Reno to take an evening train back to San Francisco. She insisted that the Blodgett son who drove her over from Tahoe should not wait to put her on the train. (These are established facts.) She then met Farnham at the Golden Hotel and drove with him to a dude ranch, the Rocking M, some distance from Reno.

That was where Logan's trail crossed with Farnham's. Farnham, having been born in Nevada and still visiting it frequently, knew the Rocking M and its reputation for—as you yourself said—"no questions asked and none answered about other guests." It was natural that he would take Bettina to a place like that, and one a fair distance from Reno.

Logan was a wanderer and might turn up anywhere. However, I did wonder if he had come to the Pacific coast simply because he wanted to see new country or if there was something else behind his choice of his next stopping place.

There was. He wanted to see his cousin, Beulah Anderson Walker. She and Walker owned the Rocking M, and Logan was in the lobby of its central building when Farnham entered it that night in July. Logan and Walker were playing cards in a corner. Farnham never got a good look at Logan and didn't recognize him later. Farnham registered under a fictitious name, but the Walkers and Logan saw him clearly. And his face—and eyebrows—were not easily forgotten.

But Bettina remained in the car. Mrs. Walker conducted her and Farnham to cabin number ten, and she got a good look at Bettina. She knew the girl was nervous and not wanting to be stared at. She was used to that sort of thing. She went back to the central building and remarked casually to her husband and Tex Logan: "They aren't married."

Logan asked: "What's the woman like?" And Mrs. Walker said: "Oh, she's pretty and blonde." She also told Logan emphatically "not to snoop."

Then she went back to the cabin just rented with a supply of towels. Before she had knocked she heard a girl crying. And she heard Farnham say:

"We've made a disastrous mistake. I can't divorce Lilian. She would never willingly consent to a divorce, whatever she might say at times. If she would, with custody of Patricia as her price, I still would never hand my child over to her. I should never have brought you here. Don't cry. Try to get some sleep. I'll bunk on the couch, and we'll leave here very early tomorrow."

And he added: "We must have been mad. Lilian would have no mercy on either of us if she ever knew of this—and particularly no mercy for you."

The conversation stuck in Mrs. Walker's mind because she thought Farnham was "a pretty decent guy." So she didn't report that conversation to her husband or Logan. And Farnham and Bettina left very early the next morning, still without Logan's having seen Bettina.

I suppose it's a rather ghastly joke that the night those two spent together was as harmless as any spent by the hero and heroine of a very strictly censored movie when they find themselves obliged to occupy a single hotel room. If that wasn't so Bettina wouldn't have declared she could, if necessary, prove she'd been no man's mistress.

Well, she says—and I believe that, too—that the affair ended then and forever. By September Mrs. Farnham had made it impossible for the Goulds to continue on their old terms of intimacy with her or Farnham, which must have been a relief to him and Bettina.

Meanwhile, Logan had tired of the Rocking M, had come to San Francisco and looked Gould up. His brief stay with Mrs. Alling followed—but he never saw Farnham there. You may call it coincidence that finally his path crossed with Farnham's again.

But if there was any coincidence it was that both Logan and Farnham knew Gould. Because as long as Gould would find jobs for Logan they would be with people Gould knew or connected with projects of his. He recommended Summit House as a resort to all his friends and acquaintances, and many of them took his recommendation. When he sent Logan to Summit House there was at least an even chance that eventually Logan would come into contact with a good many people Gould knew.

Logan returned to the Rocking M for a while after he left Esperanza de Oro, finally turned up in San Francisco again and was sent to Summit House by Gould. And, meanwhile, Bettina had "reluctantly" consented to marry Geoffrey MacNair.

Geoffrey's father was the fourth son of the Earl of Tarbet. He married against his father's wishes, came to Canada and lost touch with his family. As Mrs. Alling said: "We knew who our grandfather was but we weren't encouraged to mention him to anyone." And if you knew Mrs. Alling and her brother you'd know they aren't the sort who would ever mention a connection of that kind.

Besides, Geoffrey's father was a fourth son, and the others had married and produced offspring. Though the rate of mortality among the MacNairs was high between 1914 and 1918, Geoffrey says that he never considered the possibility that he would ever be Earl of Tarbet.

The MacNairs had twenty years of peace in which to replenish the stock, but there were deaths even in peacetime and— However, you don't want a detailed family history. It's enough to say that when the present war began the Earl of Tarbet was a man of thirty. He had no sons but two brothers, Roderick and Donald. After them Geoffrey was next in line. But they were all married and might be expected to produce heirs, so it hadn't been considered necessary to get in touch with Geoffrey.

Lord Tarbet was killed during the retreat on Dunkirk. Roderick succeeded to the title. Both he and Donald were members of the R.A.F. Donald was killed late in July. Roderick, now Lord Tarbet, was severely wounded in August but managed to land his plane in England.

After Dunkirk inquiries were made in Toronto. It wasn't difficult to locate Geoffrey, though he'd been living in California for ten years. He had married the daughter of a very wealthy Canadian. She had, after inheriting her father's money, run off with another man, returned to Geoffrey and finally killed herself. It was because of that that he left Canada. And it is important, because the burned child dreads the fire.

He said himself: "I hope I'm not too strait-laced." (He is, a trifle.) "But I couldn't face that sort of thing again. I thought that I could trust Bettina implicitly. If I'd been told of that Rocking M incident I don't know what I— But I don't think I could have faced another scandal, such as there would have been if the affair had been made public—as Lilian Farnham would have made it. . . ."

Bettina knew what his reaction would be. She had also been warned what Mrs. Farnham would do if she ever learned of Farnham's and Bettina's night at the Rocking M. We may say that episodes of that sort are treated lightly nowadays. But it's still a sin to be found out.

Mrs. Farnham's first thought would have been to tear Bettina's reputation to shreds—publicly. That sort of thing would depreciate her market value even if she hadn't Geoffrey's reactions to consider. Also, "Barney wouldn't have liked it" and would have been quite capable of tossing Bettina out of her very comfortable place in his household.

But to return to Geoffrey—a firm of lawyers in Toronto located him and wrote him several letters that made the situation quite clear. Those were the letters I read when I broke into Geoffrey's apartment. I suppose I needn't say I haven't admitted doing that to anyone until now. I had already consulted Burke and Debrett at the library, but they didn't tell me just how close Geoffrey might be to the title.

Under the circumstances there was no thought of sending a solicitor from England to contact Geoffrey, even after Donald was killed. There happened to be a "suitable" man available here, Mr. Jones of Jones, Evans and Evans. The firm is well patronized by Britishers here. Jones was born in Wales and is a cousin of the very elderly Mac-Nair family solicitor in England, so Geoffrey and Geoffrey's interests were turned over to him.

Geoffrey is a reserved sort of person who dreads publicity and abhors "swank." He was most anxious there should be no publicity at any time and, naturally, after Logan was killed and Farnham followed him Geoffrey was even more secretive about

his personal affairs. No doubt he visualized head-
lines: HEIR TO TITLE SUSPECT IN MURDER CASE.

However, he is also scrupulous and conscientious. He had told Bettina about his first marriage—also Gould—as being in loco parentis. It
was Gould he confided in when he first learned
Roderick had been wounded. He had asked Bettina to marry him, not for the first time, and she
had, characteristically, asked for time to consider
her final answer.

But, said Geoffrey, under the circumstances
had he the right to ask Bettina to marry him? He
might feel he must go to England, if Lord Tarbet
died, though, naturally, he wouldn't take her with
him. And, meanwhile, he didn't want her to be
worried.

MacNair and Mrs. Alling have kept nothing
back. Gould and Stella admit only what they
must. But from what Gould has had to admit, and
from what you know of him, you can guess that he
wanted Bettina to marry and marry well.

He had always considered Geoffrey the most
eligible *parti* who had presented himself so far. He
wasn't entirely deceived by Bettina. He was certain she wouldn't be happy married to a poor man.
But he wasn't quite certain that she didn't fancy
herself in love with Peter or that Peter might not
be able to persuade her to run away with him,

given favorable circumstances—such as too much soft moonlight.

That was why Gould returned to Summit House. He learned Peter was there and didn't think Geoffrey would be quite ruthless enough if he found Peter had made good use of his time there with Bettina.

Gould liked the sound of "my sister-in-law, Lady Tarbet." He didn't know he was playing into Bettina's hands by appearing to be rather forcibly persuading her to marry Geoffrey. And he did think it best that she shouldn't appear too eager. He is vain regarding himself and his possessions and he shied away from the idea that it was Geoffrey who was conferring a great favor. He meant to give Bettina a very respectable dowry if she married Geoffrey—and she knew that.

He reassured Geoffrey. That is, he said: "If she says she'll marry you without knowing this you can count on her sticking by when she learns about your new responsibilities." He promised to tell no one what Geoffrey had told him and kept his promise. He also, typically, tried to protect all of them later on.

Several days later Bettina unenthusiastically told Geoffrey she would marry him, presumably without knowing there was any chance that he would ever be anything but Mr. MacNair. When she was arrested I had nothing better than a hunch that she had "known everything" before she accepted him.

But we've been lucky since then. Geoffrey gave us the hour and day of his talk with Gould. And a housemaid testifies that when the two men were talking in Gould's ghastly study Miss Lawton was listening at the door. The maid thought it so strange for the well-bred Miss Lawton to be acting that way that she watched her for some time.

That, then, was the situation when Gould, MacNair and Mrs. Alling came to Summit House. Lord Tarbet had been reported severely wounded, but the report hadn't been confirmed. When it was Mr. Jones composed that very discreet wire to Geoffrey at Summit House—the "T" standing, of course, for Tarbet.

Since we knew nothing of all this, we completely misinterpreted the Honorable Maria's conversation with Geoffrey shortly after Logan's death. It wasn't until Patton called Herr Hitler a maniac and said, speaking of war, that human nature doesn't change that I saw how Mrs. Alling's similar remark might be interpreted.

As I thought that over and everything else she and Geoffrey had said and also considered Jones's telegram, I went off to consult Burke's peerage and afterward broke into Geoffrey's apartment.

I don't mean that even when I knew why he and Mrs. Alling were under some strain that I also knew who had killed Logan and Farnham. It only occurred to me that Bettina might like very much to be Lady Tarbet.

Well, Logan had ample time to observe everyone at the hotel—and to be snubbed by Bettina and to resent her attitude—before the Farnhams arrived. We don't know how quickly he recognized Farnham. Probably by Friday night. And he could also see that Mrs. Farnham could not possibly be described as "a blonde" even if you stretched a point and called her "very pretty."

If he didn't decide at once to blackmail Farnham, by Saturday afternoon he knew he could do so. Because he rode herd on Patricia Saturday morning, and she prattled to him as she did to me on Sunday. She not only defined the situation between her father and mother—she mentioned Mrs. Farnham's jealousy of Stella and Bettina.

So on Saturday afternoon Logan concocted his message to Farnham. How he did it and how he planned to have it delivered to Farnham by the bartender you know. Sullivan says the message was "fantastic," a favorite word of his when someone acts differently than he would. Personally, I think it was a rather clever approach—merely a single line—

ᴍ 🏠 VII MCMXXXIX

He put nothing into writing, yet Farnham would know it came from him, and to Farnham it would mean: the Rocking M Ranch, cabin ten, July—the seventh month—1939.

You also know why Farnham didn't read the message at once and why and when he finally turned it up in San Francisco. I don't imagine Logan worried because Farnham made no move to talk to him Saturday night. But he didn't let well enough alone. He evidently had been speculating as to who Farnham's companion at the Rocking M might have been and, very naturally, considered Stella and Bettina in that connection.

The sisters are both blonde, but "beautiful" is the word for Stella, rather than "pretty." So Logan took a chance on Bettina, probably with the idea of paying her back for having snubbed him.

She didn't know until he danced with her fairly early in the evening that her plans were endangered by him or anyone. In one way she lost her head, and in another she kept it. I suppose it's comparable to being cool under fire, without being able to do any intensive reasoning.

She couldn't pay Logan blackmail and she was afraid Farnham might not pay and that Logan would go to Mrs. Farnham. He threatened to do so, though, I imagine, merely for the pleasure of seeing Bettina squirm. Farnham was quicker, surer pay. But Bettina didn't think of that and, I repeat, she knew how much mercy she could expect from Mrs. Farnham.

Of course, she betrayed herself when Logan sprang the thing on her so unexpectedly. But he didn't tell her the way in which he had chosen to approach Farnham. He merely told her that he hoped, for her sake, that Farnham would pay up for both of them when he and Farnham had "a little talk." (She feels it was very unfair that Logan didn't tell her he'd already drawn up his message to Farnham.)

But the joke was on Logan, because she fooled him too. She begged him to meet her where they could talk more privately, and he agreed to wait at that bench around midnight until she could slip away. I'm sure he expected to enjoy that interview.

After the waltz quadrille had broken up Bettina managed to take a knife from the collection on the wall of the hotel lobby. Her dress had a wide girdle that wound twice about her waist, and she hid the knife in that. Peter's insisting that she meet him at the pool must at first have seemed a complication. But she realized that I could hear them talking and thought the fact that she had agreed to meet Peter might turn out to her advantage, so she took the risk.

She got rid of Geoffrey, ran out to the bench and said to Logan: "We can't stay here. Peter insisted on meeting me here. Could we go over to the pool?"

And Logan suggested that they take the short cut through the brush and trees behind the bench. He led the way, and she stabbed him in the back just as they came out of the shrubbery. Then she retreated into the shrubbery until she heard Peter go past the bench and on toward the pool. She followed him and came on him bending over Logan's body. . . .

She was safe from Logan, but was she safe from Farnham? She was nervous and frightened and she thought Farnham looked at her "queerly." She wondered if she might have to kill him too. That was why she decided to take my gun. It would be convenient to have, even in the city, since it couldn't be traced to her.

But I blundered into the garage. She had to knock me out—I imagine that was more good luck than a good aim—and she threw the gun away. Then she slipped back into her bedroom, lay down and wept. We're too apt to think murderers must have iron nerves, a sense of their own omnipotence and no regrets.

But she was often frightened; she often felt martyred because she'd "had to do it" and she often burst into tears. That was clear gain; it eased tension for her, and everyone thought: "Poor, bewildered little thing, trying to be loyal to her friends and relatives and protect them even when she isn't certain of their innocence."

It looked as if she had gotten away with it—until Farnham turned up Logan's message. He realized at once that it was at least possible Bettina had killed Logan. He wouldn't condone murder, however much it would cost him to make the facts known. But neither could he bring himself to turn her over to the police without first giving her a chance to explain or even a chance to escape.

He telephoned to her and asked her to come to see him. She couldn't get away until Geoffrey, who was dining with the Goulds, had left. That meant she had to come to Farnham later than he probably would have preferred. But he risked it, being fairly certain his wife would be home by ten o'clock. She did return by then. He got her to bed, and Bettina arrived shortly afterward.

Her explanation did not satisfy him, and neither did her appeals to his self-interest have any effect. He told her she had better go and got up to open the door. She remembered his gun, snatched it from the desk drawer and shot him. She went

out the back way little more than five minutes before we arrived at the house—taking Logan's message with her.

And there, I'm afraid, it might have ended
if Patricia hadn't seen and remembered parts of
Logan's message. Even so, it wasn't until I sang a
silly cowboy song to her that I realized what her
"picture of a hat" might be. We none of us have
any reason to be proud of our reasoning in this
case.

Well, you told me that an *M* on a curved line
would mean Rocking M and that there was a dude
ranch of that name near Reno. Payne went there
as quickly as possible, talked to Mrs. Walker and
heard her story. She didn't know Logan was dead.
She read only local papers, and seldom those. The
name Farnham, though his death made the Reno
papers, meant nothing to her.

She was able to describe Bettina, but that was
hardly conclusive enough. So she agreed to come
here with Payne to point her out. They were delayed in reaching here Saturday because they came
by way of Lake Tahoe and had car trouble besides.

Sullivan had discovered, more quickly than he
had hoped, that Bettina was out of the city for
three days in July. He got that from the Filipino,
though I wouldn't want to inquire into his methods. The Blodgetts, whom Bettina visited at Tahoe,

are there now, so Payne stopped by to question them and got the information I've already given you.

And so to the grand finale—disgustingly theatrical, but undermining to Bettina's morale. She knew I knew Geoffrey's story—and pedigree—from hints I'd thrown out, and that must have made her rather uneasy. Though by this time she knew it, too, officially. He had thought it "only right to confide in her" on Tuesday. It was that confidence of his, and no threat of any sort, that made them decide on an early marriage. She said that now, more than ever, he would need someone to stand beside him and that she would not think of deserting him in his hour of trial.

And shortly before Payne and Mrs. Walker arrived at Esperanza de Oro Jones telephoned Geoffrey to tell him that a cable had come, announcing that Roderick MacNair had finally died of his wounds and that Geoffrey was now Lord Tarbet.

I asked Geoffrey if he never doubted Bettina. He said: "I'm not clever about women. She seemed to me everything I wanted in a wife. But I did wonder once. That was when Peter Wallis suggested Bettina was marrying me so I would suppress some sort of damaging information I had—presumably about Stella.

"But I had said no more to her than that I had thought, that Saturday night on the third floor, that I heard someone down the hall near or in Logan's room. She said: 'Geoffrey, could—could it have been Stella?' I said: 'Of course not,' and that I'd seen no one and was probably mistaken in thinking anyone was there—as it seems now I was.

"She told Peter he had things 'twisted,' but it seemed to me she must have twisted my statement about, rather. I couldn't think she had done it intentionally. Knowing how I felt about her, I could never resent Wallis' actions too much."

Well, Bettina was still playing her part, though in that particular instance Peter got rather out of hand, and she had to back-pedal rapidly. But let us think she was marrying Geoffrey to protect Stella; let us suspect Stella or Gould or anyone, so long as she came through unscathed with what she wanted. As for Peter, I suppose his actions don't need much accounting for. He was too much in love—or too greatly infatuated—to be rational.

But even he had his moment of doubt. Gould, tiring of his antics, decided to appeal to his chivalry. He saw him Thursday and told him exactly how much Bettina would gain by marrying Geoffrey. He told him that Bettina was still ignorant of the true state of affairs but asked Peter, for her sake, to leave Geoffrey a clear field. And he told him bluntly that Bettina would not be happy for long, married to a struggling young architect.

Peter wondered if Gould might not be right. Also, it occurred to him that Bettina never quite said "yes" or "no" either to him or Geoffrey. "Had we but world enough, and time, This coyness, lady, were no crime. . . ."

But he put that thought aside as profaning his goddess. On an impulse he cleared out of the city, to think. He decided to give Bettina up, but only after one final, dramatic interview. And even at the last Bettina still played her part, still was unwilling quite to let Peter go. All along she had only to hint and leave sentences half finished, and Peter could be depended on to finish them or interpret her hints as he wished to interpret them—and as she wished him to interpret them.

As to Mrs. Farnham, she is recuperating in an expensive sanitarium, and her sister-in-law, Evelyn King, has taken Patricia off our hands. Mrs. Farnham will recover too. At least, she will be her old self again, if you can call that returning to normal. Jealousy is cruel as the grave—and I doubt that it ends at the grave.

She had brooded over Farnham's death, unable to understand it but convinced that Stella was in some way responsible for it, until she finally slipped off with the crazy idea of finding Stella. Of course her sudden appearance frightened Bettina, but then she hoped—briefly—that we would consider Mrs. Farnham mad enough to have murdered her husband.

There is only one thing more that needs explaining, and, thank God, that explanation is slightly on the humorous side. As vacation reading Stella chose two books never seen in bookstores or libraries—though these had been produced from a desk drawer by a librarian who, as Stella said, "told me I just didn't know what lit'rature was till I'd read them. When they weren't just plain nasty they were dull as dishwater and costing me fifty cents a day!"

Well, when Gould announced our suitcases were to be inspected as we left Summit House Stella was very much provoked. She didn't want anyone to see those books in her suitcases and ran to Bettina to ask how she should dispose of them. She was also exasperated because she knew she'd have to pay a stiff price for the books when she couldn't return them.

If you're still interested you may attend the trial easily enough, as Bettina is to be tried for Logan's murder in the county where it occurred. On the whole, I think the prosecution may do better there than they would here, if their attorney is fairly capable. Bettina will have the best money can buy, but that may not impress a local jury too favorably. Neither may she and her ambitions and her pale peccadilloes. As you can guess from the foregoing, she made a confession of sorts. Of course she will repudiate it, and her lawyer will try to make the jury believe the police tricked and browbeat her into damaging admissions. But I don't think a local jury will ever believe that Sheriff Payne did that.

Valerie deserted me long ago. She is asleep now, and I have typewriter's cramp. This should satisfy you, and, even if it doesn't, in the final words of the song that made me think Patricia's "picture of a hat" might be a cattle brand—"Just now I ain't a-tellin' any more."

Michael

—A—

CONVERSATION BETWEEN
MICHAEL DUNDAS AND ROCKY ALLAN,
Friday, August 30.

MICHAEL: If you saw a capital *M* written over a curved line what would that suggest to you?
ROCKY: A curved line? Do you mean a quarter circle?

MICHAEL: Yes, I suppose you could call it that.

ROCKY: That's what a cattleman would call it. Do the legs of the *M* touch the quarter circle?

MICHAEL: Yes.

ROCKY: Then, while it looks at first glance a good deal like a hat, I'd call it a Rocking M. Wouldn't you? You know we had quite a discussion of brands one time.

MICHAEL: I remembered that.

ROCKY: Yes, and I know a dude ranch that takes its name from that brand.

MICHAEL: You do? Well, I did think of Arizona but—

ROCKY: No, this is in Nevada, quite a ways from Reno. It has a reputation for no questions asked and none answered about any other guests.

MICHAEL: Oh. You don't know who—?

ROCKY: Yes, I do. A couple named Walker owns the place and they came from Texas originally. Is that the name you want?

MICHAEL: No, the name I had in mind was Anderson. But that was the maiden name of a cousin of Tex Logan's, and she might very well be Mrs. Walker now.

—B—

CONVERSATION BETWEEN
INSPECTOR SULLIVAN AND MR. DUNDAS,
Friday, August 30, 10:30 P.M.

SULLIVAN: Well, I just heard from the sheriff. It's quite a ways over to this Rocking M ranch, but he got there soon as he could. And Farnham stayed overnight there with a girl that answers Bettina Lawton's description. That was the fifteenth of July, last year.

MICHAEL: That fits in nicely. But merely a description won't do.

SULLIVAN: Well, Payne hasn't any photograph of Bettina Lawton

MICHAEL: I know he hasn't. But if they are willing to come here—

SULLIVAN: You mean the Walkers? Well, Mrs. Walker is Tex Logan's cousin, all right. And it happens she's the only one that saw the girl, though Walker and Logan saw Farnham. He signed a fictitious name to the register, but they still have that, and we can check on his handwriting. Logan also knew that Mrs. Walker took Farnham and Bettina to cabin ten, which explains the little house he drew with a number

over its door. But Bettina stayed in the
car while Farnham was making arrangements inside, so only Mrs. Walker got a
look at her since they left very early the
next morning.

MICHAEL: Oh, I see. That explains several
points that weren't clear in my mind.

SULLIVAN: That's just fine! We also ought
to clear up the point of how Bettina and
Farnham met. He could just clear out of
town, but she couldn't. I don't suppose
there's any use asking Mrs. Gould to admit her sister was out of the city over the
fifteenth. But I want to be able to prove
that before I talk to the girl.

MICHAEL: I agree with you. The evidence
should be conclusive before you act.

SULLIVAN: Yes, but God knows how long it
will take to check on that, though I'm going to work on it. Payne's staying overnight at the Rocking M, and they'll leave
there tomorrow to come down here. I want
this Walker woman's evidence to come as
a complete surprise to everyone. I'll keep
in touch with you.

MICHAEL: Yes, call me here before ten tomorrow or after one. I'll be at Gisele's in
between.

—C

CONVERSATION BETWEEN
SULLIVAN AND MICHAEL,
Saturday evening, August 31.

SULLIVAN: I finally heard from Payne. As I
told you when I called at two, when I found
out the name of the people Bettina visited
at Tahoe I called Payne at the Rocking M.
I thought, since these Blodgetts are at the
lake now, Payne might as well see them on
his way here. Well, he made a late start
from the Rocking M or I wouldn't have
caught him there. This Mrs. Walker found
a lot to do before she left things for her
husband to run over a week end. Then they
had car trouble and when they did get to
Tahoe they had quite a time locating the
Blodgetts and the boy that drove Bettina
over to Reno last July fifteenth. To take a
train home, he thought, but he didn't stay
to put her on it. Payne just phoned from
Truckee, so it's going to be a long time yet
before they get here.

MICHAEL: Well, it was your idea to send him
there.

SULLIVAN: I wish now I'd gone myself. He
takes things too slow and easy. But I had

DEATH BREAKS THE RING

no idea he wouldn't be here hours before that party of Mrs. Alling's begins.
I'd hoped maybe I could keep people here
from going down there at all.

MICHAEL: I know you did but I'm as well
pleased that it's turned out this way.

SULLIVAN: Pleased! Well, the Goulds and
Miss Lawton have already gone down—
went before lunch. I could drag the whole
bunch back here—

MICHAEL: As long as it's gone this far, isn't
it easier to bring the kettle to the teapot?

SULLIVAN: Teapot? I suppose you're thinking
of brewing a tempest in the teapot down
there?

MICHAEL: Nothing so drastic as that. I
might throw out a few hints to undermine
morale before the blitzkrieg. Of course,
that's disgustingly theatrical, but the psychological effect might be excellent.

SULLIVAN: Y-yes. It 'd be more of a surprise
to have us burst in on her at a party like
that than to bring the party back here for
questioning. Anyway, I don't like to risk
doing that until this Mrs. Walker has personally identified Bettina as Farnham's
companion at the Rocking M last year.
Say that Gould challenged our right to

bring her back here, and then Mrs. Walker didn't point out Bettina—

MICHAEL: If I were you and still had doubts
I wouldn't risk it.

SULLIVAN: Either way I'm taking a big risk.
But I'll take the one of bringing Payne
and Mrs. Walker down to Mrs. Alling's
place when they get here. And you'll go
down there yourself now?

MICHAEL: Yes, we'll start at once.

COACHWHIP PUBLICATIONS
CoachwhipBooks.com

VIRGINIA RATH

DEATH AT
DAYTON'S FOLLY

COACHWHIP PUBLICATIONS
CoachwhipBooks.com

VIRGINIA RATH
THE ANGER
OF THE BELLS

COACHWHIP PUBLICATIONS
CoachwhipBooks.com

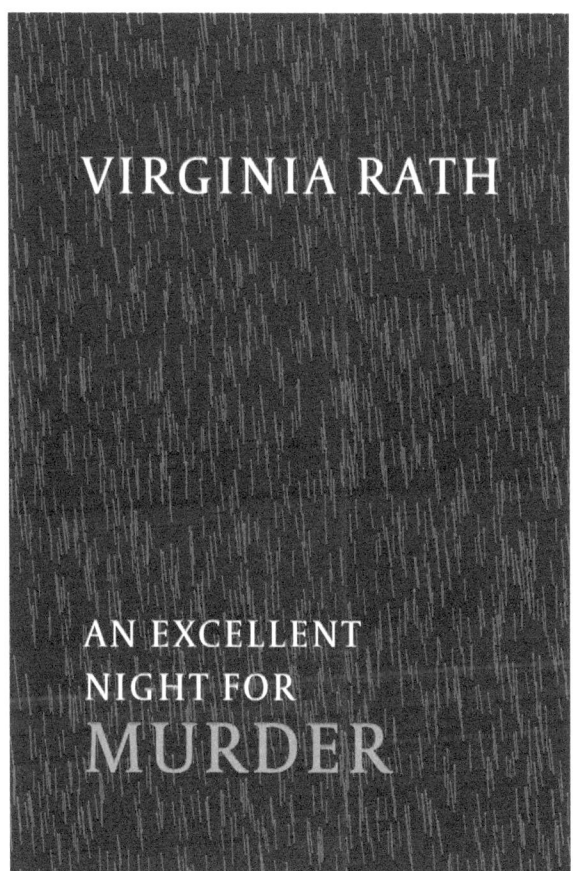

VIRGINIA RATH

AN EXCELLENT
NIGHT FOR
MURDER

COACHWHIP PUBLICATIONS
CoachwhipBooks.com

THE DARK
CAVALIER

VIRGINIA RATH

COACHWHIP PUBLICATIONS
CoachwhipBooks.com

MURDER

with a theme song

VIRGINIA RATH

COACHWHIP PUBLICATIONS
CoachwhipBooks.com

DEATH OF A
LUCKY LADY

VIRGINIA RATH

COACHWHIP PUBLICATIONS
CoachwhipBooks.com

VIRGINIA RATH

FERRYMAN,
TAKE HIM ACROSS!

DEAD
WEIGHT
ADDISON
SIMMONS

COACHWHIP PUBLICATIONS
CoachwhipBooks.com